"The gall of that Branch Walker!"

If her pa hadn't stopped her with one of them steely looks she'd have shown that puffed up, muscle-headed, son of a lop-eared mule whose table he had his feet planted under. And she'd have cut him down to size, too!

His being so big probably had a lot to do with his attitude, with most people backing down when he set them eyes that were black as Hades on them. She had no doubt he sent most women into a tizzy, too, with that bright yellow hair that shone in the sun and that smile that curled around you quicker than a whip. She could just see the women getting all aflutter the first time he rode into town.

What was it Pa had told her? Walker had three years to make his breeding scheme work, and if he didn't, he was out on his ear? Val laughed aloud. That fool didn't know it yet, but he didn't stand a chance....

MEN at WORK

MEN at WORK
ELAINE BARBIERI
STARK LIGHTNING

MEN OF THE WEST

Harlequin Books

TORONTO • NEW YORK • LONDON
AMSTERDAM • PARIS • SYDNEY • HAMBURG
STOCKHOLM • ATHENS • TOKYO • MILAN
MADRID • WARSAW • BUDAPEST • AUCKLAND

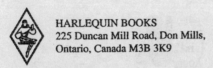

HARLEQUIN BOOKS
225 Duncan Mill Road, Don Mills,
Ontario, Canada M3B 3K9

ISBN 0-373-81038-5

STARK LIGHTNING

Dear Reader,

I'm so pleased to have *Stark Lightning* as a part of Harlequin's MEN AT WORK series, and I'm especially glad to see it reissued under my own name, Elaine Barbieri.

Stark Lightning touched me in a very special way. Totally at ease and at the top of her game in the man's world of ranching, Val found herself at a complete loss when she met up with *the rugged cowboy with a tender touch*. She tried to sort out her feelings about Branch Walker, stumbling through countless embarrassments that intensified the instant conflict and unrestrainable attraction between them. She was angry. She was determined. She couldn't let him show her up! But she was so inexperienced in affairs of the heart...and so weak in the knees. And then strange things started happening at the ranch—*dangerous things*. Where would it all end?

Val's dilemma struck a chord inside me that I think resounds in some corner of every woman's heart. How she suffered. But then, I suppose she was one of the lucky ones, because in the end, a man like Branch Walker was worth it.

I hope you enjoy the laughter and the tears as much as I did. I wrote it for the part of Val that's in all of us.

Sincerely,

Elaine Barbieri

Chapter One

Against the deep blue sky the snowy crests of the Big Horn Mountains to the west glistened in the morning sun. Shafts of sunlight lay across the valley, tinging the golden-brown grasses and spring snow with shades of pink, but Val Stark was oblivious of the Almighty's matchless canvas that stretched as far as the eye could see. Lengthening her stride, she ignored the ankle-deep mud that sucked noisily at her boots, the first harbinger of spring at the Circle S Ranch. Her fingers twitched angrily on the coiled rope she held in her hand, then tightened in a choking grip as she wished fervently that it was Wilbur Stark's skinny, wrinkled neck her hand encircled, instead.

Pausing beside the corral gate, Val glared at the unbroken bronc awaiting her rope. Her foul mood had to do with the heated conversation between her father and her that had abruptly concluded in the ranch house only minutes earlier. But, she had the feeling, as she watched the big black's nervous prancing, that she had merely traded one encounter with an unreasonable male for another.

With a grunt of disgust, Val unfastened the buttons on her bulky coat and shrugged it off her shoulders. She tossed it casually on the fence. The weather had turned unseasonably warm and she was certain the heavy long johns she wore beneath her frayed work shirt and baggy pants would be adequate against the morning chill once she began working that black devil again.

Lifting her battered Stetson from her head, Val shook an untidy brown braid down against her back, then readjusted her hat low on her forehead. She unlatched the gate, her gaze intent on the huge animal that watched her every move as she entered the corral. In her concentration, she didn't notice the cowhands who had drifted out of the barn on seeing her approach and stood just beyond her range of vision.

The great black moved nervously against the far rail as Val dropped the latch closed behind her. She approached him cautiously, speaking softly in a soothing tone.

"All right, Powderkeg, take it easy. We have some work to do together. We've been through this before, so be a good fella and neither one of us will get hurt."

Relieved that she was able to clip her lead to the horse's halter without difficulty, Val patted the stallion's strong neck. A smile touched her lips for the first time that day. Dropping back carefully to the center of the corral, she instructed firmly, "All right, boy, let's see you move."

The great black jerked at the lead, shaking his head obstinately for a few moments before breaking into a rebellious trot around the perimeter of the corral. After a difficult few minutes, the great animal began responding to her command, and the severity of Val's expression softened to cautious satisfaction. She knew she had begun to earn the stallion's respect with firm handling, patience and the relentlessness that made her the best horse wrangler on the Circle S. She also knew that she would not be satisfied until she had him purring like

a kitten. She was justly proud of her skill with horses, and
even more proud that there was not a man in northern Wyoming who could match it.

All trace of a smile faded from Val's lips as she thought of
her reputation. It hadn't been easy to gain respect in a man's
world and she had been forced to make a few sacrifices along
the way. She raised her stubborn chin a notch higher. What
did she care if most people in town disapproved of her? She
had grown accustomed to seeing women's heads wag when
she walked past on the street and to seeing their brows rise at
the way she dressed.

The truth was, very few people recognized Val as a woman
at first sight, and that suited her just fine. She had reached her
present height of ten inches past the mark of five feet at four-
teen, and she stood eye to eye with most men. Her long skinny
body lacked the usual feminine curves, at least as far as could
be seen in the baggy work clothes she wore, and her features,
while small and pleasant, were unremarkable. Her one concession to her sex was the long brown hair she refused to cut,
but wore braided and pushed up under the grimy hat that seldom left her head.

She knew the women in town gossiped about her because
she worked like a man, talked like a man and—Val rubbed
her freckled nose in annoyance—unfortunately smelled no better than the rest of the cowhands. But she had better things to
do than to worry about it. And if the smell of honest sweat
and horses offended their genteel noses, well, that was all right
with her, too. She didn't enjoy the company of women,
couldn't stand their silly games, and she was more comfortable
on the back of a horse than she would ever be in the kitchen.

"You're handlin' that big fella all wrong. You're givin' him
too much slack. He's goin' to get away from you."

Val shot a sideways glance toward the men standing in the doorway of the barn. Her irritation surged up a notch at the open challenge on the face of the big, dark-haired fellow who had called out his unwanted opinion. Damn that Aubrey Whalen! He was convinced being a man made him superior to her in every way that was important. He was too stupid to realize that a person's sex was not a measure of intelligence, ability or determination. Her terse response said it all.

"Save it, Whalen!"

Low hoots of laughter from the other cowhands flushed Whalen's face a dull red, but Val didn't smile at the good-natured teasing that followed.

"Guess she put you in your place, Whalen!"

"Yeah, that'll teach you to mess with Val when she's got her dander up!"

It was obvious that Whalen didn't share the other men's amusement at her response. Val knew he thought she was arrogant and cocky, and she was. She had earned that privilege the hard way, and she knew most of the men respected her, not only because her father owned the Circle S, but because she could outrope, outshoot and outride most of them—and because she never backed down from a fight. She was certain that she had earned the same respect from her father until two weeks earlier, when he made his unexpected announcement.

Val frowned. Some things never changed. Even at the age of four, nobody had had to tell her Will Stark was disappointed that his only offspring was female, especially after her mother left. But she had loved her pa and was determined to be the son he wanted and needed. The Circle S was now one of the fastest-growing ranches in the territory, and it was a source of pride to her that she had helped her father build it. She had thought her pa was just as proud as she was, until he told her about Branch Walker.

Val's blood boiled. There was no way in hell that the Circle S needed a ranch manager! But two weeks of constant arguments hadn't made one bit of difference. Pa's mind was set and he hadn't listened to a thing she'd said. He insisted that Walker was on his way to take over so they could both sit back and relax a bit. The only trouble was, Val wasn't ready to sit back and relax! And she didn't like the thought of anybody else taking charge of her pa's and *her* ranch, either!

"Your pa wants you back at the house, Val."

Val turned at the unexpected voice to her rear, making certain even as she did to keep an eye on the snorting stallion at the end of her lead. She frowned as Jeff Potter continued with an annoying wiggle of his hairy gray brows.

"You-know-who arrived a few minutes ago. He's waitin' in the house to meet you."

"Let him wait. I'm busy."

"But your pa said—"

"And *I* said I'm busy!"

Turning her attention back to the stallion, who was beginning to dance nervously, she cooed, "Settle down, boy. That's right, fella. *You* know who's boss here, don't you?"

A few moments later, Val heard Potter turn and squish back toward the house. A rare smile flicked across her lips. She wasn't about to cater to any new ranch manager, no matter what her pa said. Now was as good a time as any for the fella to realize it.

The sound of approaching footsteps shortly afterward started her stallion snorting anew, and Val gripped the lead tighter. "Easy, boy—that's it," she reassured the animal in a low voice. "We're not goin' to let nobody interrupt our work-out this morning, are we? That's it, keep on walkin'."

"Valentine—"

What in hell...? Had her pa called her *Valentine?*

Val turned with a snarl, only to have her jaw drop and her eyes pop open wide at the sight of the man standing at her father's side. She'd never seen a bigger, tougher-looking man in her life. He had to stand at least six inches over six feet. He had a face like granite and more shoulder and muscle than any two men put together. Oh, hell, he couldn't be—

"Valentine, I want you to meet our new ranch manager, Branch Walker."

A silent groan registered in Val's mind, a lapse of concentration that was just the opportunity the black stallion had been waiting for. Lunging unexpectedly, he dragged her slipping and skidding across the muddy corral as she struggled to restrain him.

Off balance and still fighting to resume control, Val was certain she saw an almost human glint in the huge animal's eye in the split second before he gave the lead another unexpected jerk, which lifted her off her feet and sent her sprawling facedown in the mud with a loud smack.

"Damn..."

Slowly raising her head, Val grimaced and spat out a mouthful of mud. Deliberately ignoring the guffaws coming from the direction of the barn, she flicked the mud from her eyes with exaggerated indifference, only to find herself looking up into the most intense black eyes she had ever seen.

The nervous stallion had been subdued at the far side of the corral by two grinning cowhands, and Val gritted her teeth. She slapped away the oversized hand Walker extended helpfully in her direction, and drew herself to her feet with a sharp "I don't need your help or nobody else's."

Surprise registered in eyes that assessed her too keenly for her own comfort. Walker stepped back.

"If you say so, ma'am."

Val's eyes spat fire. "I say so!"

Annoyance creased the big fellow's face, and Val saw a muscle tick in his cheek the moment before he extended his hand toward her again.

"My name's Branch Walker. I'm the new ranch manager."

Ranch manager, hell! He was salt in the wound, and Val saw bloodred. "*Branch Walker?* What kind of a name is that, anyway? It sounds like some kind of Injun shaman!"

His eyes suddenly hard as stone, Walker responded in a low, ominous tone, "Want to make somethin' of it, lady?"

"Don't call me 'lady'!"

Walker's scathing glance spoke volumes as he replied succinctly, "Sorry. My mistake."

Her eyes narrowing into slits, Val squared her stance. With balled fists, she glared up at Branch Walker's granite face. She hated looking up at any man, but she consoled herself that one well-placed kick would bring him down to size.

"Valentine, get out of that corral, damn it!"

Val turned toward her father with a snap, her eyes blazing. *Valentine,* huh? She had told him at the age of four that her name was Val and she wouldn't answer to any other. He suddenly seemed to have forgotten.

"Valentine, damn it! Valentine!"

Her pa was still bellowing as Val stomped past him without a word. She was almost to the house, when she heard his frustrated snarl and Branch Walker's infuriating response.

"That's a woman, for you."

* * *

Branch groaned silently as he stared down at the food on his plate. His stomach churned. What was that foul-smelling mess? Looking up, he scanned the faces of the cowhands gathered around the dinner table. John Wyatt, Tillman Boggs, Harvey Little, Barney Wallace, Billy Simm, Randy Smith—even that Aubrey Whalen—were spooning the unrecognizable conglomeration into their mouths without a second thought.

Were they crazy?

"Somethin' wrong, Walker?" Whalen laughed mockingly.

Branch frowned in response, again sensing that the big, dark cowhand was going to be trouble. Then he shrugged, deciding in the favor of caution. "I was just wonderin' what we're eatin' tonight."

Billy Simm's young face cracked in a smile. "Oh, hell, Red Hand don't never cook nothin' you can put a name to."

"His cookin' takes some gettin' used to, that's for sure."

"Yeah, Red Hand's a lousy cook, all right." Sitting at the head of the table, Will Stark shoved another spoonful of the nameless substance into his mouth and swallowed hard before continuing, "But he's better at it than he was when he first showed up." He lowered his spoon to the table and paused in reminiscence. "It was practically a blizzard outside that day, and that old Injun was cold and hungry as a bear. We was all hungry because the cook had run off a couple of days earlier and things hadn't been runnin' too smooth. Red Hand said he'd cook if he could eat, and I gave him a chance." Stark's full gray mustache twitched with amusement. "The only trouble is, the old coot was as thirsty as he was hungry and he found the whiskey before he finished cookin'. He made one helluva mess. He cut himself so many times while choppin' up the meat that night—" Stark laughed. "We've called him Red Hand ever since."

Branch swallowed with a gulp, and Stark hastened to add, "But he don't cut himself much no more, 'cause we keep the whiskey hid."

Red Hand chose that moment to stagger into the room with another platter, and Branch gave another silent groan.

Branch picked up his spoon. The first mouthful tasted different. The second was less of a shock to his stomach. At the third spoonful, his tastebuds went mercifully numb.

Thank you, Lord.

Branch glanced assessingly around the room as he continued eating. He had spent most of the day outdoors and hadn't had much time to look around the house, but it appeared he hadn't missed much. To say the place lacked a woman's touch was to put it mildly. Judging from the few rooms he had seen, whatever feminine touches had once graced the sprawling, well-built structure had been all but negated by time. The furniture was functional—a long table in the dining room with mismatched wooden chairs; and a threadbare couch and chairs and a scarred table and desk in the living room. The kitchen was a disaster that could not be described. The only traces of better days still remaining were the worn, unusually fine rug that covered the living room floor and the few pieces of good china that completed the mismatched dinnerware from which they now ate.

If he didn't know better, Branch would have judged by the appearance of the place that the ranch was totally devoid of a female presence.

The sound of a step in the doorway caused him to raise his head. There stood Val Stark. She seated herself at the table and shot him a black look before she picked up her fork. Branch nodded to himself in confirmation of his last thought before reaching for a slice of suspiciously gray bread heaped on the platter nearby. His hand almost dropping to the table with the unexpected weight of it, he controlled a grimace. He took a bite, uncertain the moment it touched his tongue whether Red Hand had truly surpassed himself, but Val Stark's sideways glance kept him chewing in stone-faced silence.

Branch was at a complete loss. If things had appeared to get off to a bad start between the boss's daughter and him at first, he soon learned that he had not seen the worst of it. Of all the bad-mannered, smart-mouthed, irritating women he had ever met, Val Stark took the cake. She had stuck to Will Stark and him like a pesky tick all day as Stark introduced him to the ranch, and it didn't take much brainpower to conclude that she didn't see a need for him on the Circle S. It also hadn't taken him long to conclude that she was wrong. Stark's stock consisted mostly of Texas longhorns, and the fellow obviously had no idea how to go about improving his herd. That was where he came in.

He had been working hand in hand with Alex Swan for the past five years improving range stock with the use of Hereford bulls from England. Without a shred of conceit, Branch recognized that he was as close to being an expert on breeding as there was in Wyoming, aside from Swan himself. He had worked well with Swan, had been treated well, and he had thought he was with Swan for keeps until Will Stark's arrival at the ranch.

Stark had seemed to understand clearly the growing demand for the marbled, more palatable meat of the Herefords and the greater potential for profit from a breed that was stockier and put on weight more quickly than longhorns. He had been skeptical when Stark had said he was going to make him an offer he couldn't turn down, but Stark had been right. He couldn't refuse it. As things now stood, if he kept to the schedule of progress that was a part of Stark's contract with him, he'd own a share of the Circle S at the end of three years. That thought held an irresistible appeal for a man who had worked with other men's cattle for most of his thirty-two years. However, it now appeared that there was a fly in the ointment— and that the fly's name was Val Stark.

Branch pondered that thought. He supposed he should have known the whole thing was too good to be true. How a man as likable as Will Stark could end up with such a mean-tempered, unlikely looking female for a daughter was beyond him. Not only was she a hard-nosed pain in the neck, but if he didn't know better, he'd think she was deliberately doing her best to look repulsive!

Branch darted a covert glance in the direction of the boss's daughter. Well, if the effort was intentional, she had succeeded. Val Stark didn't look or smell any better than her horse!

The obnoxious female looked up and Branch caught her challenging glance. He gritted his teeth, startled to hear himself say as the stoic Indian walked unsteadily back into the room, "How's chances of gettin' some more of that beef...or whatever it is that you got in that pot, Red Hand?"

All heads around the table snapped up in unison, confirming his own opinion of the gravity of his mistake. Certain he would pay for the gesture tomorrow, Branch watched as Red Hand refilled his plate.

Determined to show Val Stark that he could adapt to anything, Branch stubbornly scooped the last piece of meat from his plate a few minutes later and forced it between his lips. Incredulous, he stared as Val Stark mopped up the remaining gravy in her bowl with the leaden bread and stuffed it into her mouth with apparent gusto. He was still staring when she looked up unexpectedly, her mouth packed, and grated, "What do you think you're lookin' at, Walker?"

Branch replied appropriately in return. "Nothin' much, ma'am."

Snickers sounded around the table and Val Stark's spine stiffened. She swallowed with deliberation. "My name's Val, and I don't answer to nothin' else. Understand?"

Branch returned her glaring stare. "Yes, *ma'am*."

In a blur of unexpected movement, the girl kicked back her chair and was on her feet. She moved toward him as swiftly as a snake, only to be halted midway by her father's razor-sharp voice.

"Valentine, I'm thinkin' now's a good time for you to check on Powderkeg."

Val Stark snapped back a heated "My name ain't Valentine!"

Will Stark's small eyes narrowed. "Ain't it, now?"

After a moment's pause, the hot-headed witch turned abruptly on her heel and stomped from the room, leaving behind a silence that could be cut with a knife. Branch's gaze trailed the faces at the table, halting at last on Stark's sickly smile as he said, "Valentine's not herself, Branch. I reckon she'll be in a better mood tomorrow."

"But I sure enough wouldn't count on it!"

Billy Simm's candid comment raised a round of laughter, and Branch nodded. No, he didn't think he would.

Valentine? Yes, *ma'am?*

The hair on the back of Val's neck bristled. She stomped toward the corral, ignoring the purple shadows that accompanied the setting sun's breathtaking display as it rent the azure sky with dazzling streaks of orange and silver. She slowed her step as she approached the fence, not angry enough to ignore the danger in startling Powderkeg into a tantrum. Pausing with her hand on the gate, she fumed.

The gall of that Branch Walker! If her pa hadn't stopped her with one of them steely looks she'd have shown that puffed up, muscle-headed, son of a lop-eared mule whose table he had his feet planted under. And she'd have cut him down to size, too!

His being so big probably had a lot to do with his attitude, with most people backing down when he set them eyes that were black as Hades on them. She had no doubt he sent most women into a tizzy, too, with that bright yellow hair that shone in the sun and that smile that curled around you quicker than a whip. She could just see the women getting all aflutter the first time he rode into town. If she knew Marilyn Balter at all, that simpleminded piece would be out on the street in a flash, wiggling down the walk with her smile flashing. And Sally Ledman would be waiting like a patient cat at the counter of her father's store, where she knew he'd be bound to show up sooner or later.

Val's stomach tightened with annoyance. Walker probably had his way with most women just by crooking a finger at them. Well, she wasn't one of that breed, and she wouldn't—

A chorus of male laughter preceded the emergence of the ranch hands from the house, and Val turned toward the sound. Standing a full head taller than most of them, Branch walked in their midst as the men joked and slapped him on the back in the manner of old friends. Val seethed. Not only had they accepted the pretentious dolt, but they actually seemed to like him.

Damn, men were fools! How they had ever managed to attain the superior position in life was beyond her.

Watching the laughing group as they walked toward the bunkhouse, Val growled. She had worked and sweated and fought the odds for the past sixteen years to get where she was now. She was one of the most valuable hands on the ranch, and no overgrown oaf was going to give her orders, no matter how big or how smart he thought he was!

What was it Pa had told her? Walker had three years to make his breeding scheme work, and if he didn't, he was out on his ear? Val laughed aloud. That fool didn't know it yet, but he didn't stand a chance.

Still staring at the doorway through which Branch Walker and the ranch hands had exited the room, Will Stark heaved a deep sigh. He was too disgusted to get out of his chair. Nothing was going the way he'd planned.

Remembering the steaming look on his daughter's face before she'd stomped away, he closed his eyes and shook his head. When Val got herself into that hot a snit, she wasn't fit to live with for days, and it was plain that Branch Walker wasn't a patient man.

Will groaned. He just hadn't envisioned things going this way, despite Val's vehement protests. He had tried to explain things to her. He had told her that the territory was growing, and he wasn't about to find himself falling behind because he was too proud to admit they needed help.

He remembered Val's reply: "We don't need no help!"

He had responded with a statement she hadn't wanted to hear then when he said, "Look here, Val. I'm lookin' the age of sixty right in the eye. I ain't goin' to be able to keep liftin' my carcass into a saddle forever."

Will paused in his thoughts, remembering the conversation that had followed. There had been some truth in his responses, but he felt a lingering shame for some of the deceit involved. He wasn't a devious man—never had been. So why had he started this mess?

He paused—and grinned. Oh, yeah, he knew why....

Chapter Two

A bright morning sun splintered the grainy mist of roundup as Val held her gelding under tight rein at the side of the herd. Perspiring in the unexpected heat of the day, she raised the brim of her hat to wipe the sweat from her brow and looked up at the position of the sun. It wasn't past ten o'clock and she was already too warm in her coat. Cursing the continued unseasonable weather, while realizing the temperature was not the sole reason for her heated discomfort, Val slipped off her coat and tied it behind her.

A week had passed since Branch Walker's arrival at the ranch—a long, hellish week during which she had accompanied her father as he'd gone over every inch of Circle S with his new ranch manager, both on horseback and on paper. Forced to listen to Walker's high-minded plans for the improvement of their breeding stock, she had almost gagged. Her father's warnings had not been enough to stop her from offering her thoughts on the sissy English Herefords that Walker touted, as well as her reservations about the ability of that pampered breed to resist the prolonged winters of the northern Wyoming range country. In the end, her words had fallen on deaf ears, and she had not taken the dismissal of her opinions lightly.

She had saddled up with the men that morning, surprised to hear Pa beg off in order to "rest a bit" at home. Never having known her father to "rest" a day in his life, she had shot him a curious glance before riding out to begin the massive undertaking of rounding up stock from the winter range in order to eliminate the undersized steers. It was a task at which she excelled, having the best cutting horse on the spread. However, at Walker's order, she had remained on the sidelines most of the morning, a reluctant spectator as the rest of the men worked.

Her blood was beginning to boil....

As Val watched, Jeff Potter made another sweep at some wary steers, his wrinkled face shiny with sweat. Wyatt, Boggs, Little, Wallace and Whalen had been running themselves ragged at Walker's command, while Simm and Smith scouted other areas of the Circle S for strays. And she still remained observing, the princess on her mangy throne.

Her patience coming to a sudden, explosive halt, Val raised her stubborn chin. She had had enough! Walker wasn't going to get away with consigning her to the sidelines any longer!

Casting a glance in the direction Walker had disappeared a few minutes earlier, Val abruptly spurred her horse into action and rode into the fray. Everywhere at once, she was cutting, roping, herding, doing what she did best, and her spirits soared. She chased another longhorn, easily closing the distance between them as her well-schooled gelding responded without fault. Prepared for another easy target, she cast her loop just as Branch Walker rode out of a cloud of dust and into her range of vision. The rope fell short, allowing the satisfied steer the opportunity it needed to plunge back into the moving herd. Out of the corner of her eye, Val saw Walker's lips twitch, and her blood boiled up another degree. Riding back into the herd, Val easily separated the stubborn longhorn and gave chase. Within a few feet of him, she tossed her rope once more, only to pull her horse up short incredulously.

Impossible! She had missed again!

Aware that Walker was openly watching her, Val plunged into the herd a third time, her eye on the ornery steer. Left, right, she cut, finally separating him from the others. She could feel victory close at hand. She cast her rope...

God damn...!

The victorious longhorn slipped back into the herd as Val watched with disbelief. From a distance came the sound of Walker's voice as he directed impatiently, "Whalen! Get that steer for her, will you?"

Whalen—going to rope *her* steer? Never!

Charging into the herd once more, Val focused on the elusive steer, mumbling, "Prepare to meet your match, you mangy son of a—"

The dust of the chase obscuring her vision, Val did not see the low-lying brush to the side of the trail until it was too late. Her rope hooking unexpectedly upon it, she was uncertain what happened until she hit the ground with a thud.

Brightly colored stars were still spinning in front of her eyes when a dark-eyed stare penetrated the brilliant display. She felt the earth beneath her, and strong fingers probing the bump on her throbbing head. Then came the dreaded sound of Branch Walker's voice.

"Are you all right?"

Still unable to focus clearly, Val gritted out from between clenched teeth, "Take your hand off me...."

Walker's face hardened. He drew back and snapped, "Potter will take you back to the ranch."

"I'm all right. I'm not goin' back."

"You *are* goin' back."

"I am not!"

Val was still unable to pull herself to her feet when Walker poked his face back down into hers, his tone softening with growing menace. "*I'm* the boss here, and *I* say you go back. Damn it, you can't even see straight, and I'm not goin' to let you get somebody else injured just because you're too stubborn to know when to quit! Potter—" Turning to the frowning wrangler standing nearby, he ordered gruffly, "She's all yours. Get her on her feet and get her out of here. And don't come back until you've brought her home and put her to bed."

"Listen, boss—" Potter turned a wary look at Val as she struggled to her feet, and his expression turned mutinous. "I ain't goin' to—" Branch's face hardened, his dark eyes narrowing, and Potter's Adam's apple bobbed revealingly as he mumbled, "All right." He took Val's arm, and Val's fury soared as she realized that she was in no condition to argue.

Nearing the ranch house a short time later, Val squinted into the distance in an effort to identify the rider slipping out of sight on the horizon. Reluctant to admit that her vision was still blurred and that her head pounded like a fence post being driven into the ground, Val turned to Potter's carefully blank expression. Her voice was harsh.

"Is that my pa ridin' off over there?"

Potter nodded. "Seems like it is."

"He tell you that he was goin' someplace today?"

"Your pa don't tell me nothin' that he don't think I need to know."

Val growled with a familiar annoyance.

They entered the house a few minutes later and Potter's step continued behind her as she approached her bedroom. Turning with a snap that proved more painful than she could have believed, she grated warningly into Potter's startled face, "Don't you take another step."

Retreating at a pace that was almost a run, Potter was out of the house before Val had time to push open her bedroom door. Finally surrendering to her shaky knees, Val lay down on her bed as a voice in her head repeated in rhythm with its painful pounding, "I'll get you for this, Walker. I will, I will, I will...."

Will Stark looked up at the clear blue sky and gave his lagging mount an impatient kick. It was nearing noon and the weather was hotter than it had a right to be. The day was half over and the ride seemed particularly endless, especially knowing that a few hours from now he'd be riding back in the same direction from which he had just come. Damn, he was getting too old for this.

Pausing in his thoughts as a familiar house came into view, Will felt his annoyance begin to drain. He kicked his mare to a faster pace, raising his hat to wipe the beads of perspiration from his brow. The sweet scent of lilac hair tonic met his nostrils, and he smiled. He had been forced to wait until the last cowhand had left for the winter pasture and Red Hand had made his morning disappearance before dragging out that old copper tub and filling it with water. He hadn't wanted to take the time to heat the water he had pumped from the well, and he had nearly frozen to death when he'd gotten in. He had made fast work of his bath, determined to make it a monthly habit from now on. He had retrieved the hair tonic from its hiding place after donning his only fresh change of clothes and had made liberal use of it.

Will frowned. He hadn't been able to resist trying out his recent purchase from the barbershop when he had first dressed that morning, but that had been a mistake. Val had come sniffing around him like a well-trained hound the second he'd stepped into the parlor. Staring at his head, she'd asked incredulously, "What's that on your hair, Pa? It smells like buffalo piss!"

The heat had surged to his face then, and sniffing her in return, he'd replied, "I wouldn't talk about how *I* smell, Valentine Stark. How long's it been since you had them clothes off your back?"

His daughter's gray eyes had squeezed into slivers of steel as she'd returned, "How long you been wearin' yours?"

She had stomped out of the house then and joined the men. He had waited until the sound of hoofbeats had indicated they were well on their way before lowering his head to take a deep whiff of his armpit. Hummm...

Will's wandering thoughts came to an abrupt halt as a familiar figure appeared on the porch of the well-kept house in the distance, and he felt a flush of pleasure touch his wrinkled cheeks. Drawing up to the hitching rail in front a few minutes later, he dismounted as the Widow McGee walked down the steps, a smile of welcome on her pleasant, well-rounded face. He took off his hat, grateful he had taken the time to bathe, in view of the woman's impeccably clean dark dress and spotless apron, the shiny gray hair confined in a neat bun and the true pleasure in her eyes when she said warmly, "It's so good to see you again, Wilbur. My, don't you look nice today! Come right on in."

He was walking up the steps, when she smiled sweetly up

into his eyes. "How did you know that I made an apple pie this morning?"

"Aw, Mary." Will gave a little shrug. "You know it ain't no apple pie that brings me back here to see you every chance I get."

Mary's smile warmed. "I know."

In the spotless parlor Mary took his coat and hat, and suddenly awkward, Will was at a loss for words when a frown touched the widow's lightly lined face. "You know it's my hired hands' day off here at the ranch...."

Will nodded. "Yes, I do."

"Well, I've something that should be taken care of as soon as possible, if you won't mind attending to it before we go into the kitchen."

Will nodded and followed as the widow turned toward the hall. Walking close behind her, he entered the first room on the right and paused as she pushed the door closed behind them. He swallowed convulsively, familiar with the pleasant scent of flowers that permeated the master bedroom although it was barely into spring. His eyes gradually widened as Mary slowly turned to face him.

It was happening again....

As he watched, Mary's brown eyes took on a burning glow. The soft lines on her face appeared to fade away, and her cheeks took on a youthful flush. Raising hands that were steady and deliberate with purpose, she reached up to the neat bun at her nape and freed her hair with a shake of her head. Taking a step closer, she stripped open the front of her dress to display a camisole under which full breasts heaved with passion. As if possessed, Will was suddenly tearing at his shirt, as well, at his fresh smelling underwear, at his boots and socks. Soon as naked as the day he was born, he looked up to see Mary's pink flesh bared to his gaze in the second before she thrust herself tight against him and covered his mouth with hers.

His heart pounding, Will closed his arms around her, taking her kiss and returning it with a fervor stored for a score of lonely years. Together they stumbled back toward the downy-soft brass bed, together they fell down upon it and together they indulged their hungry bodies with an ardor that reflected their numbered tomorrows.

Branch strained his eyes through the dusty haze, looking again in the direction in which the two horsemen had disappeared over an hour earlier. Damn it, where was Potter! He should have returned already.

About to turn back to the work at hand, Branch saw the cowpoke he sought ride into view on the horizon. The fellow's leisurely pace tightened the knot in his stomach, and Branch was suddenly grateful that the ranch hand's scrawny neck wasn't within reach.

Potter grew gradually nearer, and Branch was incredulous at his own level of agitation. What was wrong with him, anyway? Valentine Stark, hard-headed show-off that she was, had only gotten what she'd had coming, hadn't she? He had told her that he didn't want her involved with the dangerous work of cutting and roping. Despite her lack of femininity, she was still a woman.

Branch paused in his thoughts. Perhaps that was the problem.... He had seen a surprising vulnerability in her face during those few seconds while she was unconscious. She had been absolutely motionless and he had leaned down real close, his heart pounding as he'd tried to ascertain if she was breathing. With his relief had come the sudden realization that

Val Stark wasn't as homely as he had thought at first. She was skinny and shapeless, her hair was a mess and she smelled as bad as the other ranch hands, but…

Branch stopped abruptly in his thoughts. *But* what?

Unwilling to pursue that line of thinking any further, Branch trained his attention on Potter as he drew nearer. His unwavering gaze appeared to make the fellow uneasy, and Branch was immediately suspicious and on the attack when Potter drew up alongside.

"You took your own sweet time gettin' back here."

Potter's response was too innocuous to be believed. "Val had to ride slow. She was hurtin' pretty bad."

"Hurtin' bad?" Branch tensed, his heart beginning a heavy pounding. "What do you mean?"

"Well, you know. She was havin' trouble seein' straight, and she was swaying back and forth on that saddle like a seesaw."

"Did her pa send for a doctor?"

"Old man Stark wasn't home."

"Red Hand?"

"He was off someplace, like he usually is."

"Did she seem better once she was lyin' down?"

Potter avoided his eye, his full mustache twitching. "How would I know? She turned on me like a rattler when I took one step toward that bedroom."

Branch was incredulous. "You mean that you knew she was hurt and you didn't even wait until someone came home to see to her?"

"Hell, you don't know Val Stark like I do. She's tough as nails and her head's thicker than a tree trunk. And on top of that, she's a crack shot. When she fixes them steely eyes on me, and tells me to git, I git!"

At a loss for words, Branch stared a moment longer into Potter's flushed face. Turning to a few of the other men who had gathered around them, he saw the same sentiments reflected on their faces, and he shook his head. Grown men— afraid of a woman. He didn't believe it!

Unwilling to waste another minute, he addressed Boggs sharply. "I'm puttin' you in charge here until I come back. Separate those steers that I marked from the rest and drive them back toward the south corral."

Not waiting for the cowhand's reply, Branch kicked his mount into a leap forward and headed back to the ranch.

Shafts of golden sunlight shone through windows as clear and clean as new ice. White lace curtains deflected their rays, weaving their intricate pattern against the immaculate white tablecloth on the table at which Will sat. The tantalizing fragrance of frying bacon and perked coffee hung on the air as Will pushed back the plate that had been emptied of its generous portions for the second time. His cup had been refilled with rich, black coffee, and a golden-brown apple pie awaited the knife as soon as he spoke the word.

Across the table from him, perfectly coiffed, her neat black dress buttoned up to the neck and her white apron stainless, his dear Mary smiled sweetly into his eyes. He was complete. He was in heaven.

His smile unconsciously falling, Will cleared his throat. "Mary, darlin', I've been puttin' off tellin' you this, but I gotta come right out and say it. Things ain't workin' out the way we planned."

Alarm registered in Mary McGee's eyes, and Will reached out a knobby hand to take hers as she replied softly, "What are you saying, Wilbur, dear?"

"I'm sayin' Branch Walker arrived last week, just like he said he would, but there's been hell to pay. He don't give an inch when he has his mind set, and Val's ready to bust. I tell you, they're workin' up to bloodshed, them two."

Mary's face softened. "You haven't given them a chance, dear."

"A chance to kill each other, you mean."

"No, I didn't mean that."

Pulling her toward him, Will pushed himself back from the table and sat Mary on his knee. The feel of her plump backside against his sinewy thigh was more distracting than he would have wished as he continued earnestly, "I know you didn't. And you know how bad I feel about sneakin' over here to see you every week when your cowhands have the day off. But the truth is, I don't know how Val would take the thought of me marryin' again. It was such a damned bad time when her ma walked out on us both. She was just a little squirt and she never got it straight in her head how her ma could've left her. She just started thinkin' that if females were like that, she didn't want to be one. And I'll be damned if she didn't do her best not to be."

Sympathy shone in Mary's eyes, encouraging Will to continue. "If I bring you into the house, I'm thinkin' Val will leave, you know? And even if she is more stubborn than a mule with twice the kick, I don't want to take the chance of losin' her."

"I know, dear. But this Branch Walker...you said he was the only man you ever met that would be able to handle her if they got together. Don't you think things might change if you give them a chance?"

"I think we got a better chance of Hell freezin' over."

"Oh, Wilbur..."

Tears sprang into Mary's eyes, and Will felt her pain as he whispered, "Come on, darlin'. Don't cry. We're goin' to work this out, you'll see."

Consoling her, Will stroked Mary's soft cheek, and smoothed her hair. He pressed his mouth against hers, and felt a familiar surge as she returned his kiss.

His emotions rapidly warming, Will drew back to see his own feelings reflected in Mary's eyes. Hardly believing his good luck, Will all but choked as Mary whispered, "I do love you, Wilbur."

Not daring a response, Will swallowed with a gulp and jumped to his feet. Lifting Mary into his arms with unexpected vigor, he turned toward the bedroom door, his old feet fairly flying.

The powerful horse beneath him was laboring from their long race home, but Branch leaned lower over the animal's neck, forcing the pace. His mind moving faster than his mount's flying hooves, he berated himself harshly.

What in hell had gotten into him by allowing that irritating little twit to affect his sense of judgment? Whether he liked it or not, Val Stark had been functioning as one of his cowhands and, as such, her welfare was his responsibility. He should have realized that she was a bully, that she had all the men buffaloed and that she'd end up getting her way, whether it was to her detriment or not. For the life of him, he still couldn't understand the men's reactions to the girl! Damn it, no tough-talking, nail-spitting female would ever make *him* run!

Raising his head as the ranch house came into sight, Branch spurred his horse to a faster pace. The gelding was blowing hard, but he had no time to consider the animal's discomfort.

Skidding his horse to a halt a few minutes later, Branch dropped the reins and ran for the front door, the sense of urgency inside him building. An assessing glance as he approached the house had shown no sign of life, and his anxieties were increasing. Not quite understanding his panic, he rushed through the front door with a breathless shout.

"Is anybody home?"

Silence was the only response and Branch was unwilling to waste another moment. Heading directly for the bedrooms, he paused, momentarily uncertain. He knocked on the first door, then pushed it open to find the room empty. A few steps down the hall he knocked on the next partially open door, then saw Val Stark lying motionless on the bed.

He entered the room, only to jump with a start as Val Stark unexpectedly bolted to a seated position, her voice a grating growl.

"What are *you* doin' in my room? Get out of here!"

Feeling foolish, Branch was suddenly more furious than he had ever been in his life as he growled in return, "All right, *lady*, I'll leave with pleasure. How I ever managed to convince myself that a nasty sidewinder like you might need my help, I'll never know!"

Drawing herself to her feet, Val took a wobbly step. "Need your help? Hah! When that day comes, I'll—"

Her raspy tirade coming to an abrupt halt, the girl suddenly pitched forward.

Managing to break her fall, Branch grunted under her weight as he hefted her back onto the bed and took a close look at her. Val Stark's face was colorless, except for the spray of freckles that ran across the bridge of her short nose. Beads of perspiration stood out on her brow and he wiped them away with his palm, startled at the coldness of her skin. His heart beginning a more rapid pounding, he mumbled an oath, realizing, as he pulled the blanket up and over her, that she hadn't even had the strength to take off her boots.

Turning, Branch ran out of the room and into the kitchen. He breathed a frustrated sigh at the total disorder of the place. Finally locating a chipped bowl, he flicked off the remains of a former meal and filled it with water. Grabbing a dishcloth as he passed, he raced back.

Val Stark had not moved, and Branch's panic soared. Dampening the cloth, he ran it against her forehead, her cheeks and lips. He was smoothing wisps of hair back from her face when he felt the bump on the side of her head just beyond the temple, and he swallowed hard. The damned little witch had been dizzy and in real pain, but was too stubborn to admit it. Well, if she lived through this, they would both learn a lesson.

Pausing, Branch amended that thought. No, *he* would learn a lesson. He had the feeling Val Stark would die rather than give in.

Die...? Branch swallowed hard and renewed his efforts to restore her to consciousness. Oh, damn....

An hour later Branch was still bathing Val's face. He had taken the time to remove her boots, and had praised himself for the sacrifice involved. The room still reeked. He had chafed her hands, silently wondering at the delicacy of their structure despite her heavily callused palms. He had spoken to her, pleaded, cajoled and, in desperation, had begged. She still had not regained consciousness, and he cursed every living person on the ranch who had chosen these particular hours to vacate the premises.

Leaning over the girl's face, Branch stared hard. It was as white as chalk, and her lashes were dark fans against the colorless skin. Strange, he hadn't noticed how long they were before——but, then, he hadn't noticed how smooth her skin was beneath the grime of the trail, or how her hair moved into little curls at the temples. Nor had he realized——

The girl's breathing went suddenly still, and Branch's heart skipped a beat. Panicked, he leaned closer, his face by her lips as he sought to feel a trace of breath there. He was weak with relief when she suddenly began breathing normally again.

An unexpected step at the door preceded Will Stark's sudden, room-shattering bellow.

"What in hell's goin' on in here?"

Branch jerked upright, only to find an angry response stolen from his lips by a startling reply from the bed behind him.

"Quit your hollerin', Pa. I got a headache!"

Turning toward Val with a snap, Branch was still standing, mouth agape, as the treacherous witch's bloodshot eyes met his, and she directed weakly, but effectively, "Get out of my room, cowboy!"

The blood rushing to his head, Branch felt his lip curl, but he bit back an appropriate response and turned toward the door. A furious glance at Will Stark in passing halted any further questions and set the man back a step with another of his sickly smiles.

And as he stomped down the hall, Branch thought he heard Will Stark groan.

Chapter Three

"**D**amn!"

Val moved restlessly in her bed. The subdued tone of her expletive was due far more to the throbbing pain in her head than to the depth of her frustration as she looked at the bright midday sunlight shining through the window of her room. Her patience with the unnatural restraints forced upon her after her accident was fading rapidly, as she asked herself what she was doing lying flat on her back like a weak-kneed sheep while every other self-respecting hand on the spread was in the saddle.

A sharp twinge behind her temple was the silent response, and Val groaned.

The events of the previous day returned to haunt her like a bad dream, and Val closed her eyes. There he was again—Branch Walker! She was onto his type, all right, the perfect male who was certain that the only place for a woman was either in the kitchen or warming a man's bed!

Aware that her embarrassing performance since Walker's arrival had done little to convince him any differently, Val heard her frustration soar into a growl. She couldn't remember the last time her rope had missed a critter she was after or when she had last taken a spill from a horse. And through it all, Walker's dark eyes had been measuring and watching....

Val swore under her breath, the urge to commit mayhem growing stronger. She had been shocked to see Walker standing beside her bed when the sound of her pa's voice had brought her around from that gray world in which she had been floating. Walker was the last man she wanted as a witness when she was as weak as a puppy. The only measure of satisfaction she'd had the entire day was in the tightening of his hard, square jaw and in the hot flush that rose to his face when she'd lit that fire under his tail and he'd taken off at a run.

Then Doc Pitt had come, poking his gray whiskers into her face with the smell of his whiskey-soured breath and ordering her to stay in bed. She had stayed in bed most of the day, all right, but only because she didn't have a choice with her head beating like a drum when she moved it and the world reeling around her every time she tried to get up. But she had paid a hard price.

Even now those vague, persistent shadows would not relent—the memory of a deep voice soothing her, the touch of disturbingly gentle hands as they bathed her face. She remembered the concern in that voice, the warmth in that touch. She remembered thinking how good it felt, how she—

Damn!

Val threw back the covers with a snarl. Taking a deep breath, she slowly hoisted herself to a sitting position. Gratified when the pounding in her head did not resume, she gradually drew herself to her feet. The room did a quick little whirl and Val grasped the bedpost. The room stilled and she risked a small smile. That wasn't so bad!

Val took one cautious step, only to pause as she spied her reflection in the mirror in passing. She was a sight in that old flannel nightgown someone had pulled over her long underwear, her hair sticking out in grimy spikes from the loose braid that hung down her back and dark circles under her eyes, emphasized by the whiteness of her face.

Val shrugged. Vanity was not one of her weaknesses. Pride, however...

Forcing a ramrod stiffness to her back, Val took another step, then another. She was walking with a deceivingly smooth gait as she entered the kitchen.

Red Hand turned as she approached. His skin was like weathered leather and a single feather dangled in the limp gray hair that lay against the shoulders of his ill-kept buckskins. Red Hand was a fixture in the kitchen, whom she accepted without thought.

She forced a casual tone as she held herself steady with sheer strength of will. "You're back early, ain't you, Red Hand? We don't usually see hide nor hair of you around here until after noon."

Discomfort crept up the back of Val's neck as Red Hand's rheumy old eyes assessed her. He had given her that same look too many times in the past eight years for her to mistake its meaning.

"Look here, Red Hand, I ain't stayin' in that bed another minute unless somebody ties me down." Regretting her unfortunate choice of words as Red Hand's eyes narrowed, Val released an impatient breath. "Where's my pa?"

Again Val waited for a response that did not come. So it was going to be one of *those* days.... Val's bloodshot eyes narrowed as the silent Indian turned back to the table and took his knife to a piece of beef. She was getting mad! "I asked you where Pa was, Red Hand. I'm tired of layin' in bed, and

I'm thinkin' my head might clear if I ride out for a little while. Especially if I can—''

Ugh! Red Hand cut himself and Val's stomach did a little flop as he wiped his hand casually on buckskin pants already amply stained and continued cutting the beef into chunks.

A quick assessment of the kitchen revealed a half-empty whiskey bottle on a stool in the corner, and Val groaned aloud. ''Where'd you get that bottle? You know Pa don't want you drinkin' in the house—especially *before* you cook.'' Bile rose in Val's throat. ''Red Hand, you—'' The knife slipped, and Val turned on a run.

Back in her room, Val leaned over the washstand bowl, her stomach revolting. Flopped on the bed moments later, too weak to move, she closed her eyes. It occurred to her as she finally escaped into sleep that her pa had left Red Hand at home to make sure she stayed in bed the way the doctor had ordered. And that old Injun had handled her. As always, he had handled her.

If he lived to be a hundred, Branch knew he would never forget this day. His stomach in knots, he glanced at the sky, relieved to see the sun dropping rapidly toward the horizon. He was still furious at the memory of that ungrateful twit's arrogance the previous day when she had ordered him from her room.

Red Hand and the men had returned shortly afterward. Supper was eaten and, for most, digested by the time the doctor arrived from town, although the food had lain on his stomach like a bucket of lead. Silent, furious, ready to bite off the head of anybody who came near him, he had watched the ranch house, knowing Val Stark was probably sick—sick from laughing at the way he had fawned over her as she'd pretended unconsciousness.

Damn the woman!

Forcing his mind back to the present, Branch glanced around him. It had been a long day. He had been working with the men in this section of range since sunup and they had stopped only for nature's call and their midday meal. Stark had been avoiding him, looking sheepish. He remembered Whalen's keen, silent assessment of the stiffness between Stark and himself and the feeling that the tall, dark cowhand derived a strange kind of satisfaction from it. He remembered the hidden glances he had gotten from the rest of the men: Wyatt, his lean face as noncommittal as he could make it; Wallace, mirroring Wyatt's neutrality; Little, his bulgy eyes fairly popping as Branch growled his orders; Smith and Simm, without comment; Potter, seeming to enjoy it all because he wasn't involved; and Boggs, whose main concern was his next meal.

Stark had spent most of the day working with them, and it was Branch's thought that he had probably done so in order to escape his daughter. His feelings had softened toward the old coot then, and his pity had swelled. The poor fella had as much of a chance of getting rid of her by marrying her off to some unsuspecting cowhand as tumbleweed did in the wind.

Turning at a signal from Stark, Branch nodded. Stark was going back to the ranch. A hungry rumble in his stomach indicated that it was time for the men and him to follow. They'd had a satisfactory day, despite his private aggravation, and the men had earned the good, hot meal they had waiting.

Branch unconsciously revised that last thought. A week of Red Hand's cooking had taught him that "hot" was possible, but "good"? Branch shook his head.

At his short command, the men began driving the last of the separated steers toward their temporary corral, and Branch frowned in postscript to his thoughts. If he had learned anything from the disaster of the previous day, it was that he was through making concessions to Valentine Stark because she was a woman. She claimed to be as good a cowhand as any man working at the Circle S—better than most, if he were to believe her. She wanted to be treated like one of the hands, and as soon as she sat her tail back in the saddle, he was determined she would get what she wanted.

No pushy, back-talking female was going to force him out of the chance of a lifetime! His blood was up. This was war!

Will Stark stood over his sleeping daughter's bed as the fading light of sunset streamed through the window of her room. His full gray mustache twitched with emotion as his narrow, lined face puckered into a frown. She'd given him the scare of his life the previous day, and he hadn't gotten over the fright of it yet.

The predicament he and Mary faced aside, he'd almost forgotten that his tall, strong-minded daughter was really female, after all. She had been as tough as nails after the day her ma had walked out on them. After she'd crawled up on his lap and cried for a whole day and night without stopping. He didn't think he'd ever forget the steely look in her eyes after she'd cried herself out, dried her tears and raised that stubborn little chin. She hadn't shed a tear since, and she had ridden at his side for so long without special favors that he had begun to think of her as one of the boys. But it had taken only one look at her yesterday as she lay in her bed, unable to raise her head, to scare the living hell out of him.

And it had taken only one look at Branch Walker's face as

he left Val's room for his already shaky hopes to begin collapsing around him.

Will forced away the thickness in his throat as Val's lashes fluttered and her lips moved with an unintelligible phrase. She looked like the ma she could hardly remember, with that clear skin and them eyes as gray as winter ice. Her hair was the same brown color of autumn leaves, and he knew beneath the grime of the trail it bore the same reddish highlights when touched by the sun. He had never said those words to Val because he knew she didn't want to hear them, but he was real glad that she didn't look like him. Will shuddered at the thought. But if he had suffered at losing Val's ma, for whatever reason she had left the two of them, he knew that that suffering would not compare with his feelings had Val truly been hurt in that fall from her horse.

'Cause the truth was, he loved her.

Val opened her eyes and Will was relieved when she said with a flicker of her former grit, "So you finally got home."

"That's right. I figured Branch could use some extra help gettin' the rest of them steers together today. I knew you was in good hands when I left Red Hand to watch over you."

Will turned to pick up the plate from the nightstand nearby. "Look what I got here, Val. You was sleepin' when the rest of us ate, but Red Hand saved you some of his stew." Val paled unexpectedly, and Will pressed, "Val...is somethin' wrong?"

Val turned with a groan and mumbled into her pillow, "I ain't hungry, Pa. Take it away."

"But—"

"Take...it...away."

Will pulled the door closed behind him as he stepped into the hall. His expression was puzzled as he looked down at the plate in his hand. Red Hand's stew didn't look no different than it ever did. Maybe Val was sicker than she looked.

Glancing back at the closed door, Will shrugged. Damn. He supposed he'd never really understand her.

Back in her room, Val turned to face the closing door, disgusted with the queasiness that the thought of Red Hand's stew again evoked. She closed her eyes and raised a shaky hand to her sweaty forehead. She was a sorry mess!

Taking a deep, steadying breath, she opened eyes that were suddenly hot with anger. She didn't know how all this had come about, but she knew it was tied directly to the arrival of Branch Walker. She also knew that the minute she was her old self again and back on her feet, she'd make him pay for each and every humiliation she had suffered—from the first to the last!

With the last spark of fervor in her draining spirits, Val declared in a hoarse whisper, "Damn you, Branch Walker! This is war!"

Chapter Four

Glancing out the window, Will could see the shafts of gold across the dawn-gray sky, promising a clear day to come. In the yard, the men were mounted and waiting, their breaths frosty puffs in the chill air as they conversed in low tones. Silent, sitting on his gelding a few feet apart from the men, his expression grim, was Branch Walker.

At a sound from the hallway behind him, Will turned to see his daughter step into sight, and his stomach curled into knots. Val's back was ramrod straight, her step deliberate as she walked across the parlor toward the door. All that was missing was a roll of the drums as she marched to battle. Val had not been a cooperative patient, despite Doc Pitt's warnings, and he knew it was only the severity of the headaches and the persistent dizziness that had kept her flat on her back. He also knew his daughter's mind had been working, and he didn't have to stretch his imagination far to realize what Branch Walker had in store for him.

Muttering an unintelligible phrase of frustration, Will rubbed a callused hand over his face, wondering, as he had so many times during the past week while Val had been recuperating from her fall, at the stupidity of the plan that had seemed so promising only a few months earlier. He did not, however, intend to allow things to worsen.

"Val!" His daughter turned toward him as she reached the door, and Will affixed a stern facade as he continued, "I'm tellin' you now, I don't want no trouble today. Things have been goin' pretty good for the past week. Branch's got most of the steers in the high pasture sorted out to his likin' and we've penned them that are goin' to be sold off. The calves will be ready for brandin' pretty soon, and—"

"I don't need no lesson on what's got to be done around a ranch, Pa!"

"Is that right?" Will's irritation stepped up a notch at the sharpness of his daughter's response. "Well, I'm thinkin' we all need to learn a lesson now and again, and that not a one of us should be too proud to admit it." Val stiffened, and Will pressed, "No trouble, you hear?"

Val's lip curled in a response that was little more than a snarl as she pulled open the door and marched out. She was already mounted by the time he cleared the doorway, her hat pulled low on her forehead, her lips a straight, angry line. Glancing toward Walker, Will saw that the fellow's jaw had turned to granite, and he had a gut feeling that optimism was a waste of time.

The chill of morning had evaporated with the rising of the morning sun, but the brilliance of the day was lost on Val as she sat her mount, a storm growing inside her. Again she had been relegated to the sidelines, and the knowledge that she could have turned to stone for all the work she'd done so far that day nagged at her mercilessly.

Her gaze roved the nearby rolling expanse of high grazing land, settling on Branch Walker's tall, broad frame, and she muttered an oath. She remembered their arrival at this section of winter pasture that morning and the crispness in Walker's deep voice as he gave the men instructions for the day. Her stomach did that same little flip-flop that she despised, as she recalled the way he had then looked directly into her eyes and ordered, "As for you, you sit tight! I don't want you gettin' in the way when we have serious work to do."

She remembered the strangled sound that had come from her pa as her eyes had narrowed into gray slits filled with deadly promise. In the time since, she had devised in her mind several ways of putting Branch Walker to slow, hideous death that surpassed the most innovative of Indian tortures. But try as she might, even under the most vicious of circumstances, she somehow could not envision Branch Walker begging for mercy.

Cursing her imagination for the traitorous convert that it was, Val followed Branch Walker with her malevolent gaze. He was everywhere in the group of Circle S riders, reacting with the nature of a man born to the task of command as his keen eyes took in each aspect of the work progressing around him. She saw fluid grace of movement as he sat on his gelded bay, and strength in his incredible stretch of shoulder and muscle. She saw rock-hard power as his long legs gripped his mount's sides and he wheeled in a display of horsemanship that caught her breath short. She saw, as he lifted his hat to wipe his arm across his forehead, light hair darkened with the sweat of honest work and strong features that left no question as to his grit and determination. Her heart skipped a beat, and she fidgeted, her anger suddenly erupting. If Branch Walker thought she was going to waste the day watching him, he had another think coming!

Turning her horse, Val kicked him into a sudden leap for-

ward that startled nearby cattle and riders alike. Riding away
from the herd at a pace that was just short of suicidal on the
rough terrain, she leaned low over her horse's neck, gripping
the startled gelding's reins tightly. Breathless, grinning as the
crisp air flattened against her face, feeling more alive than she
had felt for a long, frustrated week, she heard hoots of laughter
and the echo of Potter's voice as he shouted, "I win, damn
it! I knew she wouldn't sit there another five minutes!"

A glance over her shoulder at the riders she'd left behind
showed Branch Walker staring after her in motionless silence,
and it was with great satisfaction that Val heard her Pa's frustrated voice trailing, "Valenti-i-i-ne...!"

The furious knot in Branch's stomach now had a name. It
was Valentine Stark.

Watching as the hotheaded witch rode at breakneck speed
into the distance, Branch felt his hands ball into fists, and he
knew that if Valentine Stark was half the man she thought she
was, he would have already beaten her to a bloody pulp. Of
all the irritating, aggravating, thoughtless, empty-headed—

"That daughter of mine is goin' to break her neck!"

Turning toward Will Stark, who gaped in dismay after his
daughter's disappearing figure, Branch held back an instinctive
retort with supreme control. He had known from the instant
Val Stark had stepped out into the yard that morning that there
was going to be trouble. A week of peace from her acid
glances had not dimmed the memory of them, and he had
thought to nip her rebellion in the bud by showing her that *he*
was in control, whether she liked it or not. But things had not
worked out as he had planned, and there was no need to speak
the response to her father's comment that was so clearly written in his tight expression.

In the three weeks he had been on the Circle S, Stark's daughter had fought him at every turn, to the point where she had almost gotten herself stomped by an unbroken bronc and killed while trying to prove she was a better hand than she could ever hope to be. Now, in a show of bravado that was designed to tell him just exactly what he could do with the orders he had given her, she was off at a speed that showed no concern for life or limb. If he wasn't so determined not to give Val Stark the satisfaction, he'd tell old man Stark to take his job and its opportunities—

Stark's familiar sickly grin confirmed that there was no need for words, and Branch turned his head with a snap. Spotting a few cowpokes a short distance away who were grumbling as they slapped greenbacks into Jeff Potter's waiting hands, Branch barked, "Get back to work!"

The way the men jumped at his command brought his first true satisfaction of the day, and Branch rode away from old man Stark, knowing he could not risk another word.

Her first burst of elation dimming as her mount began blowing hard beneath her, Val felt a prick of conscience at her thoughtless treatment of the laboring animal. Dunbar was a valuable piece of horseflesh, and she had run the risk of losing him on an uneven terrain filled with potholes and other dangers invisible at such a speed.

Cursing her own lapse of sense, Val drew the animal back to a more reasonable pace, patted his sweaty neck and admitted to herself that the three weeks since Branch Walker's arrival had been worse than she had ever dreamed they could be. The realization that Walker put her on edge in a way she had never before experienced was difficult to accept, as was the knowledge that she had been made to look the fool more times during the previous three weeks than she had in the previous twenty years of her life.

She didn't like it.

Shivering with an unexpected chill, Val looked up at the sky, frowning. The weather was unpredictable this early in the season, and she was suddenly glad she hadn't yet shed her long underwear. That was a piece of horse sense she had learned during years of working at her pa's side through all kinds of weather. She had learned a lot more, too. She knew that the work was progressing well in the high pasture under Walker's direction and as soon as it was done, he'd be sending the men out to search for strays and for cows who had calved in the more isolated corners of the ranch, so they could begin branding as soon as possible.

Val straightened her back, her determination suddenly renewed. She knew every inch of Circle S range, every nook and cranny where a cow could hide. Walker didn't want her "gettin' in the way when there was work do be done," did he? Well, if she couldn't work *with* Branch Walker, she'd work *around* him.

A true smile lifting her lips for the first time that day, Val turned her horse northwest. She'd show Branch Walker what she was made of, and she'd make him eat his words.

At a gust of damp, cool wind, Branch reached for the brim of his hat and looked up at the sky. Rapidly moving clouds packed with rain were closing in overhead. The temperature had dropped from the balmy afternoon heat of an hour earlier, reminding him that they had a long way to go until spring was firmly entrenched in this high mountain country.

Branch glanced around him and raised his hand in a signal that started the cowhands driving the separated stock into the temporary corral so they could start the remaining animals toward lower ground. Keeping a distance from the cautiously moving herd, Branch felt satisfaction in knowing that he had men under him whom he could count on. So much depended on the first year on the Circle S. Although the ranch was growing and healthy, he knew that Will Stark didn't have the cash to waste on failed efforts.

Branch took a deep breath as uncomfortable memories returned. He had grown up with enough failed efforts to make himself forever cautious of them after his father, unwilling to face the devastation of the South at the end of the war, had taken his mother and himself West. It had been a difficult time for Branch Walker, Sr., a proud, frustrated man who was unwilling to compromise. He had maintained his ideals to the end, at a cost that had finally included his life.

Leona Walker, a frail woman whose gentility was the basis upon which Branch had compared and found most women lacking, had been unsuited to the hardships of the frontier. She had not survived her husband long, and at the age of fifteen, Branch was on his own.

Branch's unconscious frown tightened as he acknowledged the hard lessons life had taught him. He had leaned from his father's lost battles that change was inevitable, and no manner of combat, however, fiercely and loyally fought, could alter that fact. He had also learned that pride sometimes hindered a man's judgment to the point where reason failed him, but a quick, open mind learned something new every day. As a lonely young man, he had learned in the most difficult ways possible to avoid personal commitments that cut the most deeply and left the harshest scars when they went astray.

Branch had been a veteran of wars both personal and those fought on the range when he first met Alexander Swan. He had been tired of wandering and ready to settle into a niche that forced no personal obligation that he was unwilling to extend. Swan had impressed him with his dedication to improving his range stock, and Swan had been impressed in return.

Alexander Swan and he had learned the problems of controlled breeding the hard way—the high risk in breeding a Hereford bull to a first-calf heifer; the safety in taking the time to breed a longhorn or Mexican bull to ensure small, slim calves that would give the heifers little trouble. Swan and he had even begun segregating some animals so they might keep records of estimated birth weights expected from the different bulls, in an effort to protect the younger animals.

Branch paused at that thought, almost able to hear Val Stark's laughter at their efforts, and a familiar agitation grew. For all her pretense at understanding the true problems of ranching in this wild country, that shortsighted shrew couldn't see past her uppity little nose. It was damned aggravating to be challenged at every turn, to be tested and questioned like a green hand by a female who couldn't even manage to keep her tail in the saddle.

That thought brought back to mind the breakneck speed with which the irritating piece had departed that day, and Branch winced. He had felt Will Stark's eyes on him while his daughter had remained twitching with fury on the sidelines, but he had also known that if he was to make a success of this venture, he had to show her that she couldn't back him down.

Looking at Will Stark where he worked the other side of the herd, Branch felt his irritation grow. He had been hired to make a real contribution to the Circle S by setting a new standard for its stock—not to baby-sit a frustrated female! If Will

Stark said a word to him about the way he was handling things, he'd tell him so, too. The only trouble was, he knew Stark *wouldn't* say a word, as disgusted as he was with his daughter's resistance, and Branch knew that because of Stark's silence, *he'd* keep his mouth shut and suffer.

Riling him most of all was the realization that Val Stark didn't care about any of it. She would just keep pressin' on and on and on....

Val grunted with frustration as she dug deeper into her saddlebag for the work gloves normally stored at the bottom. Unable to find them, she finally dumped the entire contents on the ground, then glanced back at the bawling calf behind her that had somehow gotten penned by a fallen boulder. She resisted the urge to shout at its mother, who had been responding to the calf's cries for the past half hour with unrelenting bellows that had all but shattered Val's nerves.

Things had been going so well. She had arrived in the familiar northwestern corner of the range a few hours earlier. After taking the time to chew a piece of jerky to appease her growling stomach, she had begun rounding up the cows that returned time and again to their favorite pasture to calf. It had pleased her to know that a newcomer to the ranch would have missed many of the animals who demonstrated uncanny ability in finding crevices for protection from the weather that were almost undistinguishable to the eye. She had already rounded up an impressive number of cattle when she'd first noticed that the temperature was dropping and that thunderclouds were rapidly closing in overhead. She had started driving the mutinous animals toward lower ground when she'd heard that first bawling cry.

The calf was young, but of a good size. How it had gotten

pinned between a boulder and the rock wall of the mountain without being crushed was a mystery to her.

Val looked down at her scraped and bleeding hands. She winced, then bent to pick up her gloves. Callused as her hands were, she hadn't thought she'd need to protect them from the abrasive corners of the boulder she had been attempting to move. That had been her first mistake.

The frightened calf bawled again, eliciting another frantic response from the cow a few feet away, and Val's agitation rose another notch. The temperature was rapidly dropping and the wind was building. She knew snow, even at this time of year, was not impossible at this altitude. She also knew that the calf could not survive in a storm of any significance, pinned as it was.

A rumble of thunder sounded in the distance, and Val groaned. The storm was rolling in more swiftly than she had judged at first. Her mind began working rapidly. The boulder had been too heavy for Dunbar to move, and she had realized the moment she'd climbed over the rock to take a closer look that the calf was too heavy for her to lift by herself. She knew an attempt to haul the animal out with a rope would only cause the calf damage. She only hoped she had time to try another tack.

Quickly slipping on her gloves, Val reached for the small spade secured on her saddle. She turned back toward the calf to assess the slope of the land again. If she had it figured correctly, careful digging at the base of the rock would increase the angle on which the rock sat. She should then be able to tumble the boulder with the help of the natural grade and Dunbar's strong back. The calf would then be free...she hoped.

Darting a glance at the sky overhead, Val knew she was

taking a chance. The cattle she had gathered were grouped a short distance away, but they were getting edgy, and a storm like the one that seemed to be building could scatter them again. Also, if she delayed too long and the weather turned really bad, she'd have a difficult time driving them down by herself.

Val paused on that thought. Of course, she *could* ride for help....

Branch Walker's face popped before her mind's eye, and Val's lips twitched. Over her dead body.

Digging furiously minutes later, Val was relieved to find the dirt easier to move than she had expected. Her thoughts turned almost pleasant for the first time that day as she envisioned Walker's face when she drove this impressive herd down. She was fairly smiling, when a sudden, deafening crack of thunder sounded almost overhead, followed by a crack of lightning that struck nearby. She swore under her breath as the cattle jumped and took a few running steps. Dunbar was pulling at his tether, his eyes rolling, and Val shouted a sharp, "Stand, Dunbar!"

Relieved as her horse responded to command, Val stood up, knowing she needed only a few minutes more. Dropping the spade, she jumped up on the boulder. She was testing its angle against the rock wall, when the terrified calf gave a small leap, his slashing hooves striking her feet and knocking them out from under her. Falling with a jarring thump, Val slid into the crevice beside the bawling calf.

Thunder clapped and lightning struck almost simultaneously, sending a nearby tree crashing to the ground. Momentarily stunned, Val watched the cattle take off at a run, her heart plummeting at the sight of Dunbar galloping behind them, his reins trailing along the ground. Groaning aloud, Val realized there was not a thing in the world she could do to stop him.

The first huge drop of rain that splashed against Val's cheek almost sizzled, but the chill of the deluge that followed did not allow time for useless anger as she attempted to free her boot from the crack into which it had jammed when she fell. Pulling, straining, gasping as icy rain ran off the brim of her hat and down her neck, Val cursed with disbelief when she was unable to dislodge her foot.

She was still twisting, jerking, struggling minutes later when she realized the effort was useless. And then, like the bawling calf beside her, Val opened up her mouth and howled.

Branch swore under his breath. He had waited just a few minutes too long to run that last batch of cows to the lower pasture, and as a result they had gotten caught in the storm. And some storm it was, too. Hunching against the icy rain pelting his face, Branch adjusted his slicker and the tilt of his hat to eliminate the steady stream running down his neck, but it was no use. He was wet through, and he knew the rest of the men were, too.

Branch squinted into the distance as the ranch house came into view. He was tempted to laugh at the thought that he was actually looking forward to a cup of Red Hand's coffee. The light shining through the windows reached out into the premature darkness of the storm. It was a warm, welcoming sight that he knew would turn cold the minute he ran into the icy gray eyes of Val Stark.

Unconsciously kicking his mount to a faster pace, Branch saw his men do the same. Will Stark pressed into the lead, and Branch smiled. The old coot had a long way to go until dotage. He had worked just as hard as his hands the whole day long, and Branch had to respect him for it. He had a feeling that Stark and he could get to be real friends in time. He wished the same could be said for Stark's arrogant offspring.

Noting that Stark was suddenly pressing his horse to the limit, Branch strained to catch sight of anything that could have caused the man alarm. The house seemed quiet, almost deserted, except for the presence of Red Hand on the covered porch and Dunbar standing near the hitching post in front, still saddled, his reins hanging. Branch's lips tightened. So Val Stark hadn't even bothered to stable her horse. If she was his daughter, he'd teach her the right way to take care of valuable horseflesh and equipment, whether she liked it or not.

Stark reined to a halt and jumped to the ground with a haste that bespoke anxiety, and Branch pressed his horse forward with spontaneous concern. Standing beside Stark and Red Hand in the driving rain a moment later, he heard panic in the old man's voice.

"You say he came in dragging his reins?" Stark looked at the horse's gaping saddlebag as the Indian nodded. "Did you see the direction he came from?" The Indian shook his head and Stark gave a frustrated snarl as he turned to Branch. "I knew the minute I saw Dunbar standing here that somethin' was wrong. Val would burn the hide off any man who didn't tend to his horse before he settled himself in." Stark's anxiety deepened as he motioned to the gaping saddlebag, "What do you think this means? Do you think she met up with some kind of bandit? It looks like the saddlebag's been emptied."

Not taking the time to assess the cause for the unexpected fear that turned his blood cold, Branch responded, "Whatever happened to her, we didn't pass her on the way in, so it's safe to say she isn't able to make it to within shoutin' distance.

It's up to us to find her.'' Turning to the men who had gathered around, Branch instructed, ''You all know this spread better than I do, so fan out, and when you find her, fire two shots together at spaced intervals, and don't stop until you get back. Is that understood?''

Not waiting for reply, Branch ignored the hot coffee Red Hand was pouring into cups and turned to his horse. Oblivious to the loud claps of thunder and the ear-ringing strikes of lightning nearby that released a new deluge, he mounted. Within seconds he was heading back in the direction from which he had come.

Even the calf had stopped bawling. Turning an assessing glance toward the animal who shared her rocky prison, Val shivered anew. The rain had not relented since the sky had opened up on them, and no one had to tell her that the temperature was steadily dropping. Struggling to control her panic, Val knew what she could expect of the next few hours this time of year. It was not unusual in these mountains for the temperature to fall to near freezing through the dark hours of the night. The chattering of her teeth gaining new crescendo, Val knew what that meant. She was caught like a rat in a trap, just like the dumb animal beside her, and she had the feeling she could not make claim to any greater intelligence than his.

Incredulity swept over her. How had she gotten into this mess? Looking down at the boot wedged so firmly in the crevice between boulder and wall, Val tried once more to slide her foot free. She cursed her one extravagance of custom boots that fit her feet like a second skin. She had no idea how long she had been stuck there, but she had the feeling she had spent at least two hours calling for help that had not come. The only thing she knew for sure was that she was now so hoarse that her voice was a croak, that night would shortly fall and that even if Dunbar had returned home and everyone knew she was in trouble somewhere, no one would be able to find her in the dark in this out-of-the-way corner of the ranch. She was chilled to the bone, unable to stop quaking, her clothes were wet through, and her limbs had started to go numb. She did not want to think what the next few hours would hold.

Thunder crashed around her and Val covered her ears with her stiff hands, missing a sound that did not escape the frightened animal beside her. Suddenly picking up its head, the calf let out a low, moaning bawl, which was answered by an echoing bellow from the shadowed twilight. Straining her eyes, Val saw the calf's mother was returning, approaching at a steady pace. The calf cried out again, and the cow raised her head with a response that reverberated against the surrounding rocks despite the steady drumming of the rain.

Val groaned. As if things weren't bad enough, it would start anew, the relentless exchange between cow and calf that had made her almost crazy. But, then, maybe the two frustrated animals had already succeeded far better than she'd realized, because only a crazy woman would have tried to pull this calf out by herself, and only a crazy woman would find herself now stuck tighter than the animal she had tried to rescue. And only a crazy woman would be—

What was that? Straining to see into the shadowed distance, Val saw signs of movement. Disbelieving her eyes, she blinked and stared harder. It was a man on horseback! Someone was coming! Val called out, only to have her raspy croak overwhelmed by the calf's bawling complaints. Frustrated, she slapped at the frightened animal beside her in an attempt to silence him, but succeeded only in stimulating him to new and stronger efforts. Yet the rider was drawing closer. He was coming straight toward them.

Oh, no...it couldn't be...

Val closed her eyes, wishing with all the fervor remaining in her chattering, shivering body that she could dissolve into the muddy ground. When she opened her eyes again, an angry, black-eyed stare met hers. She swallowed as Branch Walker ordered gruffly, "Don't move—not a muscle! You're a goddamn walking calamity!"

She opened her mouth to speak, and Walker continued, "Save it! I don't want to know how you managed to get yourself stuck there, but I'll tell you that if it wasn't for old Mama here, you'd be lookin' at spendin' the night."

Val wanted to scream. She wanted to howl. She wanted to jump up and knock that denigrating look off Walker's stiff face. Instead she watched, shivering, as he affixed his rope around the boulder, tested it and turned to his horse in command. "Back, Caesar, back. That's it, boy."

Caesar? Val grimaced, her stiff face feeling as if it would crack. It figured that Walker would name his horse Caesar. An almost hysterical bubble of laughter escaped her lips. But Caesar wouldn't conquer this boulder. He wouldn't be able to move it in a million years.

The boulder rocked and swayed as Val stared at its rain-washed surface with incredulity. She was still staring as the massive rock moved with a grating sound and rolled a few feet down the incline to a sudden halt.

Val was still staring as the calf deserted her for his mother's side. She looked up into Branch Walker's face. His expression said it all. Suddenly hot with fury, she took a bold step forward, only to have her numb legs buckle.

She was pulling herself out of the mud, when Walker's

voice grated in her ear, "I told you not to move, but you never listen, do you? Well, this time you've gone too far."

Walker jerked her to her feet, and Val despaired at the stiffness in her limbs that allowed her little resistance. She attempted a reply, but her croak halted abruptly and her eyes widened as Walker drew his gun. Her eyes bulged as he cocked the hammer. She choked with a gasp the second before he turned the barrel toward the sky and fired twice.

She was weak with relief as Walker then ripped off his slicker, pushed her arms into the sleeves, picked her up bodily and sat her on his horse. Sparing only a moment to retrieve his rope, he got up behind her and kicked his mount into motion.

The rain pelted them unceasingly and Val's shuddering grew more violent as they rode with as much haste as safety allowed. She felt Walker's momentary hesitation before he drew her back against his chest, curling his body around her in protection against the abusive elements. She knew that if Walker had had his choice, he would have left her pinned by that boulder until both the calf and she putrefied. Leaning back against him, Val closed her eyes with the knowledge that if she had had *her* choice, he'd be the last man in the world whose saddle she would be sharing right now.

Silent, Val consoled herself with the thought that tomorrow would be another day.

Chapter Five

Tomorrow had come, but Val was uncertain she was up to it. The fickle weather had turned almost balmy in contrast to the frigid drop in temperature the previous night. The only trace of the storm remaining was in the deep mud through which Val squished on the way to the barn.

The slicker Walker had forced over her shoulders the night before had acted as an oven that had baked the mud against her skin as they had ridden home. She had arrived at the ranch stiff as a stick, numb, quaking beyond belief and unable to manage a decent response when Red Hand had taken one look at her and ordered, "She need to sweat!"

It had been at the tip of her tongue to respond that it was impossible for a person to sweat when she was certain she'd never be warm again, but her chattering lips would not cooperate. Instead she had allowed herself to be swathed in a blanket and pushed into a chair by the fire while the great copper tub was hauled inside and water heated to a boil.

After her second glass of red-eye, Val had lost her desire to protest that this was the second bath she had taken in two weeks, that her skin would peel off and blow away if she continued the unhealthy practice, and that all she wanted was to sleep. Instead she had stripped down and climbed into the tub, aware that her pa and Red Hand's return to the room the moment she was submerged indicated she had not gone totally unobserved.

It had galled her to admit that Red Hand was right. The steaming water and glass of red-eye in her hand raised a sweat that she had not thought possible, and as she leaned back, her head against the rim, her rigid limbs went slowly limp.

She hardly remembered the bar of soap that was dropped into the tub with her father's firm admonition to "Scrub!" She chose not to recall the giddiness that had assaulted her shortly afterward when she'd soaped her hair and submerged herself below the water until her pa had come running to the side of the tub, ready to drag her up. She was then ordered out of the tub, wrapped in a fresh blanket and guided to her room, where she slept like a log for the rest of the night.

This morning, however, she was paying in full for the liquor that had helped to relax her. Squinting as the brilliant sunlight started her head throbbing anew, Val groaned.

Breakfast had been impossible given the queasiness with which she had awakened, and she had barely managed to slip into her only change of clothing and locate her coat and hat so she could get some fresh air into her lungs. The silence of the house and surrounding yard indicated that her pa and the men had already left, and she was glad. She wasn't up to facing any one of them yet.

A familiar snorting greeted her as she entered the barn, and Val walked directly toward Powderkeg's stall, deliberately ignoring the traitorous Dunbar. She winced as Aubrey Whalen's loud voice reverberated in her pounding head.

"How you feelin' today, boss lady? The boys and me were

right worried when we found out your horse came back without you yesterday—you bein' a helpless woman and all.''

Val turned a slow, measuring look to see Potter and Simm standing nearby, unable to conceal their grins as she croaked, "I ain't no more helpless than you are, Whalen." Then she shrugged, adding in a deliberate afterthought, "But I guess that don't say much, does it?"

Whalen's smile turned nasty. "That was you the boys and me saw Walker totin' back last night, wasn't it? You was limp as a rag doll, layin' all over him."

"Liar! I was stiff as a stick!"

Potter's hoot of laughter brought her drilling gaze to his face as his gray whiskers twitched with amusement. "You shoulda seen yourself, Val! You was a sight, all covered with mud and your legs hardly workin' when Walker stood you on your feet. He slung you over his back and carried you in the house like a sack of potatoes, and you was so far out of it that you hardly knew the difference." Potter shook his head, his enjoyment increasing, "That big fella's sure cut you down to size."

Val was starting to twitch. "Is that what he's sayin'?"

"He don't have to say nothin'," Simm interrupted, his boyish face pleased. "You met your match, Val. There ain't no way you're goin' to better that big fella or back him down."

"There ain't?" Val's laughter was deliberate. "There ain't a thing that man can do that I can't do better. And I'll bet you that given some time, I can back him down to where he'll hightail it out of here like the devil was after him."

A chorus of laughter was their only response and Val's blood surged up another notch. Taking a step backward to strike a casual pose against the stall door, she knocked up the brim of her hat to expose a cocky smile. "Think that's funny, do you, boys? How would you like to put some money where your mouth is?''

"Oh, no Val, we couldn't take that bet." Potter was still laughing. "That would be stealin'!"

"Think so? What about you, Whalen? You're always shootin' off your big mouth. Want to put a month's pay on it?"

"A month's pay?" Whalen's smile was slick. "How long's this supposed to take you? A year?"

"Three months and he'll be runnin' like a jackrabbit."

"I'll take that bet."

"How about you, Simm?" Val's gray eyes were twin daggers that pinned the younger fellow's gaze. "Care to back up your big mouth with some hard cash?"

Simm's smile brightened. "Sure do!"

"Don't go gettin' in over your head, Val." Potter interrupted with the first trace of concern. "That Branch Walker is one tough fella. He ain't about to let nobody best him, especially a woman."

"Seems to me that I heard that same speech from each and every one of you fellas here, and I showed you all, one by one, that bein' a woman don't hold me back at all."

"But Walker's different."

"Put up or shut up, Potter!"

Potter suddenly grinned. "All right, I'm in."

"Done."

Reaching out, Val shook each man's hand in turn, her grip causing Simm to wince with a low "It ain't me you got to prove somethin' to, Val. It's Walker."

"Right. And his day is comin'." Turning without another word, Val headed back for the house, her step brisk. She'd have died before she'd let any one of the men left staring behind her know what each jarring step cost her. And she'd die before she'd let any of them win.

Mary McGee glanced in the mirror as she walked toward the door of her room. She saw what she normally saw reflected there, a plump, middle-aged woman dressed in black, whose gray hair was neatly pinned to her nape with the same pins she had used for more years than she cared to count. She saw clear skin showing the inevitable marks of time, brown eyes with a fine network of crow's feet at the corners and a mouth that smiled often. Without a second thought, she had accepted the changes that time had wrought at each step in the aging process, but it was only recently that she had begun wondering about the woman her darling Wilbur had brought to life inside her.

A soft giggle unbefitting the sober widow-woman that she was escaped Mary's lips. She had been married to Charlie McGee for twenty-six years, and she had loved him dearly. But she had never *lusted* after him.

Mary blushed. She remembered the first time Wilbur had touched her. It had been her ranch hands' day off, and she had decided after they'd left that she needed some things from town. She had only gotten a few miles from the ranch, when her wagon had lost a wheel. Near panic at her helplessness on the lonesome sagebrush flats, she could still remember the burst of elation she'd experienced when Wilbur had ridden into sight over the rise. She remembered his shy smile, and the twinkle in his eye that she had never noticed before in all the years she had known him. She had watched him as he'd worked, marveling at his strength as he'd fixed the wheel. She had wondered how it would feel to have his strong arms around her—to feel that soft gray mustache tickling her lips.

Mary's flush deepened. The direction of her thoughts had left her trembling when he was finished, and Wilbur had been concerned enough about her condition to volunteer to drive her back home. She had offered to make him something to eat, but before the steak and potatoes had finished cooking, she was in his arms.

Mary walked out of the bedroom and into the kitchen, a spring in her step that bespoke the day of the week—her ranch hands' day off. She had arisen at daybreak, baked a cherry pie and cleaned her house until it shined. She had been singing at the top of her lungs all through the bath she had taken using the lavender soap Wilbur had bought her. She sighed. Wilbur did love the way she smelled, and he had so many delightful ways of demonstrating his pleasure.

She had then changed to a fresh dress and apron and dreamed of the day she could dispense with black to wear the colors of a bride. Mary's smile dimmed. She knew there was the possibility that day might never come, but she did not fault Wilbur for his devotion to his daughter. The poor girl had suffered. She could still remember the expression on the child's face the first time she had come to town after her mother had run away. Valentine had been barely four, but the scars were visible even then. Mary remembered telling Mr. McGee that the girl might never truly recover from the loss, and she had wondered how the child's mother had been able to give her daughter up so easily, while she, who had remained childless all of her life, would have given anything in the world to have her.

Mary forced her smile brighter. But even if it was not meant to be that Wilbur and she should marry, she knew that he loved her as much as she loved him. Their passion was a gift from the Almighty for their old age, and she was determined they would enjoy it.

A tear slipped from the corner of Mary's eye. But she wished...

At a sound of a horse's whinny in the distance, Mary's heart began pounding. She glanced at the clock on the kitchen wall. It was close to eleven. It had to be Wilbur.

Brushing away all trace of tears, Mary took a deep breath and rushed for the front door. Out on the porch, she strained her eyes into the distance, but as Wilbur's horse drew nearer, she became concerned. Something was wrong.

Will's spirits were dragging along on all fours, but he knew he would have gone to see Mary that day if he had been forced to crawl. The McGee ranch house came into sight, and the downward droop of the many lines that marked Will's face lightened as he unconsciously urged his mount to a faster pace. He glanced up at the sun, grateful that the weather that had struck the night before had dissipated, returning to the unseasonable, almost balmy warmth of before. He only wished the aftermath at his ranch would settle as peacefully, but he had no illusions on that score.

Will shook his head, at a loss to understand the unexplained accidents his normally hard-riding, hardworking daughter had experienced of late. He had almost had a stroke the previous night, thinking that Val might be lying wounded and dying somewhere in the dark with the storm crashing over her head. She had looked like a whipped puppy when Branch had brought her back, as weak and trembling as she was, and the sight of her had shaken him. He still remembered the look on Walker's face when he'd dumped Val unceremoniously in a parlor chair and left without a word.

Will shook his head again. He had the feeling that the Circle S was going to become a battleground when Val was back on her feet, and that thought had driven him from the house as soon as he was able to sneak away.

Will searched the distance with weary eyes. *Mary...where are you? I need you, Mary.*

As if in response to his silent summons, a well-rounded figure appeared on the McGee front porch, and a smile picked up the corners of Will's lips. It was Mary.

It had been difficult to admit to himself, a man embittered by love, that he was *in* love again after so many years. He didn't truly know how it had come about. He had known Mary for so long without really knowing her at all, and then had come that day he had found her stranded with the wagon. He remembered turning around after fixing the wheel to look at Mary. She'd been shaken by the accident to the point where she was trembling, and he'd driven her home. She'd asked him in for a meal, and he had gotten more than he'd either expected or deserved.

Wilbur groaned. He wanted to marry the widow, to share his life and his bed with her, but he was not stupid enough to bring her home to live in the same house with Val. He had no desire for a premature death.

Forcing all further thought from his mind as he reached Mary's front porch, Wilbur deliberately rode around to the side of the house and slipped his horse into the barn, knowing he need do so to protect Mary's good name from gossip. But he hated the subterfuge. He hated anything that kept Mary out of his arms one minute longer than was necessary.

"Wilbur?" Will turned at the sound of Mary's voice, suddenly shy as he always was in the face of the love he felt for this woman. He walked out of the barn and onto the porch to look down into her concerned expression. "Is something wrong, Wilbur?"

Wilbur took a deep breath and said the words he had been dreading to say. "It ain't goin' to work, Mary. I ain't done nothin' but make matters worse by bringin' Branch Walker to the Circle S. Val's losin' her head, actin' crazy, and I'm goin' to have to do somethin' about it before she ends up killin' herself while tryin' to prove how good she is to Walker. I'm tellin' you, if looks could kill, I'd have bled to death already from them daggers Walker's been throwin' at me."

Mary paused to consider his words before responding softly, "Don't upset yourself, Wilbur." Sliding her arm through his, Mary drew him along with her into the house, and Will sighed at the balm of her touch. Turning as they stepped through the doorway, Mary whispered, "Don't think about it now."

Mary reached up unexpectedly to stroke his mustache, her face becoming suddenly serious as she stared at his lips and whispered, "At least we're together."

His heart pounding, Will whispered in return, "That we are, darlin'," before sweeping his loving widow-woman up into his arms with a grunt and heading for the hall.

Branch glanced up at the midafternoon sky and growled. Would this day never end? Looking around him, he saw that most of the other men had dismounted and were eating the smoked meat and sliced bread that was their usual fare when they spent the day on the range. He felt no consolation at the thought of a full stomach or the realization that the day's work was already half-done.

His mood had been less than amicable when he'd awakened that morning. He had spent a restless night after the previous day's fiasco. The memory of Val Stark splashing noisily in her bath in the kitchen as he consumed a cold supper in the dining room had given him little peace. Will Stark had been liberal with the red-eye, dispensing it freely to all the men who had spent hours searching for his daughter in the freezing rain, but the liquor had failed either to lighten his mood or to warm him. Instead his agitation had grown.

He remembered that Val Stark's body had been quaking as he'd mounted his horse behind her, the tremors so violent that he'd doubted she would have been able to remain in the saddle had he not been holding her. He remembered that he had opened his coat and enclosed her inside against the warmth of his body, wet slicker and all, and that he had pulled off her hat and tucked her head against his neck, allowing the wide brim of his hat to shield them both from the rain. He remembered the scent of her had filled his nostrils, a surprisingly pleasant fragrance of woman, earthy and warm.

Her wet hair had smelled of fresh soap, and the curling tendrils at her hairline had tickled his chin. He remembered telling himself as his concern for her had grown, as he'd pulled her closer, that she was a viper who had only temporarily lost her venom, and that he needed to beware. He remembered that he'd been angry that she had put her life at risk just to spite him, and his feelings then had become so conflicting that he had spent most of the night trying to sort them out.

He had not succeeded, and he had awakened foul dispositioned, with a headache and a driving need to take it all out on somebody, even if it was the men around him. The bad humor he had held in check had finally exploded when they had reached the corral in the high pasture where they had penned some stock the day before and found the rails kicked out and the stock gone.

Simm, Whalen and Potter had returned from the ranch a

half hour earlier, taking much longer than he'd felt necessary to bring the tools and supplies they'd needed to make the necessary repairs. He hadn't liked the looks on their faces, either, or the way they'd waited until his back was turned to conduct a conversation with the other men that set off a round of laughter.

Suddenly furious at the delay caused by the damaged corral, at cowhands who were enjoying themselves far too much not to be up to something and at the nagging scent of a certain woman that would not leave his mind, Branch drew himself to his feet. He lifted his hat from his head to run his hand through his heavy hair, allowing himself a few seconds before he barked, "All right, get back to work! You fellas have wasted enough time today."

Walking directly back to his horse, Branch was struck by the thought that because of Val Stark, the past three weeks had been the longest, most irritating three weeks in his entire life. Turning, he caught Simm's snicker, and he knew that he was not the only one who realized that he was in line for many more.

The house was silent as Will lay beside Mary in her fresh, downy bed, looking into her loving expression. Cupping her cheek with his callused palm, he pressed a wet kiss against her lips with a fervent "I love you, Mary."

Mary's response was to press her soft warmth against his sinewy frame. Will sighed at the joy of it. Tangling his hand in the long, unbound length of her hair, he tucked her face into his neck with a mumbled endearment. Mary's hair was sweet smelling and warm, just like the rest of her.

Wilbur paused, uncertain what he had ever done to deserve this late-arriving gift in life. With a low sigh of contentment, he stroked Mary's back, finally willing to risk a voice as he looked down lovingly at her once more.

"Mary, darlin', you're the best thing that ever happened to me. You're more than I could ever—"

The unexpected rattle of an approaching wagon broke into Will's words and he felt the responsive stiffening of Mary's body as she gasped, "Who's that?"

"I don't know. You'd better go out and see."

"Oh, Wilbur..." Mary struggled to her feet, grabbing her dressing gown as she dashed into the hall to peek toward the front door. Back in a moment, she was gasping. "It's Maybelle Higgins! She's the biggest gossip within two hundred miles. If she sees you here—" Mary's brown eyes filled with panic as she rasped, "You have to hide! Quick!"

Not allowing him time for response, Mary ran back into the hall, pulling the door closed behind her. Will jumped to his feet, standing stiffly, uncertain where to turn.

Taking the time for a few steadying breaths as she reached the front hall, Mary pulled her dressing gown tight around her, smoothed her hair against her head and eased the door open.

Maybelle eyed her from head to toe as she approached and entered without awaiting an invitation. When the door closed behind her, she stated boldly, "You look terrible, Mary. Are you sick?"

Nodding with an anemic smile, Mary stepped back, grateful for the excuse the woman had inadvertently provided. "As a matter of fact, I am, Maybelle. I was in bed...resting."

"Why, you poor dear, all alone and unwell."

Maybelle's small eyes took on a sense of purpose as she reached up to remove her hat, and Mary's insides cringed as she responded, "I'll be fine if I just can get some sleep."

"I'll wager you haven't had anything to eat today. Well, I'll take care of that." Maybelle removed her coat, exposing her buxom proportions as she took Mary's arm and drew her toward the hall. "Come on, we'll just tuck you into bed first."

"No! I mean—" Mary's eyes widened as she jerked back from Maybelle's compelling grip. "I'll be all right."

"Nonsense! Come on, right back in bed with you."

Dragged down the hallway, protesting every step of the way, Mary felt her face drain of color as Maybelle pushed open her bedroom door and pulled her inside. A glance around the room revealed no sign of Wilbur, and Mary released a tight breath.

Realizing she had no choice, she turned back the blanket to climb into bed, when she saw the corner of Wilbur's faded blue shirt protruding from underneath. She kicked it quickly out of sight, wincing as her toe came into contact with something that had the feel of a soft, human part. Oh, no...

"Now you just take off your dressing gown and I'll tuck you in."

Mary shook her head and swallowed. "No, I...I'm cold. I'll leave it on for a little while."

A trifle perplexed, Maybelle finally shrugged. "I'll make you some tea."

"That isn't necessary. Really, Maybelle, all I need is a little rest."

Halting midstep, Maybelle turned toward Mary, her thin lips puckered with annoyance. "It won't do you any good to protest, Mary McGee. I don't intend leaving here until you've had something to eat and I'm satisfied that you're feeling better. I don't care if it takes a week!"

Maybelle stomped out of the room, a woman with a mission, and Mary felt a swelling sense of panic. She waited until the click of the woman's heels against the wooden floor faded before whispering into the unnatural silence that followed, "Wilbur, are you there?"

A muffled "Yes, I'm here" came from beneath the deep, feathered bed.

Mary swallowed and whispered more softly, "Wilbur, she said *a week*."

"Oh, Mary…"

Two hours later, Mary forced down the last of her lunch under Maybelle's watchful eye and darted another look at the clock on her dresser. Would the woman never leave? Only infrequent words had been exchanged between Wilbur and her when Maybelle left on quick trips to the kitchen, but Mary was keenly aware that she hadn't heard a sound from Wilbur in over an hour.

Her panic a tight lump in her throat, Mary handed her empty plate back to the unrelenting woman. "I can't eat another thing, Maybelle. I appreciate your efforts, but I'd like to rest now, if you don't mind. A few hours' sleep before the ranch hands return will do me a world of good."

Maybelle's full gray brows knit over her sharp nose in annoyance as she responded, "I've been so busy catering to your illness that I haven't really had the time to tell you all the gossip you've missed in the past few weeks since I saw you. The whole town is buzzing with the news of Annie McCallum's affair with that old saddle tramp Fred Barton, you know. Can you imagine, at their age! You'd think they'd have more sense! And then there's Calvin Woods…you know him. He—"

"Some other time, Maybelle. I'm really very tired. If you wouldn't mind leaving…"

Mary's voice trailed off as her unwelcome visitor swelled to her full height with a tight "Well!"

Turning with the plate in her hand, Maybelle mumbled loudly as she left the room, "I'll take this dish to the kitchen and wash it. I wouldn't want to be accused of leaving anyone's house dirty. I'm far too good a housekeeper to let anyone think…"

Still talking, Maybelle turned into the hallway, unaware that the sound of her trailing words was suddenly overwhelmed by a harsh grating noise coming from underneath the bed. Mary froze, knowing Maybelle would be returning within a few seconds. Then she heard it again, that low, sawing sound.

Oh, Lord! Wilbur was snoring!

Maybelle's imminent return signaling time for desperate measures, Mary gave a short, hard jump on the bed, which elicited a grunt from underneath as the mattress bumped against the floor. The snoring stopped abruptly, a moment before Maybelle walked back into the room with her coat in her hand, her expression injured.

"I'll forgive you for your inhospitality this time because I know you're ill, Mary, and because I know you'll regret your short temper tomorrow." Batting her small eyes, she continued, "Neighbors are so few and far between in this country, that we must treat them wisely. I thought you had learned that lesson after all these years, but I was obviously wrong."

Pausing to allow Mary time for a response, which did not come, Maybelle added in a huff, "Goodbye, then. I'll tell your foreman that you're not yourself should I see him when I return to town, and I'll send him right home."

"You needn't do that, Maybelle. I'll be all right."

"If you say so."

Maybelle turned toward the door and Mary waited until the

woman stepped out onto the porch to call out to her retreating back, "Thank you!"

Maybelle's responding "Humph!" the most welcome sound she had ever heard, Mary waited for the sound of the wagon departing from the yard before throwing back the covers and leaping from bed. Dropping to her knees, she peered into the narrow opening between bed and floor to see Wilbur flattened there, clutching his clothes and boots, still naked as the day he was born. An unexpected giggle escaping her throat, Mary reached underneath to help Wilbur as he moved stiffly out into the open.

Drawing herself to her feet alongside him a few moments later, Mary looked into her love's pained expression, another giggle weakening the effect as she whispered sympathetically, "Oh, Wilbur, I'm so sorry."

"Mary, darlin', it ain't really so funny, you know." Wilbur could not seem to manage a smile. "I'm damn near flat as a pancake from being squashed against that hardwood floor for so long. And I think I picked up some splinters, too."

"Oh, dear…" Her smile fading to an expression of heartfelt commiseration, Mary raised her mouth to his. "Would you like me to make it all better, dear?"

Will's eyebrows popped upward as Mary's arms slipped around his neck and a familiar glow appeared in her bright eyes.

Meeting her halfway, Will was, for the brief period that followed, the happiest man alive.

Lying on his bunk after a long day on the north range, his arms cushioning his head, Branch realized he had just about reached the end of his tether. He had returned to the bunkhouse with the boys shortly after supper, his stomach filled with aggravation. Now, a half hour later, after going over the scene around the table countless times in his mind, he had come to the conclusion that Will Stark and his daughter were *both* crazy.

Not that he would truly have expected a word of thanks from Val Stark for practically saving her life the night before. Hell, no! The girl didn't have a gracious bone in her body. But neither had he expected to be treated like her worst enemy and to be shot a continual barrage of sniping remarks and challenging glances. He was getting damned tired of it.

Then there was Will Stark. A strange smile had remained on the man's lips throughout the meal. Nothing had been able to shake it. Simm had remarked that the boss seemed unusually mellow, but as far as Branch was concerned, Stark had had the look of a man who had gone soft in the head.

Suddenly disgusted with himself for having allowed Val's sniping to get the best of him earlier, Branch drew himself to his feet. His pouting behavior of the previous half hour was no more excusable than her nonsensical attitude, and he wasn't about to let that crazy female make him as crazy as she was.

Standing in his stocking feet, Branch looked at the men around him. Involved in their various nightly chores, they were conversing in low tones, carefully avoiding him. Realizing he was playing into Val Stark's hands by inadvertently alienating the men, Branch frowned. Walking to the washbowl in the corner, he poured some fresh water and splashed it on his face and hair. He then rubbed himself dry and ran his fingers through his hair. Refreshed, he turned to the men sitting at the circular table in the center of the room.

"When's that poker game you were talkin' about goin' to start, Potter? I'm feelin' mighty lucky."

Potter looked up. "I didn't think you was interested tonight.

Anyhow, Wyatt doesn't want to play, and neither does Boggs." Potter shot Boggs a sneer. "I'm thinkin' our hungry friend here is thinkin' of sneakin' back into the house to see if Red Hand threw out the leftovers yet." Branch's expression was incredulous, and Potter grimaced. "There's no figurin' some people."

Turning to the men around him, Potter inquired, "Anybody else interested in a game?" Potter smiled at the positive response of Little and Smith. "I'll get the cards."

Relieved to see an easing of the tension that had prevailed only a few minutes earlier, Branch pulled out a chair. At a knock on the door, he looked up, startled to see Val Stark enter as bold as brass.

Obviously not as surprised as he, Potter gave a short laugh. "Well, well, I was wonderin' if you was goin' to show up to play, Val. You walked out with half my poke last time, and I've a mind to get even."

Her eyes intent, Val did not smile in return as she pulled out a chair and announced, "There ain't nobody gettin' even tonight, boys—except me. So don't go puttin' any money on the table that you ain't prepared to lose."

Unable to ignore the challenge, Branch gritted his teeth in a smile. "That so, *ma'am?*"

Val's smile turned to pure acid. "That's so."

Plopping his backside in the chair with a vengeance, Branch watched Val Stark do the same. He ignored the looks the other men exchanged as he snarled, "Deal!"

More was at stake than the pot heaped in the middle of the poker table, and Val struggled not to let the others see her sweat. It had been a tough two hours, which had started off too good to be true, and she knew now that she should have prepared herself for the change of luck through which she was presently struggling. A glance at the table revealed that her funds had dropped drastically within the past half hour, and she did not have to look far to see who the big winner presently was.

Val suppressed a low curse and darted a sharp glance up at Simm as he hung annoyingly over her shoulder. His response was to step back with a widening of the grin that had been on his lips from the first moment her luck had started turning bad. She was aware that the game had gradually gained the attention of all the men in the bunkhouse as the second hour unfolded, and she knew it was not coincidental that the timing conformed to the period when Branch Walker started to emerge as the big winner of the evening. Her irritation stepping up a notch at the unconscious unity of the sexes, Val was determined not to allow herself to feel as alone as she presently was in this room full of Walker's supporters.

Glancing up again from the cards in her hand, Val surveyed the faces around the table. Potter, sitting directly across from her, was twisting the whiskers on his chin again. She knew she didn't have to worry about him this time, because that unconscious gesture meant he wasn't holding anything better than a pair. Little sat next to him, his bulging eyes betraying him. No contest there. To his right was Randy Smith, his fair skin flushed the color of his red hair. The knot in Val's stomach began to ease. Smith was set to fold. Out of the corner of her eye, Val glanced to the man seated beside her, only to come up against the same problem she had run into all evening long. Branch Walker's face was a blank wall.

A nervous jiggling started in her stomach as Val considered the cards in her hand. A full house—three tens and a pair of kings.... Realizing that at any other time she would already have considered the hand won, Val frowned more darkly. If she played cautiously, she would have enough money left for another hand should she lose this, but the sizable pot beckoned her. The time limit for the game was almost up, and she was not ready for another defeat at the hands of Branch Walker.

A nervous cough across the table turned her attention to Potter as Little nudged him impatiently. "We ain't got all night, Potter. Come on, are you in or not?"

Potter's whiskers twitched the second before he slapped his cards down on the table with disgust. "Hell, no use bluffin'. I ain't had a good hand all night."

Little shrugged. "I ain't been any luckier than you and I ain't losin' anythin' else on this hand. I'm out."

Randy Smith's fair face flushed as he threw his cards down on the table without comment, and Val released a tense breath. She'd been right about all of them. Now if she could only read Walker as easily as she could the rest.

Walker tapped his cards on the table as he looked into her eyes in direct challenge. His lips quirked in a way that set her heart to thumping as he said, "Well, I guess it's just you and me, *ma'am*. I suppose I'll have to raise you five dollars."

Five dollars! Val looked down at the bills beside her hand. The lowdown snake! He had counted her remaining cash, and he was trying to back her into a corner. Well, if he thought he was going to bluff her out now, he was wrong.

Val's smile dripped venom as she pushed her last five bills into the center of the table. Aware that all eyes were upon her, she laid out her cards and said, "Let's see if you can beat a full house, Walker."

His face never changing, Walker spread out his cards beside hers. His tone was heavy with mock regret as he drawled, "It goes against my grain to beat the pants off a lady." And as

Val stared with disbelief at a royal flush, he continued, "Excuse me, ma'am. I didn't mean you."

Val jumped to her feet, her face bloodred as Walker raked in his winnings. She stood stiffly as Walker looked up, smiling for the first time. Her heart did that annoying flip-flop as his hard features softened, but his dark eyes remained hard as flint as he said unexpectedly, "Now don't go away mad. Tell you what I'll do. I'll give you a chance to get even." When there was no response, he continued with a deliberate drawl, "You know, I've been admirin' those boots of yours. Handmade, aren't they? How about one more hand, just you and me. I'll put up all my winnings against those pretty boots."

Val knew what Walker was doing, baiting her, but he was enjoying himself too much for her not to take the chance of being able to wipe that smirk off his damned handsome face. Affixing a grin on her lips, as well, Val sat down abruptly with a short "Deal the cards."

The room was deadly quiet minutes later as Walker laid out four queens. A stream of curse words moved across Val's thoughts as she viewed the three kings in her hand and stared into those hard, mocking eyes. She slapped down her cards and pushed back her chair. Struggling, she pulled off one boot, then the other, and stood in her stocking feet. She met his gaze with a look that showed no sign of defeat as she said with barbed sweetness, "I know these boots will look damned pretty on you, Walker, so you enjoy them, hear?"

Spontaneous laughter followed her out the door, but Val realized that hers was not the last laugh as she walked through the rapidly freezing mud, her toes curling. As she entered the house, her pa looked down at her stocking feet, and she grated before turning into the hall, "I'm warnin' you, Pa. Don't ask!"

* * *

The last rumble of laughter had died down an hour earlier. The bunkhouse was in darkness, but still Branch stared at the bunk over his head as he wondered for the hundredth time why his victory over the stiff-necked Val Stark was suddenly so empty.

The reason she had shown up to play had been obvious from the first moment she'd entered. He had sensed her luck changing, and with the instinct of a predator, he had pressed for the kill. That last touch had been inspired—the direct confrontation, just her and him, the entire pot for her boots. It had been a risk worth taking just to see the arrogant spitfire walk out in her stocking feet.

But his victory had turned sour, and he was at a loss to discover why. Was it the way Val Stark had faced the humiliation of removing her boots with a proud lift of her chin? Was it that last quip that had set the men to laughing and shaking their heads at her grit? Or was it the pure pluck and determination in the set of her proud shoulders as she walked out the door in her bootless feet, without looking back?

Whatever it was, it was keeping him up, and he suddenly realized that feeling the way he did, he hadn't come out the victor, after all. Rolling abruptly to his feet, Branch reached for his pants and boots. Within minutes he was dressed and walking silently toward the door.

On the ranch house porch a few minutes later, he walked quietly to the front door and stopped, looking down at the boots he carried for the first time. Had Val Stark known exactly what she was saying when she had told him to *enjoy* the boots? Had she known that her humiliation would sit poorly on his shoulders, no matter how genuinely she had earned it?

Those questions still unanswered in his mind, he placed the boots in front of the door and walked back to the bunkhouse.

Back in bed a few minutes later, Branch breathed a sigh of relief and closed his eyes to sleep.

The first light of dawn filtered through Val's window, and she opened her eyes, realizing she hadn't had a good night's sleep since the arrival of Branch Walker. Pulling her weary bones out of bed, determined to be up and gone before the hands arrived for breakfast, she lit her lamp and reached for her clothes.

Fully dressed a few minutes later, her gun on her hip, Val walked to the mirror and took a fast brush to her waist-length hair. Two baths in two weeks—she smelled like one of them town women with their prissy dresses and flirty looks. She didn't like it. The sweet smell of cologne was all she could really remember about her ma, and she had resolved long ago never to be like her in any way. However, as she efficiently braided her hair with the skill of long practice, she could not deny the pleasure she received from its silky texture without the dirt of the trail clinging there.

Finally securing her braid, Val looked down at her stocking feet. Her hair and her boots—her two extravagances, and Branch Walker had already managed to claim one. Her stomach fluttered annoyingly, and Val frowned. Well, she'd replace her boots and she'd keep her hair, and then she'd go about the task of showing every cowhand on the ranch that she was twice as good as any one of them and a match for Branch Walker any day of the week.

Determination in the firm set of her jaw, Val arrived in the kitchen a few minutes later. She halted abruptly as Red Hand's rheumy eyes assessed her from the top of her head to the tip of her stocking feet.

Her eyes narrowing, Val grated, "I ain't answerin' no questions today, Red Hand, so don't waste your time askin'." She snatched up a biscuit and turned toward the door. "If anybody wonders where I went, tell them I said it's none of their business."

Val could feel Red Hand's look boring into her back as she walked out of the kitchen, but she shrugged it off. Having one pa was bad enough. She didn't need no Injun sticking his nose into her affairs.

Jamming her hat on her head as she walked across the parlor, Val slipped her arms into her coat and was about to step out onto the porch, when she caught sight of her boots standing just outside the front door.

Her boots? No, they weren't *her* boots anymore, and she wouldn't be caught dead wearing them.

Carefully stepping around them, Val walked across the porch, her chin high, her stocking feet silent against the weathered boards as she headed for the barn. Minutes later she was mounted and riding toward town.

Watching from the bunkhouse window as Val Stark rode out of the yard, Branch swore under his breath. Making a sudden decision, he turned, pulled on his clothes, grabbed his coat and hat and started for the door. Stopping as Potter began stirring in his bunk, he grated, "Tell Stark I'll be back later. Tell the boys to finish rounding up the rest of the strays and to make sure those critters don't get out of the corral this time."

Not taking the time for another word, Branch headed toward the barn.

The town of Clearmont came into view and Val heaved a deep sigh of relief. She'd never been so happy to see that rutted main street in her life. She kicked Dunbar to a faster pace, wincing at the pain it caused her nearly numb feet, grateful she'd soon be wearing boots again.

The prickling sensation at the back of her neck that had caused her uneasiness during the entire ride to town returned and Val looked over her shoulder. The trail behind her was empty as before, but the feeling remained. The solitude of the trail had allowed her to travel with one leg crossed over her saddle horn for a major part of the ride so she could alternately massage her nearly frozen feet with her gloved hands, a concession to the frigid morning temperature she would not have allowed herself to make if anyone had been watching.

Val glanced up at the sky. Under the difficult circumstances, the ride to town had taken almost an hour longer than usual. The better part of the day would be gone by the time she returned to the ranch, another day that she would be made to look expendable, when she knew she truly was not. There was no one who knew the Circle S better than she, no one who cared about the Circle S's future more than she, and there was no one who deserved the reins more than she when her father decided to give them up.

Realizing she was coming within view of the street, Val raised her chin and straightened her back. Her collar turned up and her hat pulled down low on her forehead, she rode directly toward the general store, not bothering to acknowledge the familiar faces around her. She was accustomed to criticism from townfolk, even ridicule, and she knew that a stiff back and a firm chin were the best protection against it.

Drawing up to the hitching post in front of the store, Val barely restrained a gasp as the stirrup cut painfully into her foot upon dismounting. On the ground at last, she swallowed against the pain in her nearly frozen feet as she turned and walked up the wooden steps.

One look behind the counter as she entered the store and Val all but groaned. Sally Ledman assessed her critically as she approached, her blue eyes widening at Val's bootless condition. Clenching her teeth against the pins and needles that made each step a true test of grit, Val waited for the inevitable question as she approached the counter.

"Valentine Stark, you're not wearing boots! What is wrong with you? Did you ride all the way from your ranch like that? My goodness! Don't you know you could get your feet frozen in these chill temperatures if you don't have them covered?"

Perspiration was beginning to dot Val's forehead as the returning circulation stirred agonizing pain in her toes. She paused, finally managing, "I need boots. Size six will do."

"Well, what in the world happened to your old boots? My goodness, did you lose them or something? You should be more careful, you know."

The pain almost more than she could bear, Val grated, "I said I need boots, not a lot of dumb questions! Get them boots now, if you know what's good for you!"

Sally took a spontaneous step backward, her face flushed. "Who do you think you're talking to, Valentine Stark? This is *my* papa's store, not yours, and if he was here right now, I'd have him throw you right out the door! I don't have to sell you boots if I don't want to, so you can just go home the way you came if you can't speak civilly to me."

Her patience and endurance expired, Val snapped her hand toward the gun at her hip, truly uncertain of her intentions in the second before a heavy hand clamped over hers and forced it away from the handle of the weapon. She closed her eyes briefly, knowing instinctively who it was even before she looked up into Branch Walker's face. But Walker was not looking at her as his rock-hard grip held her hand immobile at her side. Instead he was smiling at Sally Ledman. Val listened with disbelief at the warmth of his tone as he spoke.

"Miss Ledman?" At Sally's nod, Walker's smile widened. "I knew it had to be you because the cowhands on the Circle S are all agreed that Sally Ledman is the prettiest girl in town."

Sally's dimples flashed shamelessly, adding a tinge of nausea to Val's discomfort, and she grimaced openly. Walker's grip tightened on her hand as she sought to extricate it, and unwilling to call attention to her predicament, Val remained unmoving as Sally batted her baby-blue eyes.

"Yes, I'm Sally Ledman, thank you. And you are...?"

Val did not think she could take much more. The look she turned into Walker's face said it all, but she saw the steel behind his smile as he held her hand rigidly at her side. "My name is Branch Walker, ma'am. I'm the manager out at the Circle S. I haven't been able to get into town before or I'd have made it a point to come in sooner. The only reason I'm here today is that Miss Stark had an accident and lost her boots. I believe she said she wears size six?"

Sally's smile twitched in the moment before she responded sweetly, "I think we have a few size six boots left, right over here."

Each step an agony, Val followed Sally's wiggling walk to the far corner of the store, conscious of Walker following close behind. She dropped gratefully into a nearby chair as Sally pulled out three boxes and placed them on the floor. The jingle of the bell on the front door caused Sally to raise her head with annoyance.

"Papa stepped out for a while, so I'll have to go back to

the counter. I'll leave you to decide which boots will suit. You can pay at the counter before you leave. And, Mr. Walker—'' turning the full power of her baby blues toward him, Sally winked boldly ''—I do thank you for your lovely compliment. You're about the best-looking man who's come to Clearmont in years.''

Waiting until the girl was out of earshot, Branch dropped to his knee with an unintelligible comment and snatched one of Val's feet in his hand. Ignoring her protest, he stripped off her sock, pausing at the look of bright red skin blotched with a bloodless white. Swearing under his breath, he began rubbing her foot briskly, ignoring her gasping complaint.

''Be quiet, damn it! Do you want everyone to know what a prideful fool you are?''

''Mind your own business, Walker!'' she gasped, the incredible pain weakening her voice to a whisper. ''And leave me alone. I don't need you and I don't want your help.''

''Don't you? What did you intend to do if that girl wouldn't give you these boots? Shoot her?''

''I hadn't made up my mind.''

Walker paused, recognizing the truth in her response. Releasing one foot without a reply, he picked up the other and started the same painful process.

''Let my foot go!''

''Not a chance! Do you think I want your frozen feet on my conscience? Even if you did get what you had coming.''

''I can take care of myself. My feet will thaw out all right as soon as I get them in those boots.''

''Lady, there's no way in hell you're goin' to get these feet into those boots in their condition. You can't even bend them.''

''I said—''

"And I said sit still and be quiet or I'll carry you out of this store on my back and dump you in the doctor's office!" Walker's eyes narrowed. "And you know you're in no condition to fight me."

The pain almost more than she could bear, Val felt a tear squeeze out of her eye even as she brushed it angrily away and grated, "You're right, I ain't in no condition to fight you. Not now. But I'm givin' you fair warnin'. Present circumstances and physical parts aside, I'm twice the cowhand, twice the ranch manager and twice the man you could ever hope to be. And before I'm done, you'll admit it to me, loud and clear."

His dark eyes holding hers, Walker paused. His expression flickered and his hand curled spontaneously around her foot as he whispered with unexpected gentleness, "Lady, I don't want to fight you."

His unanticipated response all but debilitating her, Val summoned the last of her reserves with a sharp "I told you not to call me *lady!*"

Dropping her foot, Walker stood abruptly. Glowering down at her in silence for a few seconds, he finally growled, "Rub your own goddamned feet!"

Minutes later, Val was still struggling to slide her feet into her boots, when the sound of a familiar step raised her head. Crouching beside her, Walker picked up her foot and started massaging it again without a word.

Chapter Six

The gray, chilling misery of the morning was not the worst of it. Staring at the south corral where the ranch hands and he had arrived to start branding that morning, Branch was stunned at the sight that met his eyes. The corral was covered with bloody carcasses of slain calves. The tracks of a big cat, which covered the soft surrounding ground, disappeared abruptly in a nearby stand of trees. It was strange. Stark said that they'd never had trouble with mountain lions before in this area. He was at a loss to explain what had brought the animal down from higher ground.

The remainder of the stock in the corral had obviously stampeded in terror as the killing raged, because the side rails had been broken through and the animals were nowhere to be found. There would be more time lost in disposing of the slaughtered calves and rounding up those that had fled, and Branch was well aware that another corral would then have to be constructed so that the scent of blood wouldn't draw the big cat back to its feeding ground.

Releasing a disgusted breath, Branch turned to the men around him with a few short orders that set them to their tasks. His gaze moved unconsciously to Val Stark, where she remained mounted beside her father. Her hat was pulled low on her forehead and her collar was turned up in a posture he had noticed she assumed at times that she felt vulnerable and unsure. He sensed she strove to hide her reaction to the slaughter for fear of appearing weak. He had a sudden desire to tell her not to try so hard, that years on the range had not inured him to senseless butchery, either, and that he had the same sick feeling in his stomach as she did.

Turning at that moment, Val Stark met his gaze, and her face tightened into a mask of distaste that replaced Branch's softer feelings with a familiar anger. He should have expected nothing else, for things had progressed from bad to worse since that day he had followed her into town.

Even now, Branch could not explain it. He should have turned his back and canceled from his mind the look on Val Stark's face when he saw her walk out the front door that morning, carefully avoiding the boots he had left there. He should have let her cope with her problems alone, as stupid as she had been to let pride force her into risking frostbite in the freezing dawn temperature. But he hadn't. Perhaps it had been the look in her eye as she had pulled off her boots at the poker table the night before, or the tilt of her chin as she had walked off that porch onto the frozen mud in her stocking feet. Or perhaps…

Whatever, his attentions and concern had seemed to alienate Val Stark in a way caustic comments and open opposition had not. Her attitude toward him had grown progressively sharper since that day he had brought her home on his horse, until her glances were almost physical assaults and her words drew blood. He had taken just about all he could from her, and he was about to explode, but when he saw that defensive posture that inadvertently revealed her vulnerability….

Disgusted, Branch looked back at the subject of his meandering thoughts as she looped her rope around a dead calf's hooves and attached the other end to her saddle. Val Stark dressed like a man and talked like a man, and she was only satisfied when she was being treated like a man. So why couldn't he leave it at that? Was it because she insisted that she would back him down, and in her own way, she was doing just that? Or was it because he didn't want her handling that bloody cow any more than he wanted her riding into Clearmont in her stocking feet?

Damn! What was the matter with him? Val Stark wanted a contest, and a contest she would get—anytime, anywhere. She would learn that *he* was hired to be the boss here, and that what he said was law. And there was no better time to start than now.

"I thought I told you to stay out of that corral, *ma'am*. The men have work to do."

Val Stark looked up sharply, and Branch did not have to look around him to see that the cowhands' heads snapped up, as well. Her reply was almost a foregone conclusion.

"You got any objections to a person workin' on her own ranch?"

"I do when I'm the one who gives the orders." Branch advanced toward her in direct challenge. "Haulin' these carcasses out of here is men's work."

"Is that right?" Val Stark's gray eyes were shards of ice.

"You'll have to take my word for it."

"Will I." The sentence was more a challenge than a question as Val Stark's face tightened, and the urge to wrap his hands around her skinny neck was almost more than Branch could resist.

"Valentine!"

Val jerked her head toward her father. "I told you, my name ain't—"

"And I told you that we was goin' to scout out a place to rebuild the corral. And don't think you'll get away with sassin' me, 'cause you won't."

"Why don't you take your 'ranch manager'? I have work to do."

Color slowly transfused Will Stark's face, and Branch was surprised when, after a moment's pause, Stark's daughter abruptly changed her tack by snapping her rope off the calf's carcass. Coiling it as she walked, she mounted Dunbar and kicked him into motion. Will Stark followed without comment, and Branch turned to the men behind him.

"Boggs, Whalen, Wyatt—go with them and start workin' on the corral as soon as you can. I want a place to put those calves when we round them back up. I intend to start brandin' before the week is out."

The men moved to his command, and as they rode off, Branch turned to see Potter grinning. "Did you see that Val jump? I tell you, the old man ain't lost his spark yet." And then at Branch's puzzled look he added, "Val knows the look on her pa's face, and when he starts turnin' that color, she closes her mouth and ambles. There ain't nobody else that can back her down like that and I'm thinkin' the reason is 'cause there ain't nobody else she gives a damn enough about to care."

Potter turned back to work and Branch found himself angrier than ever as he stared after Val Stark and her pa as they disappeared into the distance. For the life of him, he couldn't reason why.

Playing its constant game, the temperature had taken a jump under the influence of a steady sun, but the perspiration that was beginning to mark Val's brow had nothing to do with the weather. She swung her ax again, cussing under her breath. She had come close to losing control earlier that morning. Even now the memory of those mauled calves set her stomach to churning. She hadn't been any good in the face of that kind of slaughter since she'd been eleven and her dog, Arrow, had been killed by a bear. Her weakness in the face of the carnage in the corral that morning had infuriated her, and she had deliberately forced herself to rope the nearest carcass and start hauling it out. She had almost had it beat, too, until Walker interfered.

Val swung her ax again. That was the second time Branch Walker had sniffed out a weakness and intruded, and she was not about to let there be a third. Even now the humiliation of the morning in Asa Ledman's store had not faded. She had been as weak as a kitten with the pain of returning circulation in her feet and he had not been content until she admitted to her weakness by accepting his ministrations. She would never forgive him for that. And she would never let him do it again.

Val raised her ax for another swing just as Walker's voice shattered the silence of the stand of woods with "What's goin' on here?"

Whalen, Wyatt and Boggs lowered their axes with puzzled looks, but there was no time for a response as Walker rode up to Val, dismounted, and snatched the ax from her hand.

"I told you I wanted you out of the way when there was heavy work to be done! It's not worth the risk, lettin' you handle anythin' as dangerous as an ax. Do you think I want you choppin' off your leg or somethin'?" Branch's face flushed. "We'd lose another day just gettin' you to the doctor."

Val's blood shot to her head, and she made a grab for the ax, which was thwarted by Branch's extended arm. Furious, she spat, "Not worth the risk, huh? I can match you swing for swing on any tree you pick."

Walker all but laughed in her face. "Don't go makin' statements that you don't have a chance in the world of backin' up, *ma'am*."

Val's spine turned to steel. "Think not? I'll say it again. I'll match you strike for strike." And when Branch shook his head she taunted, "Afraid of bein' shown up, Mr. Ranch Manager?"

Branch's cheek twitched as he allowed a few silent moments to elapse before shaking his head. "Forget it. I told you. It's not worth the risk."

Turning his back on her, Branch raised the ax he had snatched from her hands and started swinging at the nearest tree. Val sensed he was seeing her face on that pale bark. She knew the feeling as she walked a few steps to snatch Whalen's ax from his hands. When he appeared about to protest, she grated, "What's the matter? Afraid of losin' a month's pay?"

Whalen's snicker was snide. "Not a chance."

Walking to a tree adjacent to the one at which Branch was still chopping, Val began swinging her ax with all the skill learned in years of application. A short time later she was still matching him strike for strike, and she knew there was no denying it. Conscious of the sudden cessation of sound beside her, Val shot Branch a mocking glance. She was well aware that the other men had drifted around and were viewing the contest in curious silence as she questioned, "Givin' up, boss man?"

Branch gave a scoffing laugh as he tossed off his hat, unbuttoned his coat and tossed it on the ground. Blowing on his hands, he picked up the ax again. Mimicking him with great relish, Val tossed her hat and coat on the ground, dusted off her hands and picked up her ax. Within moments, the sound of vigorous chipping again filled the air.

Walker accelerated his pace, and Val met it. Her back screamed in protest, but she would not relent as she stared at the rock-hard bark at which she worked. She was straining desperately, certain she could not raise her arms for another swing, when the sound of Walker's ax again halted. Turning, she saw his face was studded with sweat, his hair matted to his scalp. With a low growl, he stripped off his shirt, exposing long underwear ringed with sweat as he wiped his shirt across his face. Openly mimicking him, Val stripped off her shirt, as well, to reveal her baggy long underwear, and deliberately wiped her shirt across her forehead.

The cold fury in Branch Walker's eyes momentarily numbed her in the second before he slowly, deliberately, unbuttoned his underwear and slid his arms out of the sleeves. A strangled sound from somewhere behind her sounded vaguely familiar as Val's narrowed eyes spat fire. Raising her hands to the buttons on her chest, she unbuttoned the first, the second, the—

"Valentine!"

Valentine did not turn at her father's choked call.

"One more button, Valentine, and you'll have me to face instead of Walker, and you know what that means!"

Her eyes still holding Walker's slitted gaze, Val responded, "I ain't lettin' him back me down, Pa."

"It ain't him you're facin' now. It's me." Will's voice had a fatal ring. "Drop that ax. We're goin' home."

Val's hand twitched on the wooden handle she gripped so tightly. Abruptly turning, she swung at the tree, embedding the blade in the trunk with a grunt before snatching up her clothes and walking to her horse without a word. Mounting, she was off at a run before the men she left behind had time to release their tense breaths.

As his daughter disappeared amidst the trees, Will looked at Walker and shook his head. Mounting up, he followed her out of sight, leaving silence in his wake.

Unwilling to match his daughter's pace as she rode away from the wooded grove, Will did not come within a few hundred yards of her until she reached the ranch, but he was still fuming. Even now he was uncertain how far Val would have gone to avoid being backed down by Walker again, and he groaned at the thought of what might have happened had he not been there to put an end to her stubborn stand.

Will approached the ranch to see Val disappear into the barn. He did not follow, preferring to put his horse in the corral rather than face her until they had both had a chance to calm down. She did not emerge, and he did not have to stretch his imagination to guess what she was doing. Since she was a child, she had always taken out her frustrations by cleaning the stalls. Will shook his head. How a grown woman could *still* find some measure of comfort in piled manure was beyond him.

His step dragging, Will walked back to the house. It was times like this that he needed Mary's comforting voice, her sympathetic touch. He walked into the kitchen and halted with a sigh. All he had was Red Hand.

Red Hand turned to study his face. "Hummm… Val make trouble again."

Annoyed, Will snapped, "You always hit the target when it comes to knowin' when Val's in trouble, don't you, Red

Hand? So if you're so smart, how come you never come up with a suggestion on what to do about it? You know her better than just about anybody on the ranch except me.''

"Red Hand know her better."

"Oh, you do, do you?" Resentment deepened the lines on Will's face.

"Val woman now. Time for her to take a man."

Will's face froze into stillness in the moment before he burst into wild laughter. He was still laughing minutes later, tears running down his cheeks. Finally gaining control, Will wiped the dampness from his cheek with his callused palms, his breath short as he rasped, "That's the best laugh I've had in a month, Red Hand. Goddamn it! The way things are goin', the only way Val would be able to get a man would be to kidnap him!"

"Hummm…" Red Hand nodded. "No man want woman who dress like man."

"So what am I supposed to do about it?" Will was at the end of his patience with Red Hand's feeble comments. "If I bought Val a dress, she'd wrap it around my neck!"

"Val not need dress to look like woman. She plenty woman."

Will stared at the sober Indian, finally responding with a hint of an unexpected smile, "Yeah, she's plenty woman all right." Will's smile faded. "Val looks like her ma, and I'm thinkin' that's what bothers her. She don't want to be nothin' like her. That's why she stays away from them frilly clothes her ma favored and all."

"Val not need dress."

"Well, them baggy pants and shirt she's wearin' just don't seem to bring out her femininity, now do they?"

"Hummm."

"There ain't no way to get them clothes she's wearin' off her back until they fall off, and you know she don't buy nothin' new until the old stuff's gone to rags."

"Not wait. Val ready now, and widow not happy."

Will looked up with a snap. "What did you say?"

Red Hand turned back to the stove, leaving Will incredulous. That Injun knew all about him and Mary!

A man of few words, Red Hand appeared to have said all he would and Will turned toward the parlor. He considered Red Hand's advice again.

Val was ready, all right. She was woman ripe for the pickin', and if he couldn't think of a way to wake her up to that fact, he supposed he'd have to find a way to wake somebody else up to it.

A sudden idea striking him, Will smiled. Why hadn't he thought of it before?

Val pushed her hat back from her forehead and reached for the shovel. She had moved Powderkeg out so she could clean his stall, and she was just about done. She'd scoop up the rest of the manure and spread a little hay—just a little—because Powderkeg liked it that way. A vague satisfaction stirred inside her, and she was tempted to smile. She supposed this was as close to giving vent to her female nesting desire as she'd ever come. She knew it was as far as she could possibly get from a pristine kitchen and a frilly white apron, and she was glad.

Her hands filled with straw, Val paused, truly uncertain what would have happened had her father not interfered a few hours earlier when she had faced Walker's silent challenge. Her temper began slowly climbing. Walker had deliberately baited her. It seemed he wouldn't be satisfied until he had humiliated her beyond redemption in front of the other men. But past defeats served only to renew her purpose, and Val knew the most important thing that she needed to guard against was allowing Walker to force her into pushing her pa onto his side. That would be a mistake. When all was said and done, she knew she would never do anything that could hurt the crusty old man.

Straightening up a few minutes later, Val released a satisfied breath. Suddenly realizing she was hungry, she walked to the door of the barn and took a deep sniff of the aroma coming from the house. It smelled like Red Hand was baking something. Knowing better than to deceive herself into thinking it would be conventional fare, she started toward the kitchen.

The slaughter of the calves earlier that morning had upset her and she had acted unwisely. She remembered Walker's hand closing over hers as she'd reached for her gun in Asa Ledman's store, and realized her tendency toward irrational acts had grown since Walker's arrival. Not that Sally Ledman would notice another hole in that airy head of hers.

Some women would make fools of themselves when confronted with Branch Walker's broad shoulders and dark, compelling eyes. They would giggle like idiots when flashed his dazzling smile that was all the more potent for its rarity, and would be unable to strike from their minds the surprising gentleness of his strong hands. They would allow those thoughts to prey on their minds until they were almost beside themselves with confusion.

Not her.

Branch Walker was her enemy. He would always be her enemy. She wouldn't forget it, and she would win out in the end. Or she would die trying. Her shoulders squared, Val left the barn.

Walking through the parlor and into the kitchen a few minutes later, she found Red Hand at the stove. As her pa entered the room, she looked at him in time to see his nose wrinkle as he sniffed the air. He raised his wiry brows and he gave her clothing an assessing glance. "I heard somebody come in and I knew it couldn't be nobody else but you. Good thing Maggie Winthrop will be comin' out to do the laundry tomorrow. There ain't a one of us here that's got a change of clothes left."

Tempted to respond that he'd never been bothered by a shortage of fresh clothes before, Val allowed him to continue.

"I think there's some things we should talk about, Val." Not waiting for her concurrence, Will turned back toward the parlor with a signal for her to follow.

Red Hand looked up at her for the first time as she shrugged, snatched up a piece of bread and complied.

Better days were coming. She intended to make sure of it.

Branch looked off into the distance as the sound of busy hammers and axes echoed around him, attempting to clear his mind of the turmoil in which it had circled since Val Stark had made her hasty departure an hour earlier. This was beautiful country, and as he had ridden through on his first approach, he had thought a man couldn't ask for more than to make a place for himself here.

Across the open grasslands he saw Clear Creek in the distance, its surface glittering in the sun. He knew it started high in the Big Horn Mountains, ran through Buffalo and past Clearmont before it fed into the Powder River. He knew it was still iced over, but that its beauty was deceiving because the water ran swiftly, free of ice in spots, posing a danger to yearlings who could drown in an attempt to cross. He was familiar with the drastic extremes of weather in the spring, when the temperature sometimes dropped to zero at night and soared to sixty degrees in the afternoon sun a day later, as it had that day. And he knew that tomorrow might bring snow, sleet or even another balmy day.

The thought occurred to Branch that the erratic weather bore a resemblance to the personality of one Val Stark, but he also knew that the weather was easier to accept than that woman's trying personality.

Branch's irritation grew despite his most fervent effort to keep it at bay. The events of a few hours earlier returned again to mind and he remembered the determination in Val's gaze as she had slowly unbuttoned the first button of her long johns, then the second. He remembered her long fingers working at the third, and the tone of her father's voice when he brought her defiance to an abrupt halt.

After Stark and his daughter rode off, he had finished the job he had started, turning in time to see Whalen staring at him intently as the tree crashed to the ground. A strange feeling had moved up his spine and he decided that if Whalen tried anything with Val Stark, it would be the biggest mistake of Whalen's life.

Turning to look again at the big, dark cowboy, Branch felt his agitation soar anew, and he wondered at the strength of his feelings. He also wondered at the image of long, slender fingers working at a third buttonhole, an image that would not leave his mind, when he should be thinking of the new corral that was taking shape behind him and of the difficult breeding tasks that lay before him, on which his future hinged.

There they were again, those long fingers working at that damned button....

Branch muttered a low epithet and turned back to the men. "Come on, boys, put your hearts into it!"

Turning to loop his rope over the log at his feet, he then gave Caesar a slap on the rump and picked up his ax.

Chapter Seven

Will Stark's full mustache twitched as his daughter surveyed him critically from head to toe.

"How come you ain't dressed yet, Pa?"

"'Cause I ain't ridin' out with you all this mornin'."

"Why?"

Gripping his knee with an expression he hoped was convincing, Will shook his head. "My old bones are givin' me trouble this mornin'. My knee...it ain't been right since I broke my leg a few years back." He experimented with a drooping expression, which tightened Val's lips with suspicion, following with a quick "Red Hand's got some Injun medicine that he wants to try on it. Some kind of tree bark that he's goin' to make into a poultice."

"Your leg wasn't botherin' you none yesterday."

Will took a short, limping step that he hoped was convincing. "That was yesterday, and today's today. Anyways, if Red Hand is as good at doctorin' as he thinks he is, I'll be joinin' you in a few hours."

Val stared hard into his eyes, and Will had all he could do to hold her gaze without flinching. Her eyes cut to the quick, and he was wary of them. Appearing to finally accept his excuse, Val walked toward the door as he warned firmly, "Remember what I said, Val. I don't want no more of that crazy business of yesterday."

Val turned back to him, her expression tight. "You can depend on that as long as Walker keeps his mouth shut and his nose where it belongs."

"Val, I'm tellin' you…"

Val appeared to suddenly relent. "I heard you."

Will watched his daughter walk out the door. There was a danger in allowing Val a second chance at Branch while he wasn't there to stop the bloodshed, but a conversation with Walker the night before had led him to believe that the fellow was as disgusted with his own handling of the situation as he was with Val herself. Will figured he was safe for a few hours.

His gaze moved to the riders still forming in the yard. The horses were jumpy in the cold, and it didn't take long to see that Dunbar was particularly edgy, sidestepping and bumping against the others as Val strained to keep him under control. The look on Branch Walker's face said it all, as did Val's wordless reply, and Will closed his eyes at the familiar conflict.

At the clatter of hoofbeats a moment later he opened them again to watch as the riders left the yard, breathing a deep sigh of relief. They were on their way and the rest was up to him.

Suddenly feeling a hot breath on his neck, Will turned to Red Hand's accusing eye.

"Don't look at me that way, Red Hand! You're goin' to come out on top in all this, you know. You're goin' to be a hero. Your poultice is goin' to make a new man of me—so good that I'll be back in the saddle before noon."

"Red Hand get poultice."

"Oh, no, you don't!" Will shook his head vigorously.

"There ain't nothin' wrong with my knee, and you know it. You ain't puttin' none of your crazy medicines on me. This is just another little secret you and me are goin' to share."

Red Hand nodded with a raise of his brow. "Red Hand thirsty."

"I ain't givin' you nothing to drink. It's against the law!"

The Indian nodded again. "Red Hand get poultice."

"Dammit, Red Hand!" Will took a deep breath, finally relenting with a twitch, "Well, if you're feelin' poorly, you're welcome to help yourself to a sip of the medicinal brandy I keep in the closet."

Red Hand grinned.

"*After* you cook!"

Red Hand turned without another word, and Will dragged a weary hand down his face. This was all getting to be too much. If it wasn't for his darlin' Mary...

The thought of his dear widow-woman brought a faint smile to his lips, and he turned back to the window to search the horizon. He was still there an hour later, when a wagon appeared over the rise, carrying Maggie Winthrop's familiar bulk.

Potter was having a rough time trying to conceal his grin. His gray whiskers twitched as he rubbed his hand across his mouth. He realized Val was too close to risk laughing outright. This all was doing his heart good!

Pulling his hat down farther on his forehead, Potter raised his rope and slapped the rumps of a few cows and their calves, which he and Val had just flushed out of a ravine. He drove them toward the larger body gathered nearby as he glanced at Val out of the corner of his eye. Val's face was set and hard, and he knew what that expression meant. He had the feelin'

Branch Walker did, too, by now. The only trouble was that he didn't think the fella cared.

Through his amusement, Potter could not deny his unflagging admiration for Val Stark. She had more guts and gumption than most men he knew. She had proved that fact to him the first month he had arrived on the Circle S seven years earlier. She'd been thirteen years old at that time, a tall, skinny kid in braids who was more serious and hardworking than any youngster should be. He had made the mistake of treating her like a child and she had near to burned the hide off him for his mistake. He remembered thinking that living and riding with her pa and cowhands all her life the kid would never grow up to be a lady.

There was very little about Val Stark that reminded a man about her womanhood, but he had the feeling that the men had gotten a sharp reminder of her sex the previous day when Val had stripped off her shirt and started working at the buttons on her long johns. He was certain that it was only Walker's presence in the bunkhouse that night that had kept the conversation from coming around to it, too.

Old man Stark had shown up the night before for a long conversation with Walker. Potter didn't know what had been said between them, but he did know that Walker was taking a different tack with Val today. He had allowed her to work with the herd like one of the hands, although it was obvious to all, including Val, that she was going to have to prove herself to Walker every step of the way. And it was also obvious to all that the thought rankled, for Val had been near to spitting fire since the day started.

Potter smiled. Oh, yeah, he was enjoying himself. Val Stark was too cocky for her own good, even if he did have a healthy affection for her. And if he wasn't up to puttin' her in her place himself, he was sure glad Walker was.

Waiting until Val rode up alongside, Potter could not resist a little nudge.

"About that bet we got, Val. I don't know if you've been keepin' score, but—"

Val's knife-sharp gaze sliced into him as she interrupted, "I've been keepin' score, all right."

"That so?" Potter shrugged with elaborate indifference. "Well, the way my score's been addin' up, I'd say that Walker's ahead in this little game. You ain't been doin' so good lately."

"I'm workin' the herd right alongside the rest of the hands, ain't I?"

"Well, let me see...Walker's already got your boots, and I'd say he backed you down pretty good yesterday."

"A bad run of cards don't mean nothin', and I was meetin' him swing for swing with that ax, and you know it!"

"But he's the fella that brought that tree down, not you. That's the way I see it." Potter waited for her response, his silent admiration for her growing. Val had never been one to make excuses for her sex, and she wasn't about to start now. Neither was she about to give in.

"That was yesterday, and today's today."

Certain that the devil was putting him up to it, Potter nudged again. "Are you sure you don't want to cancel out of our bet? I mean, I can talk to Whalen and Simm and tell them we took unfair advantage of you, with you bein' just a female and all."

Val's eyes narrowed. Her cheek twitched, and Potter gulped. Her hand moved like lightning to the gun on her hip, and he let out a loud yelp, kicking his horse into movement as he raced at top speed toward the safety of the main herd a short distance away.

Safe in the midst of the other men, Potter met Walker's quizzical frown with a sickly grin. Turning, he saw Val running the last of the cattle into the herd at a leisurely pace, and he responded to Walker's silent question with an inadequate "I thought I heard you call me, boss."

Behind him Potter heard Val repeat "Yeah, he thought he heard you call him, *boss.* Took off like a bat out of hell, too, didn't he? You'd think the devil was after him."

Val gave a short laugh, and Potter felt his face flush hot as she turned her horse and rode away. Walker's assessing gaze darted between Val and him and Potter twitched.

Oh, yeah, he was going to enjoy collecting his bet from Val Stark!

Potter's bleary old eyes followed Val's erect figure as she slipped back into the herd. He smiled, despite himself.

"Did you ask her, Pa? Did you?" Val shook her head, incredulous as she stared at her freshly laundered clothes lying on the kitchen table in front of her. "Did you ask her what she did to them?"

"No, I didn't! Maggie Winthrop's been doin' our laundry for ten years, and if you think I was goin' to badger that old lady just because our clothes didn't turn out too good this time, you're crazy."

"Didn't turn out too good! There's nothin' left of them!" Holding up her only change of pants, Val looked at the faded, hole-filled garment with disbelief. Dropping it, she then held up the shirt that lay alongside, her expression unchanging. "They look like she dragged them behind her wagon instead of washin' them."

"Well, it ain't only your clothes that suffered. Mine are in the same shape. I'm thinkin' it's the soap she was usin' on them—too much lye, I suppose. I guess old Maggie didn't realize it until it was too late."

"She *had* to realize it, unless her hands are tough as old leather."

Will hesitated. "Well, maybe they are. It's all over and done now, anyway, and I ain't about to hurt her feelin's by tellin' her that she ruined them clothes."

Val shook her head again. "My favorite pants and shirt...I've been wearin' them for two years."

"That right?"

"I hate breakin' in new clothes. They're always so damned itchy and stiff."

"That's so, I guess." Will looked down at the pants Val presently wore, at the spot where her long underwear protruded from a rip in the knee. "Looks like you ain't goin' to have much choice though, don't it?"

Val sniffed, and Will knew her distaste for the project was genuine. He offered subtly, "I'm goin' to town on Saturday if you want to come along."

"I was goin' to work with Powderkeg all day Saturday. I'll waste half the day if I go into town."

"Suit yourself, but *I'm* not going to walk around in clothes that can't even keep out the wind."

"You can pick up some clothes for me when you go."

"No, thank you! I remember the last time I picked up somethin' for you. I didn't hear the end of it for a month."

"What was I supposed to do with a white blouse? I ain't never worn a white blouse in my life!"

Will mumbled indistinctly, "Yeah, I know."

Val's eyes narrowed. "What was that you said, Pa?"

"I said I'm goin' to go, whether you come with me or not. But I ain't buyin' you nothin'. I learned my lesson."

"Pa—"

"I said, I learned my lesson!"

Snatching his clothes up from the pile in front of him, Will walked toward his room, aware that he left Val staring at his back. His full mustache twitched with a suppressed smile. If he knew his daughter, she'd try wearin' them clothes, anyway, but they wouldn't last past the first fifteen minutes they was on her body. And if she didn't come into town with him this week, she'd go in the next. He was smarter than anybody gave him credit for, all right. Yeah, he was *real* smart!

What had he ever done to deserve this?

Out of the corner of his eye, Branch surveyed the two riders cantering beside him. Suppressing a groan, he maintained a steady pace toward town. He had received a letter from Alex Swan, telling him that Harper Stevenson was going to be traveling their way. He had leaped at the opportunity for a Saturday meeting with Stevenson in Clearmont, believing he could get away from the irritations of the Circle S for a day while he took care of some business. The only trouble was that his biggest irritation was riding along right beside him.

Branch darted another look at Val Stark's stiff face, realizing that she was as surprised and disgusted with the unexpected situation as he. However, once she had announced that she was going to town, he knew she would not risk having anyone think that the thought of traveling with him bothered her enough to cancel her plans.

His mind returning to the last time Val and he had traveled to town together, Branch shrugged. Well, it wasn't as if he could blame her for not wanting to repeat that experience.

The memory of that day brought a frown to Branch's face. Val wasn't aware of his trailing her into town that morning, and it was a horrendous trip for him, watching her massage first one nearly frozen foot and then the other the entire way. He remembered recalling his former satisfaction at having humiliated her into losing her boots and wondering what it was about Val Stark that brought out the worst in him.

He remembered the pain which which she'd dismounted from her horse and the pride with which she had forced herself to walk up the steps to the store, her head high. He remembered hearing the sharp words exchanged between Val and that empty-headed little snip in the store. To this minute, he was uncertain what might have happened had he not stepped in to stop Val from pulling her gun.

Val Stark was determined and hotheaded, a combination that boded poorly for the future he had thought so rosy only a month earlier. Try as he might, he had been unable to undo the damage he had done by trying to back her down.

Branch paused on that thought. If he were to be truthful, he would have to admit that he had not made a great effort to undo that damage, as furious as the woman made him most of the time. His reactions that day in the store had been instinctive and his anger real when he'd taken her nearly frozen feet between his palms and attempted to chafe the circulation back into them. She'd fought him and he'd become furious, but he had taken only a few steps away from her before realizing that he could not leave her alone and in pain. He had not been prepared, however, for the feelings that had assaulted him when Val unexpectedly allowed his ministrations.

When she'd finally been able to force boots on her feet, she'd stood up with only the shortest of looks for him, but he'd seen the vulnerability there. It had touched him more deeply than he had ever been touched before.

Val had ridden stiff backed and silent all the way back to the ranch, refusing to acknowledge his presence as he'd ridden beside her, and he had suffered through alternating anger and an almost debilitating sorrow at the status of relations between them.

Now, only the anger remained. Still challenging him at every turn and thwarting him whenever possible, she was again the thorn in his side that would not be dispelled. The episode with the ax had proved to him that he was handling her all wrong, that he was, in fact, allowing her to manipulate him into constant conflict. That thought had been almost as sobering as the haunting vision of those long fingers working at that third button....

Damn!

He had forced himself to change his tactics, allowing her to work with his men. He was neither comfortable nor satisfied with it, and he knew Val Stark considered it a victory. He intended, however, to keep a close eye on her and to make her realize for herself that she was out of place there. He had merely lengthened her leash. The only problem was that he had not considered how badly that lengthened leash would chafe him.

The town of Clearmont came into sight, and Branch released a relieved breath. He'd be free of old man Stark and his daughter for a short time while they took care of their errands, and he intended to make good use of that time by reacquainting himself with his old friend Harper Stevenson. Stark was to join him later, and he had no doubt that Val Stark would come along, too. The thought plagued him.

Glancing again at the two riding beside him, Branch felt his stomach squeeze into familiar knots. Reacting spontaneously, he kicked his horse into a gallop, quickly outdistancing his companions.

Within seconds, Val Stark was again riding alongside. There was no escaping her.

The scents accosting Val's nostrils as she entered the general store were familiar, but they did not recall pleasant memories. The fragrance of lavender as she passed a display of soap, the aromas of dried apples in a nearby barrel and herbs hanging from the ceiling in the far corner of the store—all brought back memories of the mother whose image had become vague in her mind.

Her ma had loved the smell of lavender. She said it made a woman feel feminine and desirable. Val had not understood what she'd meant then, but those words had become only too revealing in the time since. The thought now made her sick, almost as sick as the scent of the herbs her ma had selected with such care in order to avoid the wrinkles she so feared.

Val recalled with familiar pain the day she asked her ma to buy dried applies for a pie. Her ma's response was that she had better things to do with her time. It was only after her ma had left that she found out what those "better" things were.

Val raised her chin a notch higher. She had neither seen nor heard from her ma after that day, but rumors had been rife and they had not missed her ears. It seemed that her ma had left with the same traveling man who had shown up at their ranch a few times when her pa was away. Val remembered him. He was tall and handsome, with blond hair that shone in the sun and a smile that sparkled. Val stiffened. Her ma had been a fool for that kind of man, but she was nothing like her ma. She had determined long ago that she never would be.

Val glanced at the counter, unconsciously grimacing as she spotted Sally Ledman's dimpled face. Her stomach churned. The memory of her earlier humiliation still burning, she tilted her hat forward and approached the counter.

"Why, if it isn't Val Stark!"

Sally Ledman's high-pitched voice grated on Val's ears.

"Did you bring that handsome foreman in with you today?"

Annoyed, Val deliberately ignored her question, stating flatly, "I need pants and a shirt."

Sally leaned over the counter, her actions exaggerated to call attention to the effort as she looked pointedly at Val's long legs. She giggled, effectively attracting the attention of nearby customers as she said, "I just *had* to look and make sure, you know. Last time you came in here for boots, and your *feet* were bare. This time you came in for pants and I thought—"

Sally giggled again, and Val's annoyance surged past restraint. "I came in for pants *and* a shirt. My legs aren't bare, but wait a minute so I can unbutton my coat and I'll show you—"

"No!" Sally's blue eyes bulged. "I mean—" The gasps of disapproving matrons around her brought a bright flush to her fair skin as she continued in a strangled voice, "Th-the pants and shirts are this way, in the corner. Follow me. You can pick out the ones you want."

Abandoning her beside the table of ready-made clothes, Sally returned to the counter with undisguised haste. Val smiled for the first time that day with the thought that even the smallest victories could sometimes be very sweet.

"If you were to ask my opinion, I'd say you put that little lady in her place very well."

Turning, Val saw the widow Mary McGee standing behind her. Unaccustomed to approval from anyone, much less a respectable widow-woman who should have been shocked by her response to Sally's taunting, Val responded, "But I *didn't* ask your opinion, did I?"

"No, you didn't." The woman's round face flushed, and Val experienced unexpected regret for her churlishness as the woman continued, "But that's the prerogative of an old woman who lives alone, you know—to enjoy a good setdown when she sees one. It was well deserved, and you accomplished it admirably."

Val sniffed and shrugged. "I've had a lot of practice."

"Yes, I suppose you have. Unfortunately there are too many Sally Ledmans in the world, although they would never believe it to be true if they heard me say it. And there are too few of us who live according to our own standards." Mary's smile brightened. "I'm pleased to have run into you today, Valentine." And then at Val's frown, "I meant to say, 'Val.' You do prefer being called 'Val,' don't you?"

Val nodded, and the woman astounded her by concluding, "Sometimes even the smallest victories can be very sweet, can't they? Thank you for sharing yours with me."

Val was still staring after Mary McGee's small, rounded figure when she disappeared between the rows of merchandise. Disturbed by the spot of warmth the woman had raised inside her, Val turned back to clothing piled on the table with a sharpness calculated to shake the woman from her mind.

Val dropped her selections on the counter a short time later, noting with particular pleasure that Sally avoided her gaze. Distracted from her satisfaction by the sound of a familiar mumbled tone, she turned to survey the crowded emporium.

She had thought she'd heard her pa's voice, but he was no-where to be seen. She paused to listen again.

"If it isn't Mr. Stark!"

Will had entered the store a short time earlier and turned with a snap at the beloved voice of Mary McGee. His small eyes brightened when he saw her standing only a few feet away, between a table filled with ribbons and notions and an-other piled high with bolts of colorful cloth. She was the pret-tiest sight he had ever seen, with her brown eyes sparkling and her thin lips curved in that smile reserved just for him. He sighed, closing the distance between them as he drew her out of sight.

"Mary…"

Mary raised a cautioning finger to her lips. "I've just seen Valentine. She's in the back of the store selecting work clothes. She looks very well."

"So do you, Mary." Will swallowed, the urge to gather his dear widow-woman in his arms almost more than he could restrain.

"But she doesn't look happy, Wilbur."

"What about me, Mary? Do I look happy?" Will shook his head, ready to pour his heart out into Mary's sympathetic ears. "It's been a helluva week, but I'm thinkin' I'm on the right track at last. With just a little luck, we won't have to be hidin' between the tables in no general store no more." Will flushed. "I hate this hidin', Mary."

"Hush, Wilbur." Mary's sweet face reflected her sincere understanding. "You don't have to say those things. I know how you feel and I know the way your feelings are torn, be-cause I've seen the suffering in your daughter's eyes as well as you have. I saw it again a few minutes ago, but she's such a fighter, Wilbur. She gives back as good as she gets. There's no backing her down.''

"Please don't say that, Mary.'' Will was beginning to feel desperate. "I'm hopin' I can change all that.''

"Oh, no, I wouldn't want you to!'' Mary shook her head, obviously disturbed by his words. "Valentine is such a strong young woman. And she's honest, too. There's no deception about her. I'd like to see her happier, but I wouldn't want to see her change, and I don't want you to do anything that you think might change her, especially not for me.''

"But Mary—''

"Promise me that, Wilbur.'' Mary's expression was solemn. "For all she's suffered over the years and for the way she's pulled through, I do love the girl, you know.''

"I love her, too, Mary, but I still want—''

"Promise me, Wilbur, please.''

Will hesitated. "I suppose it's easy enough to make you that promise, Mary, darlin', 'cause I'm beginnin' to think there's not a chance in the world that Val will ever change.''

Mary smiled and lightly touched his cheek. Will shuddered as the thrill of it ran right down to his toes. He sighed as Mary continued, "Even if Val does complicate matters between us, you should still be thankful, dear. You could have had a daughter like Sally Ledman, you know.''

Sally Ledman's ear-piercing giggle was opportunely heard over the conversation progressing at the counter, and Will grimaced. "You're right, Mary, darlin'. You're always right.''

Mary stared deeply into Wilbur's eyes for long, silent moments. "I'm tingling, Wilbur. You always make me tingle.''

Will swallowed and took a step closer. "You make me tingle too, Mary. Mary—''

"Is that you, Pa?''

Will jumped back from Mary, blinking at the sound of his daughter's voice. Mary disappeared between the aisles before he could react, and Will uttered a string of curses that still hadn't come to an end as his daughter called again, "Is that you over there, Pa?"

"Yes, it's me, damn it!" Will stepped into sight, scowling.

"Did you get them headache powders you wanted from Doc Pitt?"

"Yeah, I did."

"What was you doin' hangin' out in them aisles back there?"

"Val Stark..." Will took a deep breath. "You make your purchase and you mind your business, understand? And when you're done doin' that, you go down to the hotel and look for Branch Walker and that fella we're supposed to be meetin'. You tell him I'll be along in a few minutes."

"But I don't want—"

"Val..."

Val eyed her father's flushed face and shrugged. "Anythin' you say, Pa."

"Yeah?" Will could not resist. "Since when?"

Val shrugged again, picked up her package and turned away, and Will was never happier to see his dear daughter's retreating back.

Waiting the few seconds it took for Val to clear the door, Will followed her to peer out the window as she walked down the street. He held his breath as she paused by her horse.

Managing to smother the full-voiced cheer that rose to his lips as Val stepped to Dunbar's side and lashed her package to the saddle, Will waited with a palpitating heart as she walked slowly down the street and stepped into the gunsmith's shop. It couldn't be better. When Val started lookin' at new rifles, she always lost track of time.

With the joy of a mischievous schoolboy, Will followed Val's path down the street with as casual a posture as he could manage. Coming up alongside Dunbar, he darted a cautious glance around him before snatching the package from Val's saddle. He turned back toward Asa Ledman's store with a nervous smile that bespoke his hopes of good things to come.

The dining room of the Trail's End Hotel was quiet and filled with delectable aromas. Branch sat at a table covered with spotless white linen, a full glass in front of him and his old friend Harper Stevenson across from him. His glass refilled for the third time, he was feeling decidedly mellow as Stevenson laughed appropriately at one of his quips, then responded, "But you haven't answered my question. Are you happy at the Circle S? Do you regret leaving Swan?"

Branch's glow dimmed and his friend's keen eyes assessed his hesitation. Those eyes had been the first thing he had noticed about Harper Stevenson the day he met him several years earlier. That and the fact that he was the only fellow he had ever met whose height matched his, as different as their appearance was otherwise.

Stevenson's hair was dark and his eyes were light blue. Dressed in a dark suit that fit his muscular build too well to be bought off the rack, he was a handsome man in the prime of life. Successful in the business world as well as with the opposite sex, Stevenson was also the cattle buyer who had sold Swan his first Hereford bulls.

Stevenson and Branch had become good friends in the time since, and Branch knew that Stevenson would get him the best Hereford bulls available for the Circle S. However, those thoughts aside, Branch was not comfortable answering Stevenson's personal questions.

Stevenson smiled. "You don't have to answer me Branch. It's written all over your face."

"You're readin' me wrong, Harper. The Circle S is a real beauty with a great future—great location, good breedin' stock. Will Stark is a crusty old man, but I like him and I think we can be real friends someday."

"So?"

"So what?"

"So how come you have a frown on your face instead of a smile?" Stevenson asked bluntly. "And how come you're on the defensive now, when you were feelin' on top of the world before I pinned you down?"

The sound of approaching footsteps interrupted their exchange, and Branch turned to see Stark and Stark approaching. His expression froze. Following suit as Stevenson politely rose to his feet, Branch made the necessary introductions, the back of his neck prickling at Val Stark's cocky expression as she threw her hat on a nearby chair and sat down.

Reality met Branch's direst expectations when Val Stark focused her pale-gray eyes on Stevenson and opened abruptly, "About them sissy Hereford bulls..."

An hour later, his dinner lying on his stomach like a lead weight, Branch darted a glance between Val Stark and Harper Stevenson. It was a tight contest, and to be completely truthful, he wasn't sure who was winning. Challenging every point Stevenson had made during the past hour, Val had confused the issues enough so that nothing more had been accomplished than the consumption of a meal—and indigestion.

Infuriating Branch even more was his realization that as difficult as the past hour had been, he was fascinated by the quickness of Val Stark's mind, as devious as it was. That fact frightened him, as did the growing desire to close his hands around her slender white neck and squeeze for all he was worth.

Damn...what had he gotten himself into?

Shooting him a sideways glance, Val turned toward him for the first time in the past half hour. He was stunned to see that she actually appeared to be enjoying herself.

"Looks like you ain't got nothin' to say all of a sudden, Walker. That ain't like you." Her eyes dipped to his plate. "Off your feed, too, huh? You goin' to finish that pie?" She shrugged when he did not respond, and Branch's patience suddenly snapped.

"Well, if all the questions are finished, I think it's time we get down to business. And when we do that, I think we should excuse the *lady* from the table."

Aware that he had just said fightin' words, Branch braced himself for the onslaught, which was not delayed in coming.

Val turned on him as quick as lightning. "I know you don't mean me, Walker, 'cause I never made no pretense at bein' a lady. But just in case you was referrin' to my sex, I'll tell you now that there ain't nobody, includin' you, that's big enough to make me leave this table before I'm ready to go."

"Come on now, Val." Entering into the exchange, Will Stark made an obvious attempt to pacify his daughter's anger. "Branch didn't mean nothin'. He just figured you'd be bored with the details we have to work out—ain't that right, Branch?"

Silence.

Will fidgeted uncomfortably and Val steamed. Breaking into the tense tableau, Stevenson stood abruptly, his expression frazzled. "I don't know about all of you, but I've been sitting long enough. I think I'll stretch my legs, or maybe stand at the bar for a while and work out the kinks. I've said about all there is to say, and the rest is up to you. I'll be leaving town tomorrow morning, so you can get back to me anytime you want before that." Stevenson extended his hand toward each in turn. "Pleased to meet you all. Hope to do some business with you in the future."

Waiting until Stevenson cleared the doorway of the room, Branch stood up abruptly. His low voice barely controlled, he met Val's challenging stare. "It isn't goin' to work, *darlin'*. Harper Stevenson's too much of a man to be put off by a pesky flea like you." Pausing, he added in a low growl, "And while you're thinkin' about that, you can keep in mind that he isn't *half* the man that I am!"

"That so?"

Val's low laugh sent his fury up another notch, but Branch saw through her ploy as he responded, "That's so." He turned toward the silent Will Stark. "You got any reservations about Hereford bulls, Will?"

"No, I ain't."

"You got any objections to buyin' from Stevenson?"

"Hell, no!"

"Then those bulls are as good as bought."

With a quick turn on his heel, Branch walked toward the door, leaving an uncomfortable silence behind him that was broken by the low, exasperated voice he heard trailing behind him.

"Valenti-i-ine…"

The sympathy reflected in Harper Stevenson's light eyes as Branch approached the bar a few minutes later was reflected in Stevenson's voice as he offered, "Have a drink, Branch. You earned it."

"I'm sorry, Harper."

Harper tossed down his drink, coughed and shook his head. "I just have one question. The Circle S is the place where you're supposed to work, where you're supposed to earn a partnership and where you're supposed to live out the rest of your days?"

"That was the plan."

"You have my condolences, friend." Harper shook his head again. "I have *never* failed with a lady that badly in my life."

"You heard what she said, didn't you? Val Stark doesn't make claim to bein' a lady."

"But she is a woman, Branch. And a helluva woman under all that bristle and grit, too, is my guess. I've never been with a woman like that. I wonder what it would be like—"

Halting as hot color began to flood Branch's face, Harper gave a short laugh. "Yeah, I guess it's best if neither one of us thinks about it. I bet she's a crack shot."

The tension in Branch's gut was beginning to lessen. "To hear her talk, she is."

"I believe it."

"She says she's a better man than I am every step of the way, too—physical parts aside."

"I belie—" Harper gave a short laugh. "Sorry, Branch."

"Don't be sorry, friend, because the sale is yours, straight from Will Stark's mouth. I'll get a draft out of him within the next half hour, and you get those bulls here as fast as you can. And I'm tellin' you now, that partnership in the Circle S is going to be mine. No icy-eyed witch is goin' to run me off."

Harper stared at Branch's flushed face, then tossed down another drink. "You know what they say about all that ice on the surface and the fire underneath."

"Save it."

"You're a lucky man."

Branch's dark eyes were burning. "Yeah...."

Clearmont was falling into the distance behind them, and out of the corner of her eye, Val fought to suppress a smile. She was real pleased with herself.

She patted the package that had brought her into town that day. Her pa hadn't made any mention of Walker and him meeting that cattle buyer in town. If she hadn't decided to replace the clothes Maggie Winthrop had ruined, those bulls would have been bought behind her back. Her pa had bought them over her objections, anyway, but the real pleasure had been watching Branch Walker burn as she talked to that Stevenson fellow.

Val glanced again out of the corner of her eye. He was still burning.

Val suppressed the broadening of her smile. Sally Ledman had been put in her place, she had gotten a healthy rise out of Branch Walker and, if she didn't miss her guess, she had shocked Harper Stevenson into realizing that she wasn't just another silly twit to twist around his finger. As for Pa, well, after those bulls were delivered, he would learn that he had made a big mistake. And she'd make sure he'd never forget it.

Yeah, she was proud of herself. She had done real good.

Chapter Eight

Val was agitated and perspiring as she rushed to dress in the early-morning solitude of her bedroom. She looked out through the window into the semilight of dawn and groaned again. Sounds from the dining room indicated that the men had finished breakfast and had already gone to saddle up. She couldn't understand how she had managed to oversleep on the first day of branding.

Taking a firm hold on her patience, Val tried again. She coaxed, she pulled, she grunted, to no avail, but she was not ready to give up. She took a tighter grip. Coax, pull, grunt—ah! Her new pants were on at last!

Turning, Val viewed herself in the mirror, squinting in the dim light. Lord! That couldn't be her! She had never realized her legs were so long, her waist so small and her backside so...

Damn that Sally Ledman! She must've switched her pants for a smaller size!

Val reached for her new shirt and grimaced immediately upon unfolding it. This shirt was *half* the size of the one she had picked out! She slipped it on and pulled it closed across her chest. Her breasts were visibly well rounded to the eye, beneath the straining material, and Val gave a low snort. That Sally was far more clever and far more vicious than Val had suspected. And fast, too, considering how quickly she must have worked to switch clothes while her back was turned. If her backup change of clothes hadn't been in tatters, she might have considered it a good joke, but at the present moment, she was not at all amused.

Val searched her room in the inadequate light emanating from the small lamp on her night table. Frowning, she lifted blankets, pillows, and looked under the bed. It was getting late and she knew many of the men would already be mounted and ready to leave. Damn! Where were her old clothes?

In her stocking feet Val walked out of her room, quickly covering the distance to the kitchen. Red Hand stood at the stove stirring a large pot. It smelled awful, and she knew better than to ask what he was cooking. Instead she queried, "Where's my pa, Red Hand?"

Red Hand did not bother to turn with his response. "Him in yard, ready to leave."

"They can't leave yet! Red Hand, I looked all over my room and I can't find my old clothes. I can't wear these things. Red Hand…turn around…look at me! I'll choke to death in these pants!"

Red Hand turned. His eyes moved in quick assessment, and he nodded. "Red Hand like."

"Red Hand like? Red Hand crazy! What happened to my old clothes—the pants and shirt I took off last night? I left them on the chair."

"Your father say to wash."

"Wash! You never wash my clothes. Maggie Winthrop does the laundry."

"Your father say you not like the way Maggie do laundry. He tell Red Hand to wash."

"Forget what Pa said, Red Hand. Just give me back my clothes."

Red Hand nodded, his leathery features hardly moving as he pointed to the pot boiling on the stove in front of him.

Val shook her head. "You don't mean…"

"Red Hand get clean. Red Hand boil."

Val closed her eyes slowly, only to jerk them open as her father's impatient shout echoed in the yard.

"Hurry up, Val, or we're leavin'!"

They weren't leaving without her! Turning on a run, Val raced back to her room and jumped into her boots. Not taking the time to braid her hair, she stuffed it up into her hat and grabbed her coat. Slipping into it as she ran, she raced back to the dining room, grabbed a few slices of bread off the table and jammed them into her pocket. At the door a second later, she paused to catch her breath. Affixing a calm expression on her face, she then stepped out onto the porch. Dunbar was saddled and waiting. Relieved, she grunted a short word of thanks to her father as she mounted.

"Don't thank me. Branch had one of the boys saddle Dunbar for you. He didn't want to waste no more time waitin'."

"Oh." Val shot Branch a deadly glance where he was mounted a few feet away, and his mouth quirked cryptically.

A few seconds later, they were off at a gallop.

The grassland around them was silver with early-morning dew, and Val did not have to look behind her to know that their mounted group had left a dark-green scar as they approached the summer pasture. The air had been heavy with the smell of sage and cedar upon their approach, but the scent of pine had begun to take dominance, indication that the wind had changed direction and now was blowing from the far-off Big Horn Mountains. Reaching the crest of the hill, Val saw the mountains with their snowfields of silver and slopes of blue, and she paused, knowing that the view was as much a part of the season as the call of the meadowlark, the flashing flirt of the mountain bluebird and the arduous work that lay before them.

Grateful that the work of sorting out the dry cows and yearlings was behind them, Val surveyed the herd driven into the summer pasture where the new corral had been constructed. She knew some of the cattle had scattered and would have to be driven back out of nearby draws and corners, but she also knew the most difficult work lying ahead of them would not start until they had again succeeded in separating the bawling calves from their bellowing mothers and the branding irons were hot.

Biting back a retort as Walker signaled the men to gather around him for quick instructions, Val noted that he had deliberately chosen to ignore her presence. She gave a low snort, taking that exclusion as license to assume her usual position. Squeezing Dunbar's sides gently with her heels, she did just that.

Val tested the irons in the fire a short time later and inspected them closely. Finding them hot enough for branding, she glanced up in time to catch Branch Walker watching her. She challenged him with her stare. Her elite position of handling the irons had not come any easier than any of her other ranching skills.

She knew that a brand had to be applied just right, that a hair-branded calf would show no sign of a brand in two or three months time and could be easily rustled, and that a smeared brand was of little use. She also knew Walker would take the first opportunity to state those facts should she make a mistake, and was determined that she would not.

Turning to Potter and Whalen where they held a bawling calf a short distance away, Val ordered, "Hold him tight, boys. I want a clear brand." Ducking out of the way of a stream of manure as she approached the frightened calf, Val pressed the iron down on the calf's side, holding it with obvious expertise.

"Careful there, Val. You'll burn that calf."

Val grimaced at Potter's pitiful joke. The branding smoke boiled up hot and acid, making her eyes water as she muttered, "Very funny."

Jumping back as the calf was released, Val returned her iron to the fire. She was sweating profusely after having repeated that same procedure too many times for an accurate count, when a prickling sensation at the back of her neck caused her to snap up her head in time to see Walker's dark eyes intent upon her. Her heart leaped, but she again challenged his stare, realizing she was challenging him to criticize her work, as well.

Val could not help snickering as Branch abruptly turned his horse and moved to the opposite side of the corral. She watched the broad stretch of his shoulders as he roped a balking calf, and her stomach did an annoyingly familiar flip-flop. Off his horse in a moment, he efficiently secured the calf's hooves, and a reluctant admiration soared inside her for his undeniable skill and the strength so obvious in his quick, concise movements.

A memory of his strength tormented Val as she recalled the rock-hard wall of his chest supporting her and that warm, comfortable cranny at the side of his neck that had shielded her face from the rain. She remembered the scent of him, the steady sound of his heart throbbing under her ear and the comfort in his hands when he drew her back more closely to enclose her against the warmth of his body. She had gotten the strangest feeling then, the same feeling she'd had when he had massaged her nearly frozen feet. That same feeling had returned when she had turned to see him watching her earlier. Damn it all, she—

"Hey, Val, what're you waitin' for? You expect us to hold this calf all day?"

Whalen's impatient call startled Val from her wandering thoughts, bringing a flush to her face. Annoyed to find her hands shaking, she grabbed the nearest iron, dropping it with a low curse as it burned through a hole in her leather glove. Moving her hand up higher on the handle to find a cooler spot, she grasped it again and closed the distance between herself and the calf with a few running steps. A moment too late to move aside, she felt the full rush of hot manure spray her boots and she groaned, pressing the iron to the animal's side with a vengeance that did not go unrewarded as the calf struggled to its feet upon being released, splattering her liberally from the same, odoriferous pile.

A hearty round of laughter echoed in the corral, and Val did not have to look up to know Walker's dark eyes had witnessed the whole scene. Gritting her teeth, she dropped the iron back in the fire as Potter gave a low hoot. "You must be slowin' down in your old age, Val. I ain't seen you get caught by one of them little heifers' johnny streams since you was a kid." He laughed again, his eyes tearing with amusement. "That poor little thing. It near to fell over dead from the look you gave it."

Preferring to ignore Potter's baiting, Val turned back to the fire and grabbed another iron. She dropped it with a curse as the iron again burned through the hole in her glove, and she briefly closed her eyes at the new round of laughter that ensued. Wiping the perspiration from her brow, Val was suddenly furious with Branch Walker's black looks, Jeff Potter's unrelenting teasing, her increasingly foolish performance and the growing heat of the day, which made her position near the fire unbearable.

Stripping off her hat, Val tossed it on the ground, ignoring the long silky strands of hair that fell onto her shoulders as she ripped off her coat and tossed it on the ground, as well. Bending from the waist, she grasped the nearest branding iron as a chorus of gasps sounded behind her. Startled at the sound, she turned swiftly to see the slack-jawed, bug-eyed cowhands staring at her in astonished silence.

There was no doubt that *she* was the reason for the astonished stares each and every one of them gave her as their eyes traveled the long, curving length of her in the clothes she had squeezed into that morning. They were appraising her in a way they never had before, in a way that sent Val's anger suddenly soaring.

Taking an aggressive step forward, she tossed back her hair, jammed her balled fists onto her trim hips and demanded, ''What in hell are you all lookin' at?''

The violence of her effort popped a button from her straining shirt, and the gasps echoed again. Val's patience snapped. ''What's the matter with you fellas? You act like you ain't never seen a woman in pants before!'' She bent over to reach for the iron again and the gasps brought her upright with a snap.

Val turned with a furious look and a dire intention that was halted by the interjection of Walker's harsh command. ''Get back to work, all of you!''

Walker's face was unnaturally stiff, and Val gave a snort as she turned away from him. Taking the full length of her hair in her hands, she quickly braided it over her shoulder.

The men were all shuffling around her when she picked up the iron again. She approached the next calf and, inexplicably, found herself giving a little wiggle of her tightly clad hips as she leaned over and applied the iron. Equally inexplicably, her spirits moved steadily upward with each word from her suddenly uneasy co-workers.

Val smiled and burned another brand. Looking up, she caught Branch Walker's eyes upon her and her smile froze. Turning, not certain what possessed her, she gave a short, deliberate wiggle and continued with her work.

Branch withheld a choking gasp and turned back to his work. He was grateful there were no witnesses around as he coiled his rope with shaky hands, the image of Val Stark's unexpected physical attributes clear in his mind. The shock of it was with him still—the sight of her as she'd tossed off her coat and hat and turned toward him. Those clothes—what in hell had possessed her? They outlined every curve of her body. And that hair that had spilled down from her hat like a shimmering waterfall—he had never seen the like of it before.

Suddenly realizing that his heart was pounding, Branch took a deep, steadying breath and turned toward a lean-faced cowboy who was paying more attention to Val Stark's figure than the branding iron in his hand. It appeared that the clever woman had decided upon another tactic to disrupt the progress of work under his supervision as she postured and posed, bending from the waist in a way that elicited appreciative gasps from the enthralled cowhands. The most affected of the group appeared to be Billy Simm, who stood, openly gawking as the crafty female leaned over and applied an iron to a bawling calf's side.

Suddenly awakening to the fact that he was gawking, too, Branch felt his patience snap. Striding over to the fire where Val Stark poked at the heating irons, he took her gruffly by the arm. She struggled unsuccessfully to escape his grip, irritating him into dragging her a few steps away as he spoke in a low tone meant to be confidential. "You're done here for the day, *ma'am.*"

"What did you say?" Val questioned, her eyes narrowed shards of ice.

"I said you're done here. You're a menace. Someone's goin' to get hurt, and I'm not goin' to let it happen."

"*I'm* a menace? I'm the best hand with a brandin' iron on this spread!"

"That so? Just like you're the best horse wrangler, the best roper, the best cattle drover, the best poker player. Hell, even a first-year cowhand knows how to sidestep a johnny stream."

"You—" Val sputtered, still attempting to shake off his hand. "You go back and check my brands. There ain't a one of them that ain't perfect."

"So you say."

"So I *know!*"

Branch Walker stared down at her, certain that he was going to get Val Stark out of this corral one way or another. He'd had enough of Simm's undressing her with his eyes. It made his blood boil! It made him want to blacken both of the fella's popping eyes, then throw Val Stark over his horse and—

Oh, hell, what was he thinking?

Branch gritted his teeth. "I want you out of here—now. And I don't want you comin' back where my men are workin' until you're wearin' respectable clothes."

Val Stark went suddenly still, and Branch was struck with the thought that he was uncertain when this unpredictable woman was more dangerous—when she was cussing and in a violent fury, or when her face whitened, as it had now, and she was so unnaturally motionless that he felt he should take the opportunity to run for cover. He didn't have long to wait for the answer to the question.

"So that's it." Val's response started out low and began building. "You object to my clothes. They're not respectable, are they? Well, I'll tell you what *I* think. I think you were in cahoots with your little friend in the general store and told her to switch clothes on me. I think it was *your* idea to get me here today lookin' like this, just so's you could claim I wasn't doin' my job. And I think you did it because you're afraid I'm goin' to prove to my pa and the hands, too, that my pa made a mistake when he hired you!"

"Is that so…?" Branch's blood began boiling. Somewhere in the back of his mind he was relieved to have anger replace his confused feelings of a few minutes earlier as he continued, "Well, you're wrong, *ma'am,* as you usually are, and I want you out of here."

"No!"

"Out!"

"I'm not goin' nowhere!"

"You're goin' back to the ranch if I have to take you there myself."

Val's hand snaked as quick as lightning for her gun, but Branch's hand was just as quick as it clamped down over hers to hold it motionless on the handle.

"Val!" Branch and Val turned in unison toward Will Stark as he suddenly appeared beside them. His lined face was concerned as he continued, "This all's gone far enough."

Surprised that the old man avoided his eye, Branch watched as Stark met his daughter's enraged gaze. "Branch's right, you know."

"No, he ain't!"

"Yes, he is. You got the fellas fallin' all over themselves every time you reach for another iron. Them new clothes are interferin' with their work."

"Don't go blamin' me if them bug-eyed fools act like they ain't never seen a pair of legs and a female as—"

"Valentine! You're goin' home with me—now! You can change into your old clothes and come back if you want, but—"

Val fumed. "How in hell am I supposed to change into my old clothes when Red Hand's cookin' them!"

Branch gulped. Cooking them? He had thought there were no more surprises left in Red Hand's cooking. He groaned as Will Stark's mouth quirked oddly with a cryptic statement.

"That Red Hand. He's full of surprises."

"It ain't funny, Pa!"

Choosing not to respond, Will Stark looked at Branch, instead. "You can let Val go now, Branch. I'll be takin' her home. You're right as rain. Them damned fools act like they ain't never seen a woman before. They can't take their eyes off her—especially that Simm. He's liable to end up on the wrong end of a brandin' iron if I don't get Val out of here now."

Suddenly conscious of the fact that he was still clutching Val's arm, Branch dropped it like a hot coal. Strangely, it occurred to him as he suffered the heat of Val Stark's glare that the dark lashes that lined her incredible eyes were even longer than he'd thought. They were like fluttering fans that—

"Let's go, Val."

Val Stark faced her father squarely. "I'm comin' back as soon as I can change."

"Sure enough."

Branch stiffened as Val looked at him and rasped, "You ain't seen the last of me, Walker." She turned on her heel and within minutes, took off back toward the ranch with her father at her side.

Branch turned back toward the men to see them staring after the two departing horses, and his irritation erupted sharply. "You've had your fun for today, boys. Those calves are waitin'!"

As he stepped away, Branch heard Potter whisper teasingly to the young fellow standing beside him.

"Billy Simm, you look downright dejected. Don't you worry none. Val's comin' back. You heard her say so, and you know Val, she don't never say nothin' she don't mean."

Branch released a quiet sigh. No, blast her, she didn't.

The branding was in a turmoil, Branch Walker was fit to be tied, Val's temper was hot as a pistol, but Will Stark was a happy man. Barely suppressing a smile, he rode along beside his daughter, aware that she hadn't spoken a word to him since they had left the summer pasture a few minutes earlier. But he knew that was a temporary circumstance. Val could no more stop talking than she could stop breathing, and she'd be going full tilt again as soon as she calmed down.

Will stared at the manure-covered pants protruding from Val's coat. He had a feeling that those clothes would never be worn again, but they had accomplished their purpose. He'd never forget the look on Branch Walker's face when Val had stripped off her hat and coat. The big fella had looked as if he'd been struck by lightning—Stark lightning. Val was all woman, all right, as much as she tried to deny it, and he knew Branch was now uncomfortably aware of it. But he also knew that when it came to Branch Walker, Val was her own worst enemy. If he could only find a way to gag her for a few days.... Maybe Red Hand could come up with one of his potions—

Will halted that line of thought abruptly and shot his daughter a guilty look. He paused to study the firm line of her jaw a moment longer. No, he wasn't that desperate yet. He'd give it all a little more time.

Except for the scraping of forks against plates and the sound of smacking lips, the dining room at supper was as silent as a tomb. Still fuming, Val chewed vigorously. The meat on her plate was as tough as leather with half the taste, but she was determined to consume her share, cheated of her due as she had been earlier in the day.

In retrospect, Val realized that the fiasco in the branding corral was just another in a long line of personal disasters since Branch Walker had made his appearance at the Circle S. She had silently questioned on the long ride home, as she had so many times during the past month, what she had ever done to deserve his appearance in her life.

No response had been forthcoming, and never one to acknowledge defeat, she had almost ridden Dunbar into the ground, determined as she was to resume her place branding with the men. However, it was not meant to be. She had arrived in the kitchen to find her clothes still steeping in the pot and Red Hand nowhere to be found. She had fished out the abused garments, the skin peeling from her burned fingers as she hung the garments on the line to dry.

Furious, she had then gone to the barn and taken Powderkeg

outside for a workout. She had not spoken a word in the time since, except for the low string of curses the dark stallion evoked as he balked at her every command, behaving more the arrogant, headstrong male than he ever had before. At the end of her patience she had returned to the house, ripped her clothes off the line and retired to her room, emerging shortly after the men had arrived back from the summer corral, wearing damp clothes and a grim expression.

A quick look at her father's noncommittal expression did little to assuage Val's irritation. As for the men, she wasn't certain which was worse: the way most of them avoided her eye with embarrassment or the way Billy Simm looked at her with that mooning smile. With a low sniff of disgust, she reached for the bread, wincing as Billy offered sickeningly, "Here, let me do that for you, Val."

Val snatched at the bread, warning, "I don't need nobody helpin' me pick up a piece of bread! I don't need nobody helpin' me to do nothin'!"

Glancing up, Val saw Branch Walker's eyes upon her and her temper flared. Them damned black eyes haunted her, and she'd had all she was going to take for a day. Slapping the bread back down on the plate, Val jumped to her feet, ignoring the crack of the chair as it crashed against the floor behind her. Her pa looked up, the words he was about to speak freezing on his lips as she turned toward the door and marched outside. She was shoveling manure in the semidarkness of the barn, when she heard Jeff Potter's chuckle behind her.

"You got them all fooled back in there, but you don't fool me none, Val Stark."

Val turned a look on the grizzled cowpoke that was pure ice. "I don't fool you, huh? Why's that? Because you can't fool an old fool?"

Potter's nose twitched with annoyance. "Old fool I may be, but I'm not too old to see through you. You got three months' pay ridin' on the bet you made with Whalen, Simm and me, and I'm thinkin' you saw yourself fallin' behind and decided to do a little cheatin' today."

"Cheatin'?" Val's back stiffened and her eyes narrowed. "I ain't never cheated at nothin' in my life."

"Oh, no? Well, what would you call the way you took the wind out of most of them fellas today, showin' up dressed like you was? If Branch Walker wasn't the kind of man he is, it would've worked, too, but that fella's too smart for you. He ain't about to let you twist him around your little finger with a wiggle here and a shake there."

Val's breathing was becoming short and heated. "I'm tellin' you now, Potter, if I put my heart and soul into a wiggle and a shake, there wouldn't be no man livin' that would have a chance against me."

"Ho, ho, ho! How you do talk!" Potter was obviously amused. "The truth is, you're losin' out to Walker, Val, and you don't like it."

"I ain't losin'!"

"Ain't you? That was *you* I saw Branch Walker send home with her tail between her legs today, wasn't it?"

"Tail between my legs? You're mistakin', Potter. If my pa wasn't ridin' herd on me, I'd have shown that oversized cowpoke who was boss."

Potter raised his hairy brows. "It ain't like you to make excuses, Val." The sound of footsteps behind Potter turned him toward Whalen and Simm as they came to stand behind him, and he gave a short laugh. "Now, I'm sure Simm would be more than happy to call off your bet if you'd coax him just a little."

Val suppressed a shiver as Simm's boyish face lapsed into a sickeningly familiar smile. She gritted her teeth. "Potter..."

"But then I'm thinkin' Whalen is enjoyin' this all too much to call it quits. Am I right, Whalen?"

"Dammed right."

"And as for me—"

Unwilling to listen to another aggravating word, Val interrupted with a low hiss, "All right, you fellas, listen here, 'cause I'm goin' to set you straight once and for all." She rested her shovel on the floor with great care, when her true inclination was to swing it with all her might at the three blockheads leering at her. "I don't need no tricks, and I don't need to cheat to win our little bet. And to show you I ain't backin' out, I'm sayin' that from this minute on, I'll meet Branch Walker stroke for stroke on anythin' he does—no excuses. I'll be one step behind him, Pa or no Pa. I'll be his shadow, doin' what he does, except I'll be betterin' him every time. And at the end of three months, when he's had enough and he turns tail and runs, I'll be watchin' with a smile on my face for all of you to see."

The silence that met her emphatic statements was prolonged. Val turned abruptly toward Whalen as he shook his head and whistled mockingly. "My, ain't you tough. The trouble is, you ain't as tough as you think you are. The only thing that saved you in the past was your pa standin' behind you when you backed every one of us down. But he ain't standin' behind you with Walker, and you're goin' to be fallin' flat on your face so many times that you're goin' to be on real good speakin' terms with that mud you'll have your face in. Just so's you know it, I'll be watchin' and keepin' score, and I'm already spendin' my winnin's, *sweetheart*."

Val took a quick step forward, her hands clenched, only to

have Potter step unexpectedly between them as he turned a hard look into Whalen's dark expression. "While we're all makin' things clear, I'll speak my piece, too, friend. Just in case you got any ideas about helpin' that bet along, I'm makin' it my business to see that Val takes on only one man at a time. And right now, that man is Walker."

Holding Potter's stare for a silent moment, Whalen then turned on his heel and disappeared into the yard. Potter was still staring after the cowpoke when Val addressed him tightly.

"I don't need nobody fightin' my battles for me, Potter."

"Yeah, she don't need nobody fightin' her battles for her, Potter!" Simm's interjection jerked Val and Potter's heads toward the baby-faced cowboy as he flushed and continued determinedly, "But if anybody's goin' to stand up for Val, it's goin' to be me."

Motionless for a long moment, Val slapped her hand over her eyes with disgusted disbelief, then dragged it slowly down her face, peering at Simm's persistent smile. It seemed that in the eyes of these two men, in one short afternoon, she had gone from the toughest cowpoke on the Circle S to a helpless female—and all with a mere wiggle and a shake of her hips. Worst of all, she was certain that the road back would not be easy.

Val turned without a word and walked away. As she stepped into the yard she heard Simm utter with a sigh, "That Val, she's some woman, ain't she?"

And Potter's amused reply, "Yes, my boy, that she is."

Branch halted midstep as Val Stark marched past him on her way back to the house. Her head was high and she looked straight ahead as if he were invisible. Branch felt his lip curl with a familiar vexation. He was still fuming as Potter and

Simm emerged from the barn, and his irritation mounted as Simm stared after Val with a besotted expression on his young face.

Branch's cheek twitched. He had known more than one woman to be taken in by a baby face, and Billy Simm didn't fool him. Simm was a grown man. So was Aubrey Whalen, and it looked as if Whalen wasn't immune to Val's physical charms, either. Branch's cheek twitched again. Val Stark was biting off more than she could chew if she thought she was going to play the men against one another in order to cause him problems, because he'd put a stop to things before they began.

As for that sweet little backside and those trim, swaying hips, he was determined to consign that image to the same place he had sent the memory of those long fingers working at that third button. He'd do it, damn it, if it was the last thing he ever did! The next time Valentine Stark fell on her face, she'd pick *herself* up.

Branch turned toward the bunkhouse, seething. He was still mumbling under his breath as he slammed the door shut behind him.

Chapter Nine

The ranch buildings in the valley lay snug in the shadows as the light morning breeze carried up the crowing of a rooster and the bawl of a hungry calf. From somewhere unseen a high-pitched whinny elicited a snorting response from Caesar, and a sense of well-being swelled inside Branch at the tranquil beauty surrounding him. The knowledge that his future lay in this land touched him with a contentment that was only too fleeting as the sound of a horse making its way through the pack behind him drew his attention. He turned just as a familiar figure pulled up alongside, and his jaw stiffened.

A tick in his hide could not have harassed him more than Val Stark this past week, and he had just about had enough. Turning to Will Stark, riding a few feet away, he saw that the fellow appeared to be oblivious to his daughter's relentlessness. It was an attitude the old coot had struck since the day in the corral when his daughter had wiggled her way to the attention of the men. Simm had not yet recovered, and he had the feeling that with a crook of her little finger the conniving she-wolf would be able to turn the others' heads, as well.

Branch stiffened his spine and squared his shoulders, a posture he found himself spontaneously assuming whenever Val

Stark drew near. His breath escaped in a sound too closely resembling a growl for him not to be aware of it, and he wondered again why he allowed this woman to manipulate him so.

And manipulate him, she did. Even now the challenge in the set of her shoulders as she drew up alongside him, then deliberately urged her horse a few inches ahead of his, sent the blood racing to his face. She did not deign to acknowledge his glance, allowing him a few moments to study her profile etched against the early-morning sky. It was a pleasant profile, and he wondered how he had ever thought those small features to be unfeminine.

He had been acutely aware since that stormy night when he'd brought her home wet and quivering with cold that her cheek, where she had rested it against the side of his neck in her complete exhaustion, was clearer and softer than it had a right to be. The lone braid that trailed down her back glowed with a reddish sheen in the morning sun, and he could not recall the number of times he had awakened from dreams of that shimmering mass slipping through his clutching fingers.

Frowning, Branch jerked his gaze toward the mountains in the distance, silently wondering if he was truly going mad. The woman beside him had made his life a living hell the past week. She had returned to the branding pen the day after her expulsion with a resolution to make him eat his words written on her face as she drove herself and the men around her almost into the ground with her uncompromising pace. The men had finally balked and he had instructed Boggs to take her place with the branding iron. She had been furious, and her reaction had been none the less nettling for its predictability.

Were he not such an obstinate cuss, he knew he would have admitted to himself that she had succeeded in making him rue that day, for, free of any specific chores, she had trailed at his heels every working hour since. It had not been difficult to figure out her intention as she began matching even his slightest efforts with one of her own. She was out to prove to the hands, to her father, and mostly to him that she could do anything he could do, and do it better. It galled him to admit that she was almost succeeding.

A pheasant chuckled in the grass nearby and Val turned toward the sound, availing Branch a view of the small features motionless under the broad brim of her hat. Those eyes were like the gray mist before dawn, filled with shadows. He had the feeling a man could get lost in those eyes.

Val turned her head forward again and Branch felt a familiar despair. He was staring at her squared shoulders, when he noticed she was straining to see the pasture just coming into view in the distance. She kicked her horse into a gallop and Branch followed the line of her gaze. In a moment his mount was pounding over the ground behind hers.

Branch drew his horse to a sliding halt a few minutes later, his stomach churning at the sight that met his eyes. Dismounting, he walked to one of the many cows moaning pitifully around the water hole. Their stomachs were bloated and their breathing strained. Twenty or thirty of them were affected, as well as calves with brands still fresh. As he surveyed those still standing, another cow stumbled and fell. Will Stark's low oath broke the silence as Branch walked quickly to the water's edge. He scooped up a handful of water and sniffed, realizing as he did that Val Stark was already trailing the water from her hand, her assessment made as she mumbled, "This water is tainted. How in hell did this happen?"

Val's puzzled gaze met his and Branch shook his head. Another cow made its approach, and he shouted, "Wyatt, Little, drive that cow back. Get the rest of them out of here, too. Simm, get the vet. Smith, get yourself back to the ranch and load some tools and that extra bale of wire onto a wagon. We have to fence this water hole off. Boggs, check the condition of the nearest spring—see if it is similarly affected. We'll hold these animals in check here until you come back.''

Branch turned to Will Stark, his brow furrowed. ''All right, so tell me. Has anything like this happened before?''

Will Stark shook his head. ''Never.''

''Until *you* came,'' Val accused.

Branch turned, anger flaring at the look in Val's eyes.

Stark turned on his daughter with a look of condemnation. ''You ain't usin' your head, Val. This ain't Branch's fault, and you know it. It's just some kind of fluke, I guess.'' Will shook his head again. ''I can't see no way for it to be nothin' else.''

''We never had no 'flukes' until *he* came.''

''That's enough, Val!''

Branch raised his chin, his narrowed gaze a direct assault as he looked at Val. Angry as he was, he could not suppress a flash of admiration for the way she stood up under a look that had cowered more men than he could count. He responded with ''I don't know what happened here, but I'll find out. In the meantime, I don't need you makin' foolish accusations. And I'm tellin' you here and now, if you don't intend cooperatin' with our effort here, you can go back to the house.''

''I ain't goin' back nowhere!''

''You will if I say so, so don't step out of line.'' Not waiting for her reply, Branch mounted his horse and joined the men as they drove the remaining cattle back. He didn't need Val Stark to tell him how potentially dangerous this situation could be, that if other water holes were similarly affected they were in trouble and that if they had gone to the north pasture that day, as originally planned, instead of coming here, they might have been too late to save the entire herd in this pasture.

As Branch rode away, he did not have to look back to know that Val was glaring, her teeth clenched. He could feel the heat of her gaze and knew what it meant. It meant that he did not have enough problems, that he was going to get more.

The setting sun shadowed the deep lines in Red Hand's leathery cheek as he watched the returning ranch hands in stoic silence. His bloodshot eyes assessed the weary droop of the men's shoulders and the absence of the chatter that usually accompanied the end of the week's work at the Circle S. He had gotten the story of the sick cattle from Smith when the fellow had returned to the ranch for the wagon, and now he assessed the faces of the men, one by one, as they rode in.

His gaze returning to the tall man at the head of the exhausted group, he saw that anger vied with the weariness on Walker's face. Val was arguing with her father as she rode a few steps to the big fellow's right, and it took only one glance from Walker for Red Hand to realize the reason for the big man's anger. Val was still fighting him and things were not going well.

Turning as the men drew closer, Red Hand walked back to the kitchen and the large pot bubbling there. The silent Indian raised his head as Stark entered the room and spoke with exhaustion heavy in his voice.

"Get that food on the table as soon as you can, will you, Red Hand? The men are ready to drop."

Val walked through the kitchen without a word. Will motioned with his chin toward his daughter's retreating back as she disappeared into the next room.

"She ain't made things a bit easier today, neither. She was dammed hot when old Doc Hall finally arrived and looked at them cows, only to say he couldn't figure out what was in that water that made them sick. She called him a quack outright and the fella would've left on the spot if Branch hadn't stepped in to soothe the old quack's—I mean the old fella's—feathers." Stark shrugged. "Walker sent the men out to check all the other water holes on the ranch, but they're all right. We just can't figure out what happened in that one pasture."

Red Hand waited until he was certain Will Stark's ramblings had come to an end. Then he spoke. "Red Hand know."

Will Stark paused. "Red Hand know what?"

"Red Hand know what make cows sick."

"You do…"

Red Hand held up a stained leather pouch and turned it over to demonstrate that it was empty.

Stark's eyes widened. "Are you tellin' me that *you* put somethin' in that water?"

"No."

"Then what are you tellin' me?"

"Someone steal from Red Hand."

"You're sayin' somebody stole whatever was in that pouch and poured it into the water hole. You're sayin' it wasn't no fluke, after all. You're sayin' somebody did all that on purpose, for some crazy reason.…"

Red Hand nodded.

"What was in that pouch?"

Red Hand raised his chin and kept his silence.

Annoyed, Will pressed, "Who knew about that pouch?"

Silence again.

"Red Hand, damn it! What are you tryin' to say?"

Red Hand turned back to the stove and stirred the pot, ignoring the sounds of Stark's choked frustration. His talking was done.

Val slammed into her room, tore off her coat and hat and threw them on the bed. Resisting the urge for mayhem, she closed her eyes and counted. She was still counting when the image of Branch Walker appeared before her. She snapped open her eyes, furious. There had been a point somewhere at the beginning of this week where she had believed she was gaining on the hardheaded know-it-all who went by the name of Branch Walker, but she had begun to see the fallacy in that thought as this day drew to a close.

She was sick to death of seeing the men, her pa included, deferring to Branch Walker on every question, accepting his word, and jumping to his commands. Whose ranch was this, anyway?

The problem with the water hole this morning had been the final straw. Walker had been ineffective in determining the cause, and there was not a man on the spread who would acknowledge it. Instead she had listened with her stomach churning as her pa praised him for his fast thinking, for organizing the work so that it had been accomplished in so short a time, and all the while she knew that Walker had not accomplished anything that she could not have done in half the time—with her eyes closed!

Turning in her silent rage, Val caught sight of herself in the mirror and stopped dead. A tall, slender woman with a furious expression stared back at her, and she knew that was the source of her problem. She was a woman, and with a thoughtless wiggle and a shake earlier in the week, she had set her own cause back almost irreparably.

Val fumed. But she'd win back the credibility she had lost and she'd force Branch Walker to eat his words, too. She'd do it! She'd do it if she had to dog him every minute of the day, if it took every last ounce of strength she had, if…if…

Her head high, Val turned toward the door. Moments later she emerged from her room, renewed for battle.

Saturday was a busy day in Clearmont, and the riders from the Circle S gained little attention as they rode into town. Positioned at the head of his men, Will Stark assessed the wide main street. On one side the Loco Steer dominated the scene, the bawdy music emerging through the grayed swinging doors silent testimony to the festivity that seldom ceased in the town's most popular saloon. Next door the restaurant was filled with midafternoon customers. A few doors down, Doc Pitt's office was convenient to dissatisfied customers of both establishments, and beyond that was the Trail's End Hotel.

Will noted as they passed that the livery stable on the other side of the street appeared to be seeing a steady business with the arrivals and departures of a shopping day. Next door, the blacksmith was visible at the bellows through the open door of his shop. Then there was the barbershop with its six-foot candy-striped pole outside the door, the gunsmith and Asa Ledman's general store.

Will glanced at his daughter, who rode beside him, and winced. He had tried to convince her to stay home and let him buy the new pants and shirt she needed, despite his former refusal to do so, but she had turned down his offer. Val was certain that Sally Ledman was responsible for switching the clothes she had bought the previous week. He had not foreseen the possibility of Val's jumping to that conclusion when he had formulated the plan that had worked so well, and hours of argument about the possibility of an honest mistake on Sally's part had been unsuccessful in altering that thought in his stubborn daughter's mind.

Coward that he was, he was not ready to admit his own guilt, and he had finally determined to follow his hotheaded daughter into the store and take whatever steps were necessary to avoid bloodshed—especially his own.

The thought of bloodshed turned Will momentarily toward Branch Walker, riding behind him. It was his feeling that Branch had fallen back deliberately, unwilling to compete with Val for the lead. Considering his daughter's attitude toward the man, he had to admire the fellow's grit. He did not think for a moment that Walker was the one responsible for tainting the water hole, if the tainting had indeed been deliberate, as Red Hand had intimated.

Will paused at the thought. That crazy old Injun—he had probably lost the contents of that pouch somewhere without realizing it. Nothing else made any sense.

The general store loomed closer and Will felt his old heart jump as his daughter's eyes narrowed. He shuddered at the thought of the confrontation to come.

Then Will glanced at Branch Walker and saw the look of a man with a deep thirst. Recalling the many times he had lingered at the Loco Steer rather than return home to a daughter that drove him harder than a mule when there was work to be done, he realized it would not be the first time she had delivered a man to drink.

Will sighed. Ah, Mary...Mary... Val was his daughter and he loved her dearly, but it was time to pass her on to a younger, stronger man who was more equipped to handle her. All he wanted was the chance to spend the remaining years of his life with the comfort of a warm, sympathetic woman like his Mary. To feel her softness in his arms, to know that she—

"Pa?" The tone of Val's voice turned him toward her abruptly. "Are you sick or somethin'? You got the funniest look on your face."

"No, I ain't sick!" Will straightened his spine and rubbed his nose. "Just sick and tired is all."

Noting that his daughter chose to ignore his comment as they drew up before the general store, Will felt his heart begin a new pounding. He glanced to his rear, noting that Branch Walker and the rest of the men continued riding toward the Loco Steer. No help there. He supposed it was up to him.

Dismounting beside his daughter, Will threw his horse's reins over the rail and followed her up the steps, guilt plaguing him the entire way.

Sally Ledman, here we come....

Branch smiled for the first time that day as he approached the Loco Steer. The thought occurred to him that he had never looked forward to drowning himself in a few drinks so much in his life. Music streamed through the swinging doors on which his sights were trained, and the thought of the hardwood haven where he could escape the Circle S and everything connected with it was bliss.

The tainted water hole still bothered him. An inexplicable accident or maybe no accident at all. But who would benefit from such an underhanded act?

Thoughts of the irrational brought a familiar figure to his mind. A burr in his tail, a tick on his hide, an itch he couldn't scratch—that was Val Stark. She plagued him day and night, awake and asleep. He was never free of her, of her harassment, of her unrelenting eye and of the thought of those damned long fingers working at that third button....

She was driving him crazy!

He had almost been surprised when she'd turned her horse away from their group to head for the general store. In the back of his mind, he had begun to think that there was nowhere he would be free of her, including the sanctuary of a saloon, a man's last refuge from the weaker sex.

The weaker sex... Branch considered those words again. No, that wasn't Val Stark! Branch laughed abruptly at the thought, momentarily uncomfortable as a few of the men looked at him with raised brows.

At the hitching rail a few moments later, Branch dismounted. He turned toward the others with a smile and an announcement. "Step inside and up to the bar, boys. The first drink's on me."

His smile widening at the appreciative comments that followed, Branch watched as the hands pushed and shoved their way into the saloon. He was feelin' better already, now that he had finally shaken that pesky woman.

With a glance toward the general store, Branch mumbled, "Thank you, Lord."

He had never meant those words more sincerely in his life.

"Thank you, Lord."

Will Stark's mumbled words went unheard by his daughter as she turned away from the counter of Asa Ledman's general store with her package in her hand a short time later. He grinned. Sally Ledman, bless the fevered little darlin', was sick at home with the flu, and Asa had sadly informed them that she wouldn't be back to work for an indeterminate period.

Will's grin widened. Things were definitely looking up.

"What are you grinnin' at, Pa?"

Val's churlish comment brought him back to the present with a crash, and Will replied tartly, "Can't a man smile without givin' you a reason?"

"You looked like the cat that ate the canary."

"Well, as long as you ain't the canary, what do you care?"

Val shrugged. "You're gettin' crazier than a loon, you know that, Pa?"

"And you're gettin' bossier than—"

Val gritted her teeth. "You'd better not say bossier than Branch Walker, 'cause pa or no pa, I'll lay you out right here!"

Not doubting she meant every word, Will shook his head. "Don't go puttin' words in my mouth, daughter. Seems like you're either tryin' to put words in my mouth or thoughts into my head these days."

"I've given up tryin' to talk some sense into you, Pa. Your head's too damned hard." Val paused to glance up and down the street as they reached the door. Her gaze came to rest upon the familiar horses tied to the rail outside the Loco Steer, and Will shook his head.

"Oh, no, you don't, Val. I've put up with a lot from you in the past, but I ain't lettin' no daughter of mine shimmy up to a bar in a place like the Loco Steer."

"Ain't you, now…"

Val's eyes grew thoughtful as she stared at the broad swinging doors. Will was about to respond, when a familiar figure at the far end of the street sent his old heart to palpitating. Dammed if it wasn't Mary.

Glancing back to his daughter's pensive expression, he warned with a forced frown, "I'm tellin' you, Val, one step into that place and I'll come in and drag you out by the back of your neck, you hear?''

Val nodded. "I hear."

"That's good." Mary disappeared into the livery stable at the end of the street, and Will could stand it no longer. "I've got some things to do at the blacksmith's and all. Don't go waitin' on me if you want to go home. I just might visit Jim Parkerhurst for a game of chess."

Val's brows quirked quizzically. "You don't play chess, Pa."

"No? So you don't know everythin', do you?" Will all but growled.

Hoping he would never be called on to prove his bluff, Will started down the street. So interested in the livery stable was he that he didn't see his daughter pause and turn toward those broad swinging doors.

"You treat old Rainbow real nice now, Charlie." Mary's round face creased into the comfortable wrinkles of a warm smile as she spoke to the proprietor of Clearmont's stable. "Some oats might do her real fine right now."

Charlie Hutton nodded and winked a bleary eye. "Anythin' you say, Mary. I'll never be too busy to give your horse some special treatment, because there ain't nobody who makes an apple pie like you."

The sound of a step behind her turned Mary to the unexpected sight of Will Stark, and her heart leaped as his name escaped her lips in an excited whisper. "Wilbur! What are you doin' in town today?"

Acknowledging Charlie's nod, Wilbur waited until the fellow turned into the next stall before responding with a frown,

"What did old Charlie mean, 'nobody makes an apple pie like you'? What does he know about your apple pie?"

Mary flushed. "Charlie had some of my pie at the last church social." And when Wilbur remained silent, she sniffed, a tear coming to her eye, "What did you think he meant?"

Suddenly contrite, Wilbur darted a quick look around them and took her hand. "Oh, I don't know what I meant, Mary, darlin'. It's just that…" He took a deep breath, "I'm jealous, and I was thinkin' that maybe you're gettin' tired of waitin' for an old man like me to set his house in order."

Mary's throat constricted at the pain she saw in his eyes. "An old man, Wilbur? You'll never be an old man to me. Why, when I look at you my heart begins to pump, and my palms get sweaty, and the tingle that starts in the center of my stomach goes right down to my toes." She blinked and momentarily averted her eyes. "You think I'm shameless, don't you, Wilbur?"

Wilbur's gaze was worshipful. "Never, darlin'. Never. I just wish we wasn't in public, right now. I wish we was someplace where I could show you what I'm thinkin'."

Mary paused, the drumming of her heart approaching staccato as she said, "You didn't ask me what I'm doing in town today, Wilbur."

Will smiled, penitent and anxious to please. "What *are* you doin' in town today, Mary, darlin'?"

Mary trained her eyes on Wilbur's face, observing the warmth in his eyes as he gazed down on her, the creases in his cheeks that curled into his precious smile, the little wiggle of the marvelous mustache that tickled her so. She closed her eyes as her heart raced faster, then opened them to respond.

"Well, you see, a lady from the East was traveling through town last week when she became ill with some kind of poisoning of the blood. She's at the Trail's End Hotel. She can't get out of bed while she's recuperating and Dr. Pitt has been visiting her twice a day. The ladies from the church have been taking turns coming to town to spend time with her and bring her meals. It's my turn today, and I spent most of the morning with her. I just came back to check on Rainbow before getting some things for the poor dear at the general store and returning with her supper. I told her I would be leaving her food with her this time, because I have to get back to the ranch shortly, and she understands. Dr. Pitt will check on her again tonight, you see.''

Wilbur looked puzzled at her lengthy explanation, and Mary became anxious. She tried again. ''You see, Wilbur, I'll be going up to the hotel in a little while to drop off the poor woman's supper. I had intended to leave immediately for home, but who knows how long I'll be detained there. I mean—'' Mary looked hopefully into Wilbur's eyes ''—who knows what will pop up to keep me there...in the hotel...somewhere...?''

The light that dawned abruptly in Wilbur's eyes grew to a molten glow as he nodded enthusiastically. ''That's right, Mary. Who knows what could come up to keep you there.'' Wilbur's breathing was becoming rapid. Mary felt her heart reach out to his and she wondered, as she had so many times in the past, how this marvelous miracle had come about—this love that had leaped into flame between them.

She was unable to speak when Wilbur continued with an emotional rasp in his voice, ''That poor old lady. She sure enough is needin' your attention, and I'm thinkin' you should be gettin' back to her as soon as you can. Uh...what room did you say she's in?''

''Number 9...on the second floor...in the back.''

"That's good, Mary." Wilbur rubbed a callused knuckle against her cheek as he continued in a whisper, "'Cause I've been needin' you, darlin'."

"Oh, Wilbur…"

Moments later Mary walked swiftly along the boardwalk toward the general store. She was a woman with a purpose, and her heart had wings.

Val walked through the swinging doors of the Loco Steer to the sound of Billy Simm's startled words of welcome.

"Well, lookee here! If it ain't Val! Come on over and join us."

Val was aware of the exact second Branch Walker turned to glare in her direction, and her purpose grew bolder as she accepted Billy's invitation, smiling. "Don't mind if I do, Simm."

"Your pa know you're in here, Val?"

Potter's question set Val's teeth on edge as she responded, "Don't matter much if he does or he don't. I'm my own boss."

"Are you?" Whalen's sarcastic interjection turned Val to his sneer. "That ain't the way it looks to me."

"Well, maybe that's because you ain't seein' straight these days, Whalen. Either that, or you're too dumb to know what you're seein'."

Whalen's expression darkened. "There ain't nobody who calls me dumb, not even you."

"That so? I guess it's hard to face the truth, ain't it, boy?"

Potter interrupted, darting a glance between Whalen and Val, cautioning, "Watch yourself, Val. You're goin' to push this fella too far."

"He don't scare me none."

"Bigmouthed female…"

Billy Simm turned on Whalen with true venom. "You watch what you say about Val, Whalen."

"I don't need nobody to stand up for me, Simm." Val knocked back her hat and stared Whalen down with fire in her eyes. This face-off with Whalen had been a long time in coming, and she was readier than she had ever been. The knowledge that Walker watched the scene from a few feet down the bar added to her bravado, as she continued, "I can take care of myself."

Simm's sudden smile was unexpected, "Maybe that's so, Val, but I sure would like to change the subject now by buyin' you a drink. What'll you have?"

Whalen responded mockingly in her stead. "The lady drinks tea, Simm. What else would a *female* drink? Only a man's got the stomach to handle a real drink."

Val smiled. Whalen was as transparent as glass. He was also ignorant of a fact that most of the other Circle S wranglers had learned in an all-night poker session a few years before he signed on. She had a hollow leg. There wasn't nobody who could outdrink her.

Val's smile broadened. "Just set 'em up, and we'll see who's got the stomach and who don't."

Whalen's eyes took on a demonic glow as he turned to the bearded barkeep. "Harry, give the *lady* a glass, fill it up and keep it filled."

Val smiled as the glass was placed before her, and her smile turned to a grin as the barkeep filled first her glass and then Whalen's. Seeing the bartender's concerned expression, she reassured him confidently, "Don't worry, Harry. You just keep count." She laughed again. "Loser pays, Whalen. You sure you got enough in your pocket to cover?"

Not waiting for Whalen's response, Val reached for her glass, only to have a heavy hand close unexpectedly over hers, pinning it to the bar. Branch Walker's tight voice sounded in her ear.

"You don't have the sense you were born with, do you?" Then he added, in response to Whalen's angry grunt, "You're askin' for trouble, Whalen. And I'm makin' you a promise that you'll get just what you're askin' for if you keep it up."

Val fought to dislodge Walker's hand. Realizing it was impossible, she faced Branch hotly.

"It galls you to see a woman betterin' you every step of the way, don't it, Walker. And if my pa wasn't such a hardhead, he'd admit it, too. I don't need you standin' up for me any more than I need Simm to fight my battles. Whalen's no match for me, no way—nohow, and neither are you. And the sooner you admit it the better it'll be for the Circle S, 'cause that's the day I'll be waving goodbye to your back as you ride off into the sunset!"

Branch paused, his dark eyes brittle as stone when he finally spoke. "I'm not leavin' the Circle S, and the sooner you get that through your head, Val Stark, the better it's goin' to be for all of us. Now you get your backside out through that door and don't come back."

"Let go of my hand."

"Are you leavin'?"

"I said, let go of my hand."

"And I asked you if you're leavin'."

As fast as lightning, Val snaked her gun from her holster with her left hand. The cold muzzle pressed a notch below Walker's belt, she purred, "I said, let go of my hand, Walker, or I'll raise your voice to a higher pitch—permanently!"

Walker's eyes silently challenged, *you wouldn't.*

Val's gaze responded, *oh, no?*

The tense standoff came to an abrupt halt as Walker freed her hand. Smiling, Val picked up her glass and tossed down its contents in a single gulp. She wiped her hand across her mouth and ordered, "All right, Harry, set up a glass for Walker here. Him, Whalen and me are goin' to enjoy ourselves—glass for glass. Ain't that right, Walker?"

Val waved her gun in Walker's direction, only to have it slapped away by Walker's casual hand. "Put that thing away, *ma'am.* You don't need it, because all of a sudden, this is somethin' I wouldn't miss for the world."

Picking up his glass, Walker tossed down the contents and signaled the bartender. "Fill 'em up!"

Simm's uncomfortable "I don't think this is a good idea," was met with Val and Branch's simultaneous "Who asked you?"

Relieved to see Potter step back, as well, Val stared at the sparkling amber liquid in her glass. She felt Walker's rock-wall presence at her side, and she all but laughed with glee. This was going to be fun!

Mary picked her way across the busy street, carefully balancing the tray and a small paper sack in her hands. She entered the Trail's End Hotel and paused to survey the lobby. Her round face creased with concern, she nodded toward the desk clerk and started up the stairs. It had taken her longer than expected to buy the few things the sick woman upstairs had requested and to collect a simple dinner for her. She had been relieved to hear that a relative would be coming to pick up the poor dear by the end of the week, and the problem of caring for her would be solved.

Mary reached the top of the staircase, ridden with guilt.

Since when had she been so niggardly with her time that she couldn't spare a few hours for a poor woman who was sick and alone? Mary lowered her head. She supposed it was since she had discovered Wilbur and each day had become more valuable than the previous one. Time was such a cherished possession at her age. She did not wish to squander it wantonly.

Mary giggled. Poor choice of words.

Serious once more, Mary continued down the hall, more disturbed than she cared to admit to find the corridor empty. Surely Wilbur had not misunderstood her. Perhaps she should have made herself more clear. Pausing before room number nine, Mary knocked and entered. She returned the smile of the woman who welcomed her warmly.

Back in the hallway a short time later, Mary surveyed the area once more, disappointment a hard lump in her chest. She adjusted her coat and hat and walked toward the staircase, her step lagging. It had been a foolish notion, in any event. She had recognized Dunbar, Valentine's gelding, tied to the hitching rail nearby as she returned to the hotel. She knew that one slip in discretion and all the precautions that Wilbur and she had taken would be wasted. There would be a scandal, and she supposed she—

A sound from behind the closed door to her left interrupted Mary's thoughts a split second before the door opened abruptly and an arm reached out to snatch her from her feet. Inside the room, with the door slammed shut behind her before she had time to catch her breath, Mary could do no more than utter a shocked cry as she looked up into Wilbur's excited smile.

"Did I scare you, Mary?"

Mary paused to catch her breath. "I suppose you did, a

little. I've never been swept off my feet by a man before, you know. But it was thrilling.'' She blushed. ''You always thrill me, Wilbur.''

''You do more than thrill me, Mary.''

The husky timbre of Wilbur's voice was music to her ears. Mary could not get enough of it. He was the virile young man of her dreams, the knight in shining armor who had merely been a few years late in arriving. She wanted him and she knew he wanted her, too. The power of that knowledge set her voice to quivering.

''I love you, Wilbur.''

Wilbur's loving expression was more eloquent than words as he swept her up into his arms. Entwining her arms around him in return, Mary discovered to the delight of her aging heart that fairy tales really did come true.

''Aw, come on, Val...''

Billy Simm's low entreaty elicited a grunt and a resounding burp from Val as she slapped down her empty glass and turned toward him with a lopsided smile.

''Are you countin', Simm? How many does that make?''

''I ain't countin'.'' Simm groaned. ''I can't.''

''Leave her alone, Simm.'' Whalen's tight response was slightly slurred. ''We're goin' to see who the better man is, once and for all. Set 'em up, Harry.''

''That's right, Harry, set 'em up.''

The challenge in Branch's tone was not lost on Val as she turned toward him with a knowing smile. Choosing to withhold a response, Branch tossed the contents of his freshly filled glass down his throat, coughed and glared, but he was not immune to a nudge of conscience as Val mimicked him by tossing down her drink, as well. From the corner of his eye,

Branch watched as Whalen downed his drink and slapped the bar for another, aware that Whalen's bragging was not the reason for this ridiculous contest in which he was indulging.

Self-reproach swelled inside him. What was happening to him? He had come to the Circle S for the opportunity of a lifetime. The work he had started had been seriously threatened by a natural disaster only a day earlier—the poisoning of a water hole that could neither be explained nor ignored. It had happened once without warning, and he knew it could possibly happen again. With the arrival of the new bulls imminent, a similar incident could spell the end of his plans for the future.

That thought had haunted him during the long night, and had finally driven him to the Loco Steer so he might attempt to escape his troubles for a few blissful hours. So—he paused to ask himself confusedly—why did it now seem that while his future lay hanging by a thread, the most jarring note in his life was presently provided by the unlikely female standing beside him at the bar?

He must be going crazy! There was no other explanation for the feelings he had experienced when Val Stark walked through those swinging doors. The long-legged, baggily clothed, freckle-faced female was beginning to look so good to him, it was frightening! The fact that she looked better and better to Simm and Smith, as well, had not skipped his notice, and he had begun to simmer at Simm's too-friendly invitation for her to join them when the friction between Whalen and her began.

Branch shook his head and reached for his glass. He downed its contents without giving a thought to the cheers of the growing crowd of observers, his mind beginning to reel as he looked at Val again. She had stripped off her hat and coat, and had loosened the top two buttons on her faded shirt. The action had titillated him, even though only a patch of worn long johns was revealed.

Branch watched as Val again raised her glass to her lips and drained the amber liquid. Branch's stomach did a serious flip-flop as the final drop clung to her upper lip like a drop of dew on a rose.

Dew on a rose...? Oh, Lord.

Why couldn't he get it through his head that Val Stark despised him, that she thought he was unneeded on the Circle S and that she didn't want him interfering with her life? What was it that made him want to reach out to touch the brave, hurt little girl underneath that hard exterior who was threatened by his presence? Why couldn't he just have stood by as she made a fool of herself, pitting herself against Whalen? Why had he suddenly determined that if any man was to back her down it was going to be him? And why was his reason for that thinking so confused in his mind that it was driving him to drink?

Branch closed his eyes, only to snap them open a moment later at the sound of Val's taunting "Whatsa matter? You dizzy, Walker? Ha! This is goin' to be easier than I thought." She turned to Whalen, who stood rigidly beside her. "Bottom's up, *boy*."

His anger erupting with a restrained belch, Branch slapped the bar for a refill. He held Val's eyes with a wicked stare as he again drained his glass.

Val's hoot was followed by a hearty punch in his shoulder as she shouted almost approvingly, "Well, what do you know! The man's got grit!"

Branch glared at Val's gray, slightly unfocused eyes, her soft, flushed cheeks, then at that damned third button where her long fingers unconsciously played. His breath emerged in a snarl.

Yeah, he had grit. Val Stark was going to see just how much grit he had before the day was done. And when she was ready to eat crow, he was going to spoon-feed it to her, bit by bit. He could hardly wait.

The sun was a golden glow against the drawn shades of the hotel room as Will lay beside his silent Mary. Propped on his side, Will stared down into her motionless face, his lips curved in a soft smile filled with love. Mary's hair streamed across the pillow in long, shiny strands streaked with silver, and he leaned down to sniff them, then sighed. Sweet—everything about Mary was sweet. She looked sweet, smelled sweet, tasted sweet.

Will remembered his moment of gut-wrenching jealousy earlier in the day when he had seen Charlie Hutton talking to Mary with a wink in his eye and a tease in his voice. He had been ready to tear the fella's old bones apart, so frightening had been the sudden thought that he could lose her. But his Mary loved him, only him. She had told him so only minutes earlier.

Still staring at his beloved Mary, Will whispered, "I don't ever want to leave this place—or you, Mary."

Mary snuggled against him. "Neither do I, Wilbur."

"It's hell knowin' that when we leave here, I won't be seein' you for days and days."

"I know."

Will took a deep breath. "Maybe I should just tell Val that we're goin' to get married."

Mary drew back, and Will read the reply on her face before it left her lips. "She'll hate me, Will. She doesn't like women—any women—and if you bring me into the house, she'll not only hate me, she'll begin hating you because she'll think you betrayed her. I don't want to come between your daughter and you, and I don't want you to resent me if Valentine should leave."

Will frowned, and Mary nodded. "You see? Even the thought has stolen the joy from this afternoon."

"No, it hasn't, darlin'." Gathering her close, Will whispered against the softness of her shoulder. "There ain't nothin' that can take the joy out of us bein' together for me. You've given me new life, Mary."

Mary drew back and looked up into his eyes, and the thought that she might be gauging the depth of sincerity in his statement cut like a knife. The tear that trickled from the corner of her eye struck a similar moistness in his own as she responded softly.

"You *are* my life now, Will. And I want you to know that I'll wait as long as it takes to work things out. Val may not know it, but she's my daughter now, too. It can't be any other way."

Momentarily unable to speak, Will finally questioned with sincere wonder, "How did an ugly old cowpoke like me ever rate a woman like you?"

"By being you." Mary's smile was tremulous. "Just by bein' your wonderful self. You're the man of my dreams—didn't you know that, Will?"

Will paused, filled with incredulity as he shook his head. "That so, Mary?" Another pause. "That so?"

A silent affirmation in her eyes, Mary stroked his cheek. "And you've shown me that reality is better than my dreams could ever be."

And then, the loving woman that she was, Mary moved closer and kissed him once more.

"'Oh, my dar-r-r-lin' Clementine...'"
Branch winced as Val strained for a high note, singing at the top of her lungs while she clutched the bar with a steadying hand. Her head back, her eyes closed, she had been howling at the ceiling, making the damnedest racket he had ever heard, for the past five minutes. He had just about had all his heavy head could take.

Drawing her painful serenade to a halt, Val opened her eyes and looked up into his face, suddenly frowning. "You are damned tall, you know that, Walker? And I don't like lookin' up at you. I don't like lookin' up at no man!" She laughed. "You hear that song I've been singin'? It ain't about no hard-ridin', fast-shootin' fella. It's about a *woman*." She paused, her lopsided smile slipping. "This country don't give a woman a break nohow." Her smile suddenly bright once more, Val picked up her chin. "But *I'm* goin' to change all that."

"That so?" The words emerged through Branch's stiff lips. It galled him to admit that he was feeling his liquor, especially since Val Stark was still standing. There was a refilled glass in front of him, and one in front of Val, as well. He knew the contest was not yet over, but if he got much stiffer...

Speaking of stiff... Branch glanced at the table in the corner where Aubrey Whalen sat rigidly, staring forward as if transfixed. The big cowhand had been sitting that way for the past half hour, unmoving, a filled glass in his hand. As Branch watched, Smith sauntered over to wave his hand in front of Whalen's face. The young cowpoke then turned with a hoot of laughter that turned his fair skin as red as his hair.

"Looks like Whalen's out of the game! There ain't nothin'

behind them eyes no more. It's down to just Val and Walker, now!"

"Yahoo!" Val's piercing hoot was still echoing in the saloon as she raised her glass to toss the contents down her throat in one gulp. All eyes snapped toward him, and Branch growled his annoyance at the silent call to empty his glass, as well. Squinting as the liquor burned all the way down to his gut, Branch wiped his hand across his mouth as Simm slid next to Val at the bar.

"Come on, Val." Simm's youthful face was concerned. "Little and Boggs was talkin' about gettin' up a game of cards. Want to join us?"

Val tilted back her head, swaying as she attempted to focus on Simm's face. Branch's stomach squeezed into a knot at the way Simm stared at her lips as she responded, "I got a little game goin' here already, Simm. But if you want to wait until Walker's laid out as stiff as Whalen, I'll be happy to join you."

"You don't have to prove nothin' to nobody here, Val." Simm shot Branch an accusing glance. "Everybody knows that you was your pa's right hand."

The smile fell from Val's face as she shifted to square her stance. "You said *was,* didn't you, Simm? You said I *was* my pa's right hand!"

Simm flushed. "I didn't mean nothin' by it, Val. You'll always be number one with me."

But Val was no longer listening as she muttered, "I'll show 'em. I'll show 'em all!" She turned to the frowning barkeep. "Fill them glasses, Harry. And keep 'em filled until Walker is sittin' it out right next to Whalen over there."

"Val." Simm put a conciliatory hand on her shoulder. "Don't go actin' crazy. I didn't mean nothin', I swear."

"Hands off, Simm!" Hardly realizing the words had escaped his lips, Branch took a wavering step toward the startled cowpoke. "This is between Val and me. As she said, we're goin' to settle this here and now."

"I can't believe that's you talkin', Walker!" Potter's exclamation cut unexpectedly into the moment, turning all heads toward him as he spoke. "I've been waitin' for you to come to your senses, or for Will Stark to come walkin' in here to put an end to this business, but I ain't waitin' no longer. I'm goin' to find Stark and tell him that his daughter and his ranch manager are both crazy!"

"Oh, no, you ain't!" All heads snapped toward Val as she drew her gun in a flash and leveled it in the old cowhand's direction. "Nobody's doin' nothin'."

"Put that gun down." Branch's command turned Val toward him the split second before he wrested the weapon from her hand with an unexpected twist of his wrist. She was seething as he handed it to the bartender, ordering, "Put that gun someplace where it won't get this *lady* into trouble. And while you're at it, fill those glasses. I'm gettin' tired of stringin' this thing out."

The glasses were being refilled, when Branch saw movement out of the corner of his eye. He warned softly, "Stay where you are, Potter. You're not takin' one step out of this bar until I'm ready." Potter's wrinkled face twitched, and Branch pressed, "Understand?"

"I understand, all right!" Potter turned back to the bar.

Satisfied that Potter was no longer a threat, Branch looked down into Val Stark's flushed face.

"Bottoms up, *ma'am.*"

With a look that was pure venom, Val tipped up her glass.

* * *

The shadows of the silent hotel room were lengthening as Mary stirred. She opened her eyes, momentarily disoriented, then smiled as the warmth of Will's steady breathing brushed her cheek. He was asleep, and Mary smiled at the thought of the loving afternoon they had shared. Her smile waning, she realized she must soon awaken him so they could leave—but she could not bear to separate from him just yet.

Her love rising, Mary resisted the temptation to stroke her lover's handsome mustache and trace the creases that networked his cheeks. She had changed her plans several times in the course of the afternoon, and she knew the lateness of the hour would now demand that she remain in town overnight, at the home of one of her friends. Grateful to the poor stricken woman down the hall for providing an opportunity for Wilbur and her to be together, Mary mentally prepared an explanation should the woman inadvertently reveal that Mary had not remained with her.

Mary's smile faded as she considered her own deviousness. But that was the way it was when you were in love.

Taking a deep breath, knowing she could delay no longer, Mary whispered, "Wilbur, wake up." Will opened his eyes and she smiled. "It's time to leave, dear."

"Just five minutes more, Mary, darlin'." Will's voice was husky with emotion. "I ain't ready to part from you just yet."

Swallowing tightly at the realization that Wilbur's feelings echoed her own, Mary responded softly, "Well, maybe just five minutes."

But in her heart, Mary wished fervently for so much more.

Uncertain how many times he and Val had emptied their glasses since that short altercation with Potter earlier, Branch fought to focus his eyes. The room around him had become unnaturally bright, the faces close by slightly blurred, but there was one face he saw even more clearly than before. What he saw left him uneasy. Val's color was high now. Her eyes were half-closed and her movements heavy and awkward. She was no longer leaning against the bar—she was clutching it for dear life as she swayed like a leaf in the wind. She was ready to go at any minute.

But that wasn't all he saw. With every glass he downed, the clarity of Val's skin had become even more appealing, the color of her eyes more intriguing. He had become increasingly fascinated by the graceful line of her throat each time she tilted back her glass, and he had begun wondering how it would feel to nuzzle the soft little hollow at its base. A few heavy strands of reddish brown hair had escaped her braid and he unconsciously raised his hand to stroke them back from her face, only to stop himself abruptly as Val slapped the bar with the flat of her hand and slurred, "Harry, you're lettin' me down. Walker's still standin', and I got a card game waitin' on me. Come on, fill 'em up!"

Harry reached for the bottle and started pouring, and Branch was suddenly startled to hear himself say, "No. The *lady's* had enough."

Val turned slowly, her expression growing outraged. "*I've* had enough? *You're* the one who can't even stand up straight!" She turned an unfocused glance around her. "Everybody in the whole room is swayin'. Ain't nobody sober here but me?"

Val's eyes suddenly widened and she clutched the bar tighter. "Watch it! Earthquake! Everythin's startin' to spin. We're goin' down!" Val blinked. She blinked again, then gave a whoop. "You're drunk, Walker!"

"*I'm* drunk?" Branch held two fingers up in front of Val's face. "How many?"

"How many what?"

Branch shook his head, disgusted. "That's it. You're goin' home."

"I ain't goin' nowhere! I got a card game waitin'. Simm—" Val looked around her, suddenly smiling as Simm popped into her line of vision. "There you are, you cute little fella."

Simm beamed. "That's right. I've been waitin' for you, Val." Simm took Val's arm. "How about—"

"I told you to keep your hands off her, Simm!"

Simm turned on Branch angrily. "You ain't my boss off the ranch, Walker, and I ain't about to let you take advantage of Val no longer."

"Take advantage of me?" Val laughed uproariously, the effort almost knocking her from her feet. "Simm, honey, you got it all wrong."

Simm, *honey*...

Growling, Branch thrust Simm from Val's side and glared down at her. "The contest is over."

"It ain't over till I say it's over!"

"Then say it!"

"Say what? Oh, yeah. Pour, Harry!"

Branch studied Val's face a moment longer, gauging her strained effort to hold herself upright and fix her gaze. Deliberately echoing her, he instructed, "Yeah. Pour, Harry."

Watching as the amber liquid rose to the brim of Val's glass, then his, Branch turned to Val. "Well?"

Val laughed loudly as she picked up her glass. Waiting only until he did the same, she quipped, "Say goodbye, Walker, 'cause you ain't goin' to survive this one!"

Tossing back her head, Val emptied the glass, slapped it on

the bar and turned, her lopsided smile challenging. Branch raised the glass to his mouth and drained it. He slapped it back on the bar.

Val's eyes widened. Her gloating shout, "There he goes!" was still echoing in his ears as she pitched forward, right into his arms.

Val was limp as a Chinese noodle as Branch grabbed her coat, jammed her arms into the sleeves and pushed her hat down on her head. Flipping her over his shoulder, he reached into his pocket to slap a wad of bills down on the bar.

"If that isn't enough, get the rest out of Whalen. The whole thing was his idea in the first place."

Val beat feebly at his back, her words slurred. "Put me down, Walker. I don't want you carryin' me. You're drunk!"

Ignoring her, Branch turned toward the door, only to have Simm step out to block his path, his boyish face flushed as he stated flatly, "Val wants you to put her down."

"That's right, I want you to put me down!"

Simm nodded. "She wants *me* to take care of her."

"The hell I do!"

Branch would have grinned had he not been so angry. Instead he snarled, "Hear that? Now get out of my way, Simm, or I'll walk right over you."

"Where are you takin' her?"

"Out of my way you little piss ant! Now!"

Thrusting Simm aside, Branch started resolutely toward the swinging doors of the Loco Steer. Feeling stronger with every step, he burst onto the street, grateful that the light of day was fading as he walked across the street with Val hollering and beating at his back every step of the way. Ignoring the stares of disapproval from passersby, he turned into the nearest alley.

Val pounded harder. "Where're you takin' me?"

Branch slowed his step momentarily. That was a good question. Suddenly certain he would know where he was going when he got there, Branch resumed his stride. He had gone only a few steps farther, when Val went unnaturally quiet. He heard a warning gag, and flipped her off his back in time to hold her head as she paid the price of her folly in full.

Totally limp, Val moaned as Branch looked up to survey their surroundings. He was behind the livery stable, and it took only a minute for him to locate the solution to his problems. Propping Val up with one arm, Branch dragged her toward the horse trough. Realizing he had no recourse, he bobbed her face into the cold water, grimacing as she came up sputtering and swearing, and he wished from the bottom of his heart that such a drastic measure hadn't been necessary.

Val was still muttering incoherently when Branch realized he wasn't feeling so well himself. He groaned and took a few staggering steps to the nearest dark corner. Emerging moments later, he thrust his head into the trough. Breathless but relieved, he turned to look at Val. Her head was resting against the trough and she was fast asleep, looking more innocent and vulnerable than he had ever seen her.

Scooping her up into his arms, he staggered to his feet, cursing his stupidity for allowing this angry, obstinate young woman to put him at such a disadvantage.

A mound of hay in the corner of the livery stable beckoned to Branch as he swayed through the back door. With mercifully few steps, he was beside it. Dropping to his knees, aware that he would not have been able to walk another foot, he lowered Val onto the hay, flopped down beside her, closed his eyes and cursed again.

Moments later, he forced open his eyes and saw that Val slept peacefully beside him. Turning toward her, he threw a heavy arm across her chest and drew her close. He needed to make sure she wouldn't escape him, and he needed to sleep for a few minutes. He'd be all right then. Just a few minutes…

An echo of drunken laughter aroused Branch from his wild dreams to the darkened corner of the livery stable. His arm tightened spontaneously around the warm figure beside him, and an unconscious relief overwhelmed him as Val moved restlessly in his grip.

Evening cast its shadows over them as Branch strained to assess Val's condition. Her clear face was smooth, showing no sign of discomfort, and her body was relaxed. Her ragged braid was twisted under her head, and he dislodged it gently and smoothed it with his hand. Its silky texture sent chills down his spine.

He looked back at Val's motionless face. Her skin had that same silky look up close. Submitting to impulse, he trailed his fingertips against her cheek, swallowing as Val's lips separated with an incoherent murmur. She was so young. It must have been truly difficult for the little girl who had worked so diligently beside her father most of her life to face the fact that when all was said and done, her father was looking to a stranger to run their ranch. He supposed he couldn't really blame her for reacting the way she had, and he wondered why he had been so blind to her feelings before.

Branch searched his mind for the answer to that question. It could be because Val Stark irritated him more than any woman he had ever known. It could be because she had stopped him cold every time he attempted to extend his friendship. It could be because he had never known a woman to challenge him so directly, to taunt him so unmercifully or to drive him so crazy with a glance. Branch took a deep breath.

And it could be because she had made him sit up and take notice of her from the second he stepped foot on the ranch, and had made him so aware of her that barely an hour passed when she did not enter his thoughts.

Branch paused, finally admitting to a disturbing reality that could no longer be ignored. It could be because he was increasingly drawn to her, while she seemed only to be repelled.

Val frowned in her sleep, and Branch could not resist a smile. She was one tough woman. He hadn't been willing to accept either her ability or her accomplishments at first, and he'd been wrong. He had thought that there was nothing new he could learn about women, but he'd been wrong there, too. It seemed that there was much more Val Stark had to teach him, too. Without the shield of her bluster, he now saw a different side of Val Stark, an innocence that was previously as invisible as that little dimple that darted in and out at the corner of her mouth as she mumbled again. He was suddenly fiercely protective of that innocence without truly knowing why.

Branch's gaze lingered on Val as he drew her a comfortable inch closer. Patience was needed now. Branch's nimble fingers worked unconsciously at Val's braid. He would have to demonstrate more patience with Val's resistance than he had in the past. He would have to stop reacting and start thinking. He would have to teach her that he realized how much she had accomplished and that he did not intend to shut her out of participation in the future of the Circle S.

The heavy dark mass of Val's hair freed at last, Branch leaned down to rub his cheek against it. Lord, it felt good... Val turned unexpectedly toward him, her eyelids fluttering as she mumbled again. Her parted lips were so close, and Branch felt an unexpected dryness in his throat, an ache in his gut, then a driving hunger that guided his mouth toward hers with a fierce intensity that had him shaking.

His mouth only a hairsbreadth from hers, Branch froze abruptly, then jerked back as if stung. What was he doing?

Branch jumped to his feet, the sudden movement setting his head to pounding as he stared down at Val Stark's sleeping form with incredulity. He *was* going crazy! That woman was about as helpless and vulnerable as a rattler, and she would've separated him from his manly parts with the blink of an eye if she had seen where he was heading a few seconds earlier. Being understanding and sympathetic was one thing, but... Branch looked again at Val's moist lips. But...

Damn...!

Turning on his heel, Branch stormed out of the livery stable. He returned to the rear door a few minutes later with Caesar and Dunbar in tow. Taking a deep breath, Branch leaned down and shook Val roughly.

"Wake up...Val, wake up."

Val opened her eyes. Disoriented, she stared wordlessly up into his face. Those damned gray eyes were unguarded and they tore at him, adding an unintended gravel to his tone as he pulled her roughly to her feet and held her a few inches from him. "We have to get back to the ranch."

"But where...what time is it?"

"What the hell do you care what time it is? It's time to go home, and I'm takin' you there."

Val's silence was unspoken testimony to her condition as she allowed him to jam her hat on her head, drag her the few steps to the rear door and boost her up onto her horse. Mounting, as well, Branch turned with a few words of command that never left his lips. Val's face was a sickly green, her shoulders were slumped, and if he didn't miss his guess, her stomach was about to revolt again.

Cursing aloud, he leaned over and snatched Val's reins out of her hands. He wasn't sure if he was angry with Val for her stubborn pride, with Will Stark for choosing this particular afternoon to get lost, or with himself for his own foolish part in this most recent fiasco. Growling "Hold on!" he kicked his horse into motion.

On the road home, Branch halted again in response to a whimper from the sagging figure riding at the end of his lead. He watched as Val slid from the saddle and staggered to the side of the road. Although they hadn't been riding for a full hour they had stopped twice before. Unable to bear the misery inside him that had nothing to do with the quantity of liquor he had consumed, Branch finally dismounted. Walking to where Val was crouched by the roadside, he waited until her retching spasms halted, then drew her to her feet. An unexplainable emotion tugged somewhere deep inside him as he looked down into her pale face. The physical distress reflected in those dulled gray eyes melted the last of his resistance.

Boosting Val up onto Caesar, he mounted behind her, pulled her hat off her head to hang it over the saddle horn and drew her back against his chest. The feel of her weight resting against him was warmly familiar and more pleasing than he cared to admit as he instructed briefly, "Go to sleep."

A slight shudder and the fanning of her warm breath against his skin as she turned her face against his neck were Val's only responses. Gathering up Dunbar's reins, Branch spurred Caesar into motion.

Chapter Ten

Branch held Caesar motionless with a firm hand as he surveyed the new green of the empty pasture around him. His gaze came to rest on the long line of fencing nearby that had been trampled into the ground, and a muscle in his jaw tightened with suppressed anger. He turned abruptly toward the silent group of mounted cowhands behind him.

"All right, Potter, you were responsible for this section of fencing. What happened?"

Potter shrugged. "Your guess is as good as mine. All I know is that me and the boys jammed them posts tight in the ground and they was steady as a rock."

"But they're down, aren't they?"

"It wasn't Potter's fault."

Branch turned toward Val, where she sat her horse a few feet away. His eyes narrowed as she continued.

"This country wasn't made to be fenced in. I told you that when you first started cuttin' up the grazing land into all them little pieces, for this kind of stock and that kind of stock. We ain't never separated stock before, and we got along just fine."

Branch assessed Val's pinched face, aware that her father maintained his silence a few feet to her rear. She had hardly spoken a word to him since he'd delivered her home from town that day a week earlier, and he had begun wondering which was worse, their former conflict or the silent treatment that somehow made him sad and edgy at the same time. It appeared, however, that the silence had come to an end. He responded cautiously, aware of the fragility of relations between them.

"Things have changed, Val, and they're not going back the way they were."

Val's eyes sparked with long-absent fire. "Oh, they ain't, huh?"

Deciding to leave his response to another time, Branch turned back to Potter, his brow darkening. "I don't know how this happened, Potter, and I guess it doesn't matter much because it won't change the result. We had prime breedin' stock in this pasture and now they're long gone. That means we're goin' to lose a lot of time findin' them and cuttin' them out of the main herd again, and we don't have the time to waste. I want you, Wyatt and Boggs to get busy repairin' that fence right now, so it'll be ready when we drive the stock back in."

"Val's right, you know." Potter's raspy voice bore a note of resentment. "It ain't my fault."

"Who's fault is it then?"

"I'm just sayin' that it ain't *my* fault!"

Turning his horse abruptly, Potter signaled to Wyatt and Boggs, and within minutes the three men were riding toward the farthest point of downed fencing. Unwilling to waste time attempting to sort out Potter's cryptic statement, Branch waved the men forward.

When they reached the main herd a short time later, the difficult process of selection and cutting began again. The men worked with precision under Branch's direction, but the unrest among them did not go unobserved by Branch's keen eye. They were mumbling and he was not unaware of the reasons for their disquiet. Some of them resented being made to do the same work over and again as the result of recurring "accidents." Some of them believed, like Val, that it was unnecessary work, that controlled breeding was a fad that would see a few hours in the sun and then fade away. But for some of them, like Simm and Val, the resentment was more personal.

Annoyance pulled at Branch's mouth as he watched Simm working efficiently within the herd. If he had ever seen a man with a purpose, it was Simm. Simm didn't fool him with those mooning eyes, and he had just about had his fill of the fellow's trailing after Val. He knew what that baby-faced cowhand was after. Simm had been all but salivating since that day in the branding corral when Val had taken off her coat and bent over in those tight pants, and he hadn't stopped sniffing at her heels since. How Stark put up with it, he'd never know, but Branch did know he wasn't about to suffer that behavior much longer. He also knew that if Stark didn't have the sense to protect his daughter from Simm's intentions, he would.

Branch's thoughts came to a jarring halt at the thought of Val's reaction to his interference in her private life. Well, it was too late for her objections. He had interfered with her life merely by accepting her father's proposition. He had interfered with her life by unconsciously accepting the challenge she had issued him from the first day. He had interfered with her life by viewing the surprisingly innocent and vulnerable young woman behind her tough facade, and he was now more heavily burdened by that knowledge than he could ever have believed. He admired her grit, he had come to feel responsible for her and he'd be damned if he'd let that Simm sneak behind her defenses with his crafty ways.

Pressing Caesar into motion as a steer bolted from the main herd, Branch turned it back, then returned to his former position. Submitting to a tendency he had fought to curb all morning long, he searched out Val's slender figure as she worked with the men, following her skillful movements with a mixture of admiration and regret. He didn't want to see her working as hard as the other hands, but he didn't know how to stop her. He wanted to make her understand that she didn't have to fear him in any way, that he wanted the best for her and the Circle S. He wanted to tell her that he wanted to see a smile on her face, instead of that perpetual frown; that he wanted so much more for her than she seemed to. He wanted...

Val moved quickly, as she spurred her horse after a bolting steer. Bending low over the saddle, she pushed her mount to a faster pace as she prepared to rope the animal. She was rapidly gaining on her quarry when Dunbar suddenly stumbled on the uneven terrain. Watching with helpless horror as the big horse struggled to keep his feet, Branch gasped as he fell to one knee, almost tossing Val over his head as he did. Miraculously, both animal and rider were upright in a second, but suddenly furious, Branch kicked his mount into motion.

Val turned toward him as he reined up beside her, her expression belligerent, and the power of his fury suddenly drained. She was all right, and he felt an almost irrepressible urge to reassure himself by taking her into his arms and holding her tight until his heart resumed its natural beat. This whole thing was impossible, the way she hated him and the way he was beginning to feel!

Val's clipped tone cut into Branch's whirling thoughts. "What do you want, Walker?"

Momentarily at a loss, Branch responded, "I wanted to

make sure you were all right. I think you should check Dunbar out. He had a pretty bad jolt.''

"I don't need your advice. I know how to take care of my horse."

Branch hesitated, his gaze fixed on Val's face as the grainy red dust settled around them. Aware that several cowhands had gathered nearby, he saw the tension in Val's frame, the perspiration that dotted her forehead and upper lip, the shadows in those cool eyes that he longed to explore. Unwilling to be led down the same path he had been led so expertly before, he surprised them both by responding, "Just as long as you're all right."

Wheeling his horse, Branch made his way back to a point of detached observance. He did not turn as Will Stark rode up behind him and muttered, "That girl is goin' to shorten my life by twenty years!"

Appearing to realize that there was no response forthcoming, Stark continued in a voice lowered to a more confidential tone, "I'm thinkin' we should have a talk, Branch." Branch turned toward him and Stark glanced cautiously around them. "I'm thinkin' Val ain't my only problem here. Potter was right, you know. It didn't look to me like that fence back there in the pasture was knocked down accidentally. What do you think really happened?"

Branch met Stark's keen scrutiny and his jaw hardened. "Some kind of fluke."

"Another fluke?"

Refusing to consider the thought that had been nagging him since the day the water hole had been tainted, Branch raised his chin. There was only one person who stood to gain from the steady chain of accidents that was threatening his position on the ranch. But Val couldn't hate him that much...could she?

"Answer me, damn it! Do you really think it was just another fluke?"

Branch stiffened his spine with a growling "Yeah..." that dropped Stark's jaw. Turning his horse without another word, Branch rode off, aware that Stark could not be any more surprised at his response than he was.

The sun, now at its zenith, shone relentlessly down on the three cowhands repairing the fencing in the quiet pasture. Pausing, Potter wiped the perspiration from his forehead with his sleeve, frowning as Boggs's stomach growled audibly for the second time.

Potter looked up at the sun in the blue sky overhead. "Yup, it's noontime. We don't need to ask what time it is when we're workin' with you, Boggs. That stomach of yours is better than an alarm clock."

"You ain't foolin' me none." Boggs's jowled face reflected his resentment. "You're as hungry as I am, and you were just lookin' for an excuse to quit workin' for a while."

"That's where you're wrong, partner." Potter pulled on his grayed whiskers. "I seen the look on Walker's face when he seen that fence was down and them cows was gone. He's goin' to be expectin' this fence to be up and waitin' for him when he drives them cows back, and I ain't about to disappoint him."

"It ain't goin' to hurt none if we stop to eat for a few minutes." Wyatt's interjection drew a nod from Boggs that encouraged him to continue. "I ain't about to go hungry for no man."

"Suit yourself." Potter picked up his shovel. "When Walker comes back snortin' fire 'cause this here fence ain't fixed yet, I'll turn him over to you.''

Wyatt paused to consider his response, but Potter's attention was drawn from the uncertain cowpoke by the outline of a solitary horseman coming into view on the horizon. Lifting his hat to scratch his sweaty head, Potter mumbled, "Well, if it ain't Red Hand.... What's he doin' out here? I've been workin' on this spread for seven years and I ain't never seen him ride out where we was workin' before.''

Red Hand drew closer and Potter called out, "What brings you here, Red Hand?''

Red Hand returned Potter's stare as he approached, his dull black eyes unblinking, and Potter frowned as an uneasy feeling stirred in the pit of his stomach. Somehow the old Injun always looked harmless and kind of pitiful in the kitchen and he'd never given the fella much thought. He supposed that was because the old geezer kept to himself so much and hardly spoke a word to anybody. He knew Will Stark and Val had a healthy respect for the fella and even sought his advice in some quarters, but the reason had always been a mystery to him. Now, facing the old Injun out here in the open where he was in his element and sittin' his pony with an imperial grace, Potter was beginning to understand. But that didn't hinder his curiosity. "What're you doin' out here, Red Hand?'' he asked again.

The Indian's creased leather skin hardly moved as he responded, "Trouble last night. Fence down. Red Hand come to look.''

"How did you know the fence was down?''

When Red Hand did not respond, Boggs snorted, "That ain't hard to figure out. Walker probably sent one of the boys back to the ranch for somethin'.''

Potter scrutinized Red Hand's face. "That so, Red Hand?" There was no response, and Potter gave an angry snort. "Well, you can look all you want. We're fixin' to take some time to eat. We're almost done, anyways."

Sprawled on the heavy grass a few minutes later, Potter chewed his stringy smoked beef and took the opportunity to watch as the old Indian walked slowly along the fence, his eyes on the ground. Potter squinted assessingly as Red Hand suddenly squatted, appearing to study the ground closely. What was the old fool doin'? There wasn't nothin' to see there but some churned up ground where all them cows had plowed across the fence.

His eyes still trained on Red Hand, Potter reached for his canteen. He was thankful that Boggs and Wyatt were engrossed in conversation and did not see the old Indian's expression as he suddenly drew himself to his feet, mounted his pony with surprising dexterity and rode off without a word.

A funny feeling crawled up the back of Potter's neck. Shaking it off, Potter decided then and there not to say a word about Red Hand's curious antics—not to nobody, nohow.

Val's gaze did not wander as she walked toward the barn. It had been an exhausting day, and were she not so keyed up, she would have considered that she had worked hard enough to merit a long snooze. She knew it was fortunate that things hadn't turned out to be as difficult as first expected when the downed fence had come into view that morning. The cattle hadn't run far, and it hadn't taken the hands long to sort them out again and run them back to the fenced pasture.

Walker had been upset when he first saw the damaged fence, and she knew why. The Hereford bulls would be arriving any day, and he didn't want anything to go wrong. But, strange as it seemed, something had happened again.

Refusing to follow the natural progression of that thought, Val entered the barn and turned toward Powderkeg's stall. She had taken a chance and shed her long underwear a few days earlier because of the discomfort it had been affording her in the heat of the afternoon. She couldn't afford any more discomfort than she had been made to bear lately, with the way the ranch hands had been riding her about that disastrous contest in the Loco Steer the previous week. She was beginning to believe she'd never live that incident down.

Val's small nose twitched with annoyance. The worst part of it all was that her memory of that afternoon was less than sketchy. She remembered Whalen taunting her into a drinking contest, and Walker getting into the act. She remembered matching both of them glass for glass, and she remembered seeing Whalen sitting stiff as a statue at the table in the corner. A smile tugged at Val's lips. That damned cowboy had been petrified....

Whalen had been keeping his big mouth shut all week, even though the rest of the men had been riding her pretty hard, and that satisfaction alone was worth part of the price she had paid. The only thing that really bothered her was that she couldn't remember how Walker had fared through the whole thing.

If she was to believe all that Potter had told her, Walker had drunk her under the table, and she'd made a real fool out of herself. She had gotten vivid descriptions from the men of Walker carrying her out of the Loco Steer, slung over his shoulder like a sack of potatoes, but she didn't believe a word of it. She could never have been that drunk!

Val considered that thought again. Potter tended to exaggerate, and she had the feeling that the rest of the boys were enjoying themselves too much at her expense to worry about stretching details a bit. As for Walker, he had been surprisingly quiet about the whole thing.

Then there was her pa. Val gave a low snort of disgust. She couldn't rely on him to tell her the truth because it seemed he had been too engrossed in his chess game with Jim Parkerhurst most of the day even to miss her. According to Potter, her pa hadn't shown up until after she'd been long gone, but Val had to admit that she was glad she'd been asleep in bed when he'd come home that night—even if she couldn't remember how she got there.

The only thing about which she was certain was the immense size of her aching head the morning after and the regularity with which shadowed images from her dreams returned to haunt her. A familiar heat flushed Val's face. Those dreams had been so real. To her chagrin, she remembered almost *feeling* the tightly muscled length of Walker's body pressed against hers, his arm wrapped around her like a band of steel. In those dreams, his face had been so close to hers that she could see the gold tips of his thick eyelashes and the stubble beginning to sprout on his chin. Haunting her, also, was the feeling of his heavy hands stroking her hair, of his fingers moving through it, and his breath against her lips....

Then there were fragmented pictures of a horrendous ride home and agonizing moments at the side of the road, where she paid her dues over and again. Finally there was a memory of tranquility, strongly associated with strong arms supporting her and the scent of Branch Walker in her nostrils.

It had been several days before she had finally swallowed her pride and asked Red Hand how she had gotten home. The old Injun, however, wasn't talking.

Bothering her most of all was the subtle change in Walker during the past week. She was uncomfortable with it and she had let him know of her discomfort by ignoring him as much as she had taunted him before. If she had expected to get a rise out of him that way, it hadn't worked. Even a return to her old baiting had failed. Walker wasn't being overly friendly, but he had stopped sending her those black looks, no matter how hard she tried to earn them. She had noticed him watching her at times, too...such as when Simm hung around her, which he tended to do of late. She wondered what Walker was waitin' for her to do. She didn't trust him.

In front of Powderkeg's stall at last, Val could not resist a smile at the stallion's whinny. Her uncomfortable thoughts of a few minutes earlier drained away as she looked at the handsome animal, who eyed her with caution. She had been neglecting the big fellow of late, and she was about to make up for it. Already feeling better, she reached for his halter and held him fast.

"Hey there, Powderkeg. Glad to see me, ain't you? Well, you and me got some things we got to do today. I'm goin' to put a saddle on you, and we're goin' to ride around a bit, just like we did the last time."

"You ain't really goin' to try ridin' that big fella again today, are you, Val?"

Val jumped at the unexpected sound of Simm's voice and turned sharply in the cowhand's direction. "What are you tryin' to do, sneakin' up on me like that, Simm? You damn near scared me out of a year's growth!"

Simm flashed his boyish grin, unaffected by her sharpness. "That so? Well, I guess that means you won't be changin' and you'll stay just the way you are then...perfect."

Val went momentarily motionless. *Perfect*...her?

Convulsed with laughter, Val slapped her knees and doubled over, unable to contain her hilarity. Her amusement finally under control, she wiped the tears from her cheeks as Simm took a step closer. Reaching around her, he placed the flat of his hand against her back and made comforting circles as he looked at her with his big brown eyes and spoke in a low, soothing tone similar to the one she often used to calm Powderkeg.

"It ain't really so funny, Val. You're as close to perfect as any woman I ever knew. You're smart and you work as hard as a man, even though you're a fine figure of a woman. And you're real pretty."

Val raised her brows. Pretty?

"Don't believe me, do you, Val? Well, just look at your hair. It's bright and shiny as a new penny. And your skin is soft…"

A sudden sound from behind them turned both their heads toward Branch Walker as he interjected sharply, "You didn't mention her eyes, Simm. How would you describe them? Like gray velvet—or the way they look now, like storm clouds on a rainy day?"

Simm's young face flushed. "What business is it of yours, Walker? Val and me were talkin' some private business that ain't none of your concern."

"Everythin' that goes on here on the Circle S is my concern."

"That's where you're wrong, Walker!" Showing him her back without another word, Val opened the door of Powderkeg's stall and grasped his halter firmly as she turned. "Now both of you can get out of my way. Powderkeg and me are goin' outside."

"Wait a minute, Val…"

Simm's low protest turned Val toward him with a frown.

"I was hopin' I might get a chance to talk to you for a while."

"Later."

"Maybe we can go for a walk after supper."

Val turned toward the cowboy as if he had two heads. "Walk? Simm, I ain't *walked* nowhere since I learned to ride."

Annoyed at the smirk lingering at the corner of Walker's lips, Val ordered, "Out of my way!"

In the corral a few minutes later, Val lost all thought of her former discomfort as she approached the wary Powderkeg with a saddle. "Easy now, boy. We done this before and it didn't hurt none. You know I'm light as a feather on your back and gentle as the breeze as long as you behave yourself."

Powderkeg snorted nervously, but did not move as she adjusted the saddle blanket and flopped the saddle in place. Val smiled. "See that? I even got a new saddle for you, a real nice one." She tightened the cinch. "It looks real fine."

"You'd better tighten that cinch a bit."

Branch's clipped instruction turned Val toward the corral fence where he observed with a frown. Simm's expression wasn't any lighter, and Val felt a spurt of annoyance.

"I don't need no advice from you, Walker. I'm the best horse wrangler—"

"On this ranch." Walker nodded with a wry smile. "I know."

That smile, as wry as it was, made Val's heart do a little flip and she cursed under her breath as she turned back to her horse. It didn't help any to realize that Walker was right as she pulled the cinch a notch tighter.

Looking up at the big stallion as she gathered the reins in

her hand, Val whispered comfortingly, "Steady now, Pow-derkeg. We're goin' to have some fun."

A careful foot in the stirrup and Val mounted easily. Her eyes widened with surprise. The big fella was as gentle as a kitten! She pressed her heels into his sides. "Come on, let's walk now." The stallion did not move except for the twitching of his ears and a low snort. She nudged him harder. "Pow-derkeg, come on. Powderke-e-g-g-g!"

Suddenly bucking wildly, the big stallion danced across the corral, his back arched, his head down, putting as much space between the earth and his hooves as his strength would allow. Stuck to the saddle like glue, Val maintained a firm grip on the reins, shouting with glee as the world jerked and bumped around her. She laughed breathlessly, having the time of her life! She hadn't had so much fun since—

At the sound of an unexpected snap Val went flying head over heels in a blur of dizzying motion. A crack sounded loudly in her ears as she met the ground with a breathtaking thud.

The darkness around Val was filled with noise. She heard loud shouts and a horse's excited snorts. She heard the sound of footsteps and angry words. She heard a familiar voice mur-muring and felt the touch of gentle, probing hands. The dark-ness gradually faded to light and was replaced with the image of Branch Walker's face filled with concern as he leaned over her, his hand stroking her cheek.

"Are you all right? Can you hear me, Val? Talk to me. Say somethin'."

She had never truly realized how black Branch's eyes really were, his mouth was so close. She wondered how it would taste. Warm…sweet…comforting…? No, not comforting….

"Say somethin', Val!"

There was panic in his voice, but Val felt nothing but the touch of Branch's hand against her cheek, the way he stroked back her hair, the way…

Pa's face popped into Val's line of vision, and she blinked, then blinked again.

"Val…" Branch's voice held a pleading note as he urged again, "Say somethin'."

Val swallowed, finally managing a croaking "What happened to my horse?"

Branch froze, then gave a short, relieved laugh. "He's fine. Simm's holdin' him on the other side of the corral."

Val struggled to get to her feet despite the warnings, realizing as she did that she would not have remained there for long without the support of Branch's arm. She blinked again as she looked up into Branch's tight expression. "What happened? Did Powderkeg fall?"

Branch shook his head. "The cinch broke."

Her pa responded with the same words that had not managed to reach her lips. "That's a brand-new saddle! How did that happen?" And then he directed two words harshly at Branch's concerned face. "Another fluke?"

Val took a step forward, but little stars still danced in her line of vision and she closed her eyes with relief as Branch scooped her up into his arms. She did not protest at all as he carried her into the house and lay her down on her bed. And as disoriented as she was when Branch crouched beside her and stroked her cheek with his callused hand, Val realized she might even have smiled.

"Another fluke? Is that what you're sayin'?" Will's face was hot with color as he faced Branch over Powderkeg's saddle in the rear of the barn. "This cinch was cut and you know it!"

Old Doc Pitt had come and gone, Val was sleeping in her room, but Branch had not yet stopped trembling inside. The image of Val lying limply on the ground as the stallion's hooves slashed dangerously around her would not leave his mind. He had never been so shaken.

"Yeah, I saw it. It could've been cut...."

"Could've been?"

"We can't be sure."

"Can't be sure? Don't you think this is one accident too many around here?"

Branch shook his head. "I don't know."

"What?"

"I said I don't know!" His frustration erupting, Branch took a deep breath and shook his head again. "I'm sorry, Will. It scared the life out of me seein' Val lyin' there like that."

"How in hell do you think I felt? She's my daughter!" Will paused to study Branch's face, then continued, "But it ain't goin' to do no good goin' over it all in your mind. It's time we got down to the bottom of all that's been happenin' around here."

Branch's face tightened with tension. "I've gone over it again and again, but I can't think of anybody who'd profit from the things that've been happenin'...most especially from hurtin' Val."

Will's eyes narrowed. "I can think of one."

"Who?" And then at the penetrating quality of Will's stare Branch added hotly, "You don't mean me!" He took a step back at the silent accusation in Stark's eyes. "You don't really think I'd hurt Val? Don't you know that I..." He paused, stunned at the words he had been about to speak.

Branch started again. "Look here, Will. I'm not so attached to this place that I'd try to kill somebody to get a part of it! The thing that's been drivin' me crazy was the thought that maybe it was Val who was arrangin' for all these accidents, so I'd get discouraged and leave, or so you'd change your mind about havin' me breed those bulls."

"That's crazy!" Will's color heightened. "Val wouldn't do nothin' to hurt the Circle S. She loves this ranch."

"Yeah, well, the only thing I know is that I can't dismiss everythin' as coincidence now." Still shaking inside with the thought of what might have happened in that corral, Branch added, "But I think we should be careful about what we say. I think we should keep this business about the cinch quiet. I'll get it fixed, and we'll keep our eyes open. That all right with you?"

Will stared into Branch's eyes a bit longer, then nodded. "I guess we don't have no choice. But I tell you now, if anybody is tryin' to hurt my little girl, I'll have his hide!"

Mentally reinforcing that threat with another of his own, Branch swallowed the lump that had formed in his throat. Turning toward the door without a reply, Branch looked at Stark as he fell into step beside him, the commitment in his gaze clearer than the spoken word.

Waiting until the two men had cleared the doorway of the barn, Red Hand crept out of the shadows at the rear entrance. In a few silent steps, he stood beside Powderkeg's saddle. He took the cinch into his hand and ran his scarred finger against the torn edge. His lined face showed no emotion as he gave a short nod, then disappeared as silently as he had come.

Chapter Eleven

The bulls were restless, walking the fence and bellowing, and Val knew that if circumstances were different, she would have openly admitted that she had been wrong. These Herefords were not sissies.

Urging Dunbar on, Val skirted the edge of the pasture, making certain to keep in line with the other men as they moved the bulls steadily toward the gate. She hated driving bulls, and these Herefords looked to be a dangerous lot with their long, curving horns. She knew bulls were particularly rambunctious in late spring, full of energy and orneriness, and she didn't relish the thought of getting caught among them if a fight broke out.

Val's mind dropped back to the occasion a few weeks earlier when she had been thrown from Powderkeg. Her recuperation time had been short, but she had been humiliated at suffering another in the long line of accidents that had occurred since Branch Walker had arrived at the Circle S. She knew it made her look foolish and inept, but that wasn't the worst of it.

A familiar weakness struck Val's knees, and her stomach clenched into tight knots as her heart began a wild palpitation.

There it was again, the same affliction that she suffered each time she recalled the way Branch Walker had crouched beside her bed after she'd been thrown, stroking her cheek and mumbling words of comfort that she could not fully recall. She had faded in and out of consciousness, but Branch had remained by her side until the doctor arrived. The comfort she had gained from his presence had been enormous, though she had been unwilling to make that admission even to herself.

She had returned to the job within a few days, and realized immediately that she had somehow lost a strategic battle as a result of that injury. Uncertain how it had come about, she knew that as far as Branch Walker was concerned, the war between them was over. In the time since, she had been unable to bait him, and even her most abrasive attitude toward him earned her nothing more than a glance or nod. He was endlessly kind and gentle with her in a way that made her want to weep and scream with fury at the same time.

Val took a deep, steadying breath. She was at a loss to discover what was wrong with her. She didn't want to concede victory to Branch Walker. She didn't want anyone other than herself to run the Circle S and to make decisions that should be hers to make. She had spent sixteen years of her life earning that right. Still, she could feel her opposition to Walker draining each time he looked into her face with his steady gaze.

The situation with Billy Simm was another matter entirely. Simm was driving her crazy. If she turned around one more time to see his cow eyes mooning in her direction, she was certain she would howl like a banshee! She was so tired of hearing that her freckles were a dusting of gold on her silky cheeks…that her eyes made him think of clear ice on a moonlit night…that her mouth teased and beckoned him.

Teased and beckoned? Val groaned. Damn those tight pants

that had awakened Simm to the curve of her backside and the sway of her hips! She'd get Sally Ledman for that yet!

A loud belligerent bellow brought Val sharply back to the present as the younger of the two bulls trotting nearby challenged the other. A sharp snap of her rope set them both back in line as Dunbar sidestepped agilely. The bulls had arrived earlier in the week, and the excitement was such that she'd been surprised when her pa announced that morning that he was going into town for the day instead of riding out with the men to scatter the bulls. She suspected Branch would have held off another day to accommodate him if he could, but the bulls were becoming too difficult to restrain any longer.

It was almost June, and Val knew that meant they could expect a few calves in late February and March, although most would be born in April and May. If these bulls did all that was expected of them, each of the five would sire from thirty to forty offspring the following year.

The direction of Val's thoughts caused her sudden dismay. When had she begun accepting the infusion of the Hereford breed into the Circle S herd? If she kept it up, she would become her own worst enemy!

Looking toward Branch's broad frame where he worked the other side of the corral, Val saw that he was watching the bulls carefully. Her lips twitched with vexation. He was probably running a mental count of the calves they would sire and licking his chops at the thought of what the new year would bring. Well, breeding was one thing, but the success of the breed up here in this high mountain country was another, and Val consoled herself that these bulls had a long way to go before they were secure on the Circle S.

Val released a ragged breath as the last of the bulls slipped through the gate and out into the open, knowing that it would be easier to handle the stubborn animals where there was more room to maneuver.

Val's relief was short-lived, however, as the same two bulls abruptly turned to clash again, bellowing loudly. Pushing heads, they backed apart, allowing the older of the two the opportunity to charge with a thrust that sent his opponent staggering backward on the rough ground. Before his action could be anticipated, another bull ran over to join them, bawling angrily, and Val moved forward in an instinctive attempt to thwart the melee that appeared about to ensue.

Val swung her rope, realizing a bull whip would be far more effective and cursing Walker and herself alike for the lack of foresight that left them poorly prepared for this situation. The bulls were struggling, the younger one being pushed steadily backward as she guided Dunbar carefully toward the fray. She swung her rope again, shouting, only to have Branch ride unexpectedly between her mount and the snorting bulls as he called over his shoulder, "Whalen, Boggs, get over here!"

Nudged aside in the rush that followed, Val took a deep, angry breath and urged Dunbar forward again just as the younger bull broke and ran. Wise to the ways of bulls, Dunbar wheeled and leaped sideways, escaping the huge animal's sharp horns, but Caesar was not as lucky as the older bull swung his head upward, catching him on the flank. Frightened and in pain, Caesar bucked wildly, effectively putting an end to the exchange and sending the bulls racing out into the open.

Val took off after the running bulls and began circling them as they came to a halt. Turning, she saw that Simm was not far behind her. It was obvious that all the fight had gone out of the huge animals, but Val's sigh of relief was cut short by Branch's sharp command as his horse slid to a halt beside hers, and he shouted over his shoulder, "Little, Wallace, get over here and get these bulls moving again."

The resentment Branch's words evoked was cut abruptly short as he looked directly into her eyes, then dismounted to check Caesar's flank. Dismounting beside him before she realized it was her intention, Val saw a streak of red muscle where the skin had been peeled back from Caesar's hide. She assessed the wound as superficial at the same moment Branch mumbled, "It's not serious."

At a loss for words as Branch turned toward her unexpectedly, Val nodded. "I'm glad."

She was about to remount, when Branch suddenly grasped her arm and held her fast. His face drawing into tense lines, he held her gaze, speaking softly.

"I don't want you putting yourself in danger again, Val. Leave that work to the others. That's what they're paid for."

There it was again, that debilitating weakness that made her want to weep and scream in anger at the same time as Branch looked at her with that strange softness in his eyes. He was crippling her, and she wouldn't let him get away with it!

Tearing her arm from his grasp, Val responded, "Really? Well, I go where I want, and I do what I want on this ranch, and nobody's going to tell me otherwise."

Val mounted her horse and resumed her former place with the men. She did not have to turn to see that Simm had again taken up behind her and that Branch's gaze rested on her enigmatically for long moments before he called out, "Get these bulls moving!"

Raising her chin, Val spurred Dunbar forward.

Will stared at Mary's back as she stood at the stove in her sunny kitchen, certain it was impossible to love any woman more than he loved her.

Sensing his perusal, Mary turned toward him with a smile. "I knew you were looking at me, Wilbur, dear. I could feel your eyes on me. It was as if you were touching me."

Pushing himself away from the table, Will walked the few steps to the stove, slid his arms around Mary's ample waist and ducked his face into the warm crease of her neck as he whispered, "I love lookin' at you, Mary."

Mary turned in his arms, the hash she had been stirring momentarily forgotten. "I know you're telling me the truth, because I've never known you to tell me anything else, but I can't imagine why you should enjoy looking at me, Wilbur. I've never been a particularly pretty woman."

Appearing offended by her remark, Will frowned and stroked Mary's cheek. "Now that ain't true, darlin'. You always was a pretty woman. I remember thinkin' that to myself the first time I saw you and Charlie come into town. Your skin was so clear and your eyes so bright—you looked like a little chickadee chirpin' at the start of a new day."

"Oh, Wilbur—a chickadee?"

"A beautiful chickadee."

Mary's smile deepened as she turned reluctantly back to the stove. A whisper trailed over her shoulder. "We've lost so many years."

The sadness in Mary's voice brought a mist to Will's eyes as he drew her closer. Their lovemaking only a short time earlier had been passionate and satisfying, but he could not seem to get enough of holding this woman in his arms. He did not want to hear anything but joy in the tone of her voice, and the realization that their love was bringing her any less, even for a moment, tortured him.

"We ain't goin' to lose much more time, Mary. I'm sure of that."

Mary turned a hopeful glance toward him. "Do you mean things are gettin' better between Mr. Walker and Valentine?"

"Well, not exactly...." Mary looked puzzled and Will shrugged. "There don't seem to be much progress there. They're just toleratin' each other, but I'm thinkin' that Billy Simm has a real case on Val. He follows her everywhere. She can't turn around without bumpin' into him."

"But, Wilbur...Billy Simm?"

Will's expression became defensive. "What's wrong with Billy Simm?"

"If Valentine and Simm ever married, Val would chew him up and spit him out the first week."

Will could not resist a chuckle. "Mary, how you talk."

"You know it's true, dear. Just as you said, there's not a man within a hundred miles who can handle Valentine other than Branch Walker. I could tell that the first time I saw him."

Will's nose twitched, severely out of joint as he quipped, "You seem to think pretty highly of Walker, knowin' him as little as you do."

"A woman senses some things. It's the way I knew the moment you rode up beside my wagon when I was stranded that day that things were goin' to be different between us from then on. My heart pounded like a drum."

"Mine did, too, Mary."

"Well, that's what I see when I think of Val with Branch Walker."

Will sighed. "It's too bad Val and Walker don't see it that way. Oh, it ain't that they're arguin' like they used to. Val can't get a rise out of Branch, no matter how hard she tries, and that's what makes me think it's a lost cause. He's treatin' her real kindly since we've been havin' them problems at the ranch—kinda like a kid sister who can't abide him.''

"But you said nothing has happened since that day when Valentine's cinch broke."

"That's because Branch's seen to it that there ain't been no chance for anythin' to happen. He's got the fellas on watch, takin' shifts.''

"What do the cowhands have to say to that?"

"Branch didn't give them no chance to say nothin'. He just told them that he's heard about things bein' robbed from nearby ranches, and he ain't takin' no chances of our place sufferin'.''

"Did they believe him?"

"Max Colley's place got robbed, didn't it?"

"But that was his ex-wife. She just came back and had her new boyfriend move some things out when Max was gone."

"That ain't general knowledge, you know."

Mary nodded in silent assent. "Well, maybe if things settle down and you find out that the accidents were really accidents, after all, Mr. Walker's mind will be relieved enough to think of other things.''

Will's lined face drooped. "I don't think there's much chance of that, darlin'. I don't think Branch's got any interest in Val at all—not the way we was hopin', I mean.''

"But Billy Simm—" Mary looked pained. "He's little more than a baby.''

"I've got a feelin' that Simm's baby face is deceivin'. You should see the way he looks at Val. He looks at her like...like...''

"Like you look at me, Wilbur?" Mary turned in his arms and pressed herself against him. She whispered again, "Like you're looking at me now?''

Will gulped. "Hell, no, Mary! I'd kill the fella if he looked at Val that way."

"Then he's not the man for Valentine, because there's more to loving than just making cow eyes and such."

"I know that, Mary." Will smiled down into his lover's sweet face. "But I'm doin' the best I can."

"Well, if Mr. Walker isn't the man for Valentine, I just hope she can find a man as wonderful as you. She couldn't ask for more."

"She couldn't?"

Will's throat thickened with emotion as Mary whispered, "Not in a million years."

Holding her as the fragrance of Mary's hash permeated the kitchen, Will stroked her back and whispered, "That's the problem, Mary, darlin'. We ain't got nowheres near that much time."

Branch gritted his teeth, certain he could not take another minute of this unbelievably aggravating day. Glancing up at the position of the sun in the afternoon sky, he gave a relieved sigh and looked back at the cowhands working on the fencing nearby. There had been several more fights between the bulls before they arrived at their destination, the last of which had resulted in a whole section of fence being torn down by the powerful animals. But the downed fencing didn't bother him, or the fights between the bulls, or the fact that he had been forced to extricate Val out of the middle of each one, his heart pounding with fear that she might be injured.

Branch looked toward Val again where she stood beside her horse. The knots in his stomach tightened mercilessly as Billy Simm slid a casual arm around her shoulder and squeezed it lightly. He couldn't take much more of that. If Simm didn't get his hands off Val soon, he was going to pulverize him.

Branch took a deep breath and a hold on his flaring temper. What did Billy Simm have that he didn't have? He considered that question for a long moment and was unable to come up with an answer. But he knew that it really didn't make much difference what he thought, because Val obviously saw something in Simm that he didn't. What other reason could she have for allowing Simm to follow her around like a puppy dog and for suffering his pawing hands and his mooning gaze, when it was obvious to Branch that he couldn't do or say anything right in her eyes. He had tried to be her friend, but she didn't want his friendship. He had tried to give her sympathy, but she wanted no part of it. She wanted no part of him at all, while he wanted—

Turning away from the picture of Val and Simm together, Branch shouted, "Boggs, Whalen, get that extra wire over here. We're goin' to have to reinforce this spot, too, before we're done for the day."

Boggs grumbled, and Branch squinted angrily at the fellow's full face. "What did you say, Boggs?"

"I didn't say nothin'."

"You said somethin'."

Boggs looked up resentfully. "Yeah, I did say somethin'. I said it's gettin' late and I'm gettin' hungry."

"Hungry?" The thought of food made Branch's stomach turn, but no further response was necessary as Boggs turned to do his bidding. Branch was still shaking his head as he turned to see Simm whisper into Val's ear. He started a slow burn. She was enjoying that fool's nonsense—every single minute of it!

* * *

Val cursed under her breath as Simm's whispered flattery hissed into her ear. Turning slowly toward him, she responded through clenched teeth, "Simm, if you don't get out of my way, I'm goin' to mow you down."

"I might enjoy bein' mowed down by you, Val."

Val groaned and stared at Simm's relentless smile. "What's the matter with you, Simm? How many times do I have to tell you that you're barkin' up the wrong tree? I ain't interested in hanky-panky. I got my mind set on other goals for the future."

Simm moved a step closer. "What goals might that be? You ain't goin' to have a real heavy hand in the runnin' of this ranch, 'cause Walker's goin' to be takin' over that chore."

Val bristled. "You're wrong."

Simm's young face looked pained. "Why can't you just face it, Val? Walker's here to stay, and your pa wants it that way. I'm more than willin' to take up the slack. As a matter of fact, I'd consider it a privilege."

"There ain't goin' to be no slack."

The sound of Walker's voice from across the corral turned Val toward his frowning figure as he barked, "Forget about that extra wire! We're done for today. Leave everythin' the way it is. We'll pick up where we left off tomorrow."

Val turned back to Simm's surprised quip. "Well, ain't that somethin'! Walker's lettin' us off early. I wonder what tick got under his hide."

Val shrugged. "His hide's so thick that there ain't a tick alive that could manage it."

"Maybe so." Simm unexpectedly squeezed her arm. "But I sure appreciate him lettin' us go back a little early. Maybe we can go for a walk, just you and me, so we can talk."

Val stared speechlessly at Billy's unshakable smile. Wasn't

there any way to get through to him? She tried once more. "I told you, I ain't walkin' and I ain't talkin'. You're wastin' your time, Simm."

Simm's cow eyes did not lose a fraction of their glow. "I'd sure like it if you started callin' me 'Billy.'"

A silent, incredulous second passed before Val turned on her heel and headed for her horse. Mounting, she kicked Dunbar into motion. A moment later, she shivered at the sound of Simm following close behind.

Will pushed himself away from the supper table, a contented smile on his face as he drew himself to his feet. Suddenly realizing he was getting curious stares from some of the hands, he gave a little sniff and turned toward the door. He heard the sound of chairs scraping backward behind him as he stepped out onto the porch. The western sky blazed with the brilliance of a glorious sunset, but his thoughts were all of Mary. He had returned to the ranch with his heart full. Mary always did that for him.

The sound of footsteps turned him to the men as they emerged from the house one by one. His smile dropped as Branch stepped out onto the porch, his face stiff. There were questions Will needed to ask, although he did not relish the thought of the answers he would receive, for he could only judge by Branch's face that there had been problems in scattering the bulls that day.

"Branch, I been meanin' to talk to you."

Will released a quiet groan as the big fellow returned his gaze with a raised brow and a note of agitation in his voice.

"About what?"

"About how things went today with the bulls."

"No problems to speak of. A few fights, but we got them in hand quick enough."

"Oh. From the look of you, I thought that there might've been more trouble."

Branch's expression tightened. "From the look of me?"

"Well, you ain't exactly in the best mood I ever seen."

The men were still trailing past, and Will saw the spontaneous stiffening of Branch's frame as Val emerged, followed closely by Simm. He saw the tightening of Branch's brow and the balling of his fists. A spark of hope sprang to life inside him as Branch growled, "There's nothin' wrong with my mood."

Will nodded. "That so? Hummm…well, if everythin's all right, I guess I'll just go take myself off for a walk. I ate too much today."

Realizing Branch hadn't heard a word he'd said, Will stepped down off the porch, making certain to go in the opposite direction from Val and Simm as they walked toward the barn. Not daring to look back, he walked swiftly as a voice in his mind sent a few words of heartfelt entreaty up toward the darkening sky overhead.

Pausing at the door of Powderkeg's stall, Val jerked her hat off her head, her face flushed with vexation as she threw it on the floor. Her eyes were blazing as she grated, "I'm gettin' sick and tired of tellin' you, Simm—"

"Call me 'Billy.'"

"I'm gettin' sick and tired of tellin' you, *Simm,* to quit followin' me around! I don't need your help when we're workin'. I don't need your help with Powderkeg. I don't need your help no time, nowhere!"

Simm shook his head. "You're real pretty when you get

mad, do you know that, Val? Your eyes get so bright, and you get that pink color in your cheeks.''

Val closed her eyes.

"And you got the longest eyelashes. I ain't never seen none longer."

Val's eyes popped open with a snap. The fella was drivin' her crazy! She stared at his hand as he grasped her shoulder and squeezed it warmly. She attempted to shrug it off. She slapped at it repeatedly, only to find that it stuck there like glue.

"Don't you like me touchin' you, Val?"

Val's hand halted in midslap. "I was beginnin' to think you wasn't gettin' my message."

Simm's hand remained adhered to her shoulder. "I like touchin' you. Maybe I could teach you to like it. Maybe I could teach you—"

At a sound remarkably similar to a growl, Val looked up to see Branch Walker appear behind Simm the split second before he slammed Simm backward against the stall. Simm's eyes bulged as Walker towered over him and poked his face down into Simm's to snarl, "I thought I told you to stick to your job and stay where you belong, Simm. You don't belong here now, and your hand doesn't belong where I just saw it a few minutes ago."

Val looked from Simm to Walker and back again, stunned. Then she exploded. "I don't need you watchin' over me, Walker! I've been tellin' you since you came to this ranch that I can take care of myself!" She darted a glance at Simm where he struggled to regain his composure. "You all right, Billy?"

Simm's youthful face brightened at the use of his given name. Val cursed the obstinacy that had caused her to give him that small encouragement as he straightened up and said,

"I told you before, Walker. I'm my own boss when I'm on my own time, and where I go is my business."

"Not on this ranch, it isn't! Get back to the bunkhouse."

"Val and me were talkin'."

Walker gritted his teeth. "I said, get back to the bunkhouse."

"Go back to the bunkhouse, Billy." Val all but twitched as she used Billy's given name again. "I'm goin' to be busy here for a while. I'll see you in the mornin'."

"But, Val—"

"*Out*, Simm!"

The lethal note in Branch's voice turned Simm toward the door, and Val waited only until he stepped from sight before turning on Branch in a fury. Her heart did a little jump at the peculiar look in his eyes, and she felt a sudden weakness in her knees that was belied by the tone of her voice.

"When I want to make Simm git, *I'll* make him git, you understand that, Walker?"

"It looked to me like you weren't doin' so well when I came in, and I wasn't about to let that soulful little pup maul you."

Val was having trouble maintaining the fire of her response as Walker's dark eyes took on a mesmerizing quality that began melting her insides. His handsome face was so close that she could feel his breath. It had a pleasantly familiar scent and she fought the desire to breathe deeply of it, to draw it within her. She swallowed hard and firmed her resolve.

"I don't let no man maul me unless I want to. And what I do is my concern."

A pained expression moved across Branch's face before it softened unexpectedly. When he finally spoke his voice was only a notch above a whisper. "Look, Val, all this fightin' isn't gettin' us anywhere. I don't know what went wrong when I came here, but I have a feelin' it was as much my fault as yours that we got off on the wrong foot. I'd like to change all that now.''

Val fought to still her sudden trembling, forcing harshness into her reply. ''There's only one way you can change things—by goin' back where you came from. There ain't no room on this ranch for you and me both.''

''You're wrong, Val.''

Branch unexpectedly raised his hand to stroke a wisp of hair back from her cheek. A shiver moved down her spine as he continued.

''I want a chance to show you that I can be your friend. I *want* to be your friend.''

''I got all the friends I need. I don't need another one who thinks he's goin' to take over my pa's ranch like it was his own.''

''The ranch will always belong to you and your pa.''

''You're damned right it will!''

''I'll only own a small part of it.''

''Oh, no, you won't!''

Val's throat was thick, her eyes full. She was shuddering, and she was disgusted with herself for the shambles Branch Walker had made of her defiance with a soft word and a warm glance.

''Just give me a chance to prove to you that I only want what's best for you, Val.''

''*I* know what's best for me. And what's best for me is for you to leave this ranch now!''

''I don't want to leave.'' The simple statement was almost a caress as it emerged from Branch Walker's lips. ''I want to stay.''

"Is that so?" Val was breathless as Walker moved a step closer. "It looks like we can't both have what we want then, don't it?"

Walker was breathing heavily, and he swallowed tightly with his hoarse response. "I think we can, if you'll just let me—"

Val shuddered, her eyes widening as the last of her resistance began draining away. Panicking, she shoved hard at Branch's chest. The suddenness of her move caught him off balance, knocking him back a few steps as she rasped, "You ain't goin' to work your wiles on me. I'm wise to you and everythin' you're tryin' to do. So I'm tellin' you now that there ain't nothin' that's goin' to change things here, except the sight of your back when you ride off, never to return. I don't like you, Branch Walker. I don't want to be your friend. I don't want nothin' from you and I never will. And I'll win, you know. You and your bulls will never last the time it takes to earn a part of the Circle S. You'll see...."

Unable to bear another moment of looking at Branch Walker's tortured expression, Val turned abruptly away. Putting one foot deliberately in front of the other, her step grew steadier as the distance between Walker and herself widened.

In the yard, Val took a deep, shuddering breath and headed for the sanctuary of her room. As she closed the door behind her moments later, she realized she had come close to sacrificing all she had worked for to the plea in Walker's deep voice and that soft look in his eyes.

And to her despair, she could not help wondering how it would have been if she had.

Chapter Twelve

Val had been riding for almost an hour. The morning nip in the air had warmed, and the sun shining relentlessly on the unshaded trail had raised a sweat on her brow that she wiped away with her sleeve as she questioned again, for the hundredth time since starting out, what she was doing.

Squinting into the distance, Val reviewed the events of that morning in her mind. She had awakened exhausted after a long, sleepless night that was little different from the three previous nights since her encounter with Branch in the barn. Branch's husky whisper echoed again in her mind.

We can both have what we want if you'll only…

Only what? Sacrifice everything she had worked for to the ache deep inside her that would not abate? Give vent to the steady gnawing in her stomach that had no relation to a hunger for food? Allow Branch Walker, her enemy, to show her what he truly meant by "being her friend"?

Even now, his mesmerizing stare held her captive. Even now she could not shake the memory of the shape of his lips, the strength of his arms, the sheer power of the man and the gentleness of his whisper.

We can both have what we want if you'll only…

Lifting her hat, Val smoothed back the flying wisps of hair that had escaped her heavy braid, allowing the sun to warm her unshaded face for a few moments. She closed her eyes and tilted up her face to the fiery orb, waiting for a sense of relaxation that did not come. There was no escaping her turmoil.

It had been sheer misery riding out with the men in the few days since their encounter, avoiding Branch's gaze, maintaining her determination not to allow him to supplant her completely in the running of the Circle S, even though she had begun losing heart for the battle. She had even changed her attitude toward Simm in an effort to distract her mind, but it had been to little avail. All she had achieved was a deep sense of guilt for encouraging an affection from Simm that she could never return.

What had happened to her? Why did she watch Branch covertly, studying the stretch of his shoulders, the power in his muscular frame and the golden glint of his hair, when she truly wished she never had to see him again? Why did she spend each waking minute with a lump in her throat? Why did she hurt so badly?

Needing an answer to those questions before she went mad, Val had first thought to turn to her pa, but the words would not come. In desperation, she had even wandered into the kitchen, where she had hovered around Red Hand, but when the old Indian had looked up, the words had stuck in her throat. That morning her misery had been too acute to ignore, and she had made a mumbled excuse about remaining behind when the hands rode out.

And here she was.

Replacing her hat on her head, Val tugged at her coat and slipped it off her shoulders. The breeze cooled her skin, and she wished the fire inside her could be cooled as easily. She flopped her coat across the saddle, her heart beginning an accelerated beating as the house she sought came into view. Taking a determined breath, she urged Dunbar into a canter.

Reining up beside the hitching rail out front a short time later, Val dismounted. The front door opened to reveal the Widow McGee's smile as she stepped onto the porch.

"Well, Valen—Val, how nice to see you! This *is* a surprise."

Val nodded, searching the woman's face. She saw sincerity in her welcome, and an unexpected concern. Confused, she responded cautiously, "I suppose it is. I just happened to be passing and I thought I'd stop by."

"I'm glad you did." Widow McGee motioned her forward. "Come inside. I'm alone right now. My cowhands are out working in the high pasture. I was just going to have a cup of tea and a piece of pie. Will you join me?"

Val nodded, squinting as her eyes adjusted to the change in light as she entered the house. She looked around as the widow led her toward the kitchen. She had never seen a house like the widow's before. It was spotlessly clean and exuded a warmth that she could not define. A few minutes later as she sat at the kitchen table and the widow turned toward her with a piece of pie, it occurred to her that the house had taken on the personality of the woman who had made it a home. Val's spirits fluctuated between relief and a strange sort of anxiety. She did not know where to start.

Pouring a cup of tea for herself and sitting across the table with a smile, the widow relieved Val's uneasiness by opening the conversation for her.

"You're such a pretty girl, Val. Mr. McGee and I never had children of our own, and I must admit that I watched you grow up with a bit of envy, wondering what it would be like to have a daughter like you.''

Val shrugged, embarrassed by the compliment and by the woman's directness. ''Oh, I don't know that it would have been so great. My pa says I was always a handful of trouble. Things haven't gotten much better now that I'm older.''

''Oh, that isn't what I heard. Most people around here figure your father would've been lost without you after your mother left.'' Val's head jerked up at the mention of her mother, but the widow continued evenly, ''That was a sad day for him, but I think you made all his hard work worthwhile the way you worked along with him, valuing everything he was trying to build as much as he.''

Val's mouth twitched. ''You wouldn't think so the way things turned out—with him bringin' in a ranch manager and all.''

The widow's small eyes saddened. ''I think you're being a bit hard on your father, Val. I can't really speak for him, but it was my thought that he might have hired a ranch manager for you as much as himself.''

''He didn't do it for me!'' Val raised her chin, her cheeks flushing. ''He knew what *I* wanted. I wanted to take over when he was too old to handle things anymore. I wanted to take care of him like he took care of me, and I wanted to make the Circle S my life like he made it his.''

The widow was silent for a moment before she whispered, ''Don't you think he knew that, too? And don't you think he might have wanted something more for you than he had most of his life—like someone to love and marry—''

''I ain't goin' to marry nobody!'' Val put her fork down on the table, the thought of eating impossible. ''I ain't goin' to trust somebody with my love just so he can throw it back in my face like my ma did to my pa. And I ain't goin' to bring a kid into this world so somebody can run off and leave it like my ma did to me.''

"Oh, Val..."

Mary McGee's warm hand covered hers, and the woman's warmth dulled the edge of Val's pain.

"It isn't always that way. Nobody really knows what happened with your mother or why she left."

Val nodded, her lips tightening. "I know why she left. She didn't want to live on the ranch no more, and she didn't want to live with my pa and me. She wanted that traveling man who was always tellin' her how pretty she was—with his blond hair that shone in the sun and that smile that made her feel like she was made of pure gold. But his type don't love nobody for long."

"You saw the man? You knew who he was? I didn't think anybody knew."

"I knew. I remember him. He came to the house a few times. He was real big and blond, and my ma was always smilin' and laughin' when he was around. She couldn't do enough for him."

"Big, handsome, and blond—like Mr. Walker."

"Yeah." Val's heart began drumming. "But I ain't nothin' like my ma. Walker ain't goin' to wrap me around his little finger."

Mary McGee's smile was tentative. "Has he tried?"

Val pulled back her hand, her lips tight. "Yeah, he tried. He says he wants to be my friend. He says we can both have what we want."

"What do you both want, Val?"

"The Circle S."

"Is that all?"

Val's lips tightened, barely allowing her whispered response. "I don't know."

"Val, dear..." Mary McGee leaned over to hug Val briefly against her soft body. "You had such a terrible experience. If I could change it all for you, I would, so you would never suffer another day for your mother's mistakes. But I can't change it, dear. All I can tell you is that you can't shut yourself off from life. You're a grown woman now, and a grown woman begins yearning. She wants her life to be full of more than good, honest work. A grown woman wants to love, even if the thought is frightening at first. She wants to have children."

"I ain't never havin' no kids!"

"Don't say that, Val. Children are life's greatest blessing."

"Not to my ma they wasn't."

"You're not your mother, Val." Mary McGee's brown eyes were suddenly firm. "Don't ever think you're like her, because you aren't."

"How do you know I'm not? Maybe I am, down underneath."

"No. You aren't. You're good and you're constant. You've never run away from anything difficult. Your father is proud of you."

"Yeah, proud. That's why he hired Branch Walker."

"I don't think your father's pride in you had anything to do with the reason he hired Mr. Walker. I heard your father say that he wanted to improve his herd and that Mr. Walker was an expert in those matters, and that he wanted another person to share the burden of running the ranch."

"But we don't need nobody else, Mrs. McGee."

"Please call me 'Mary,' Val."

Val's eyes suddenly filled. "I don't know what's wrong

with me. Everything seems to be going wrong. I don't even know what I feel, except that I feel real bad.''

"I think you're trying to deny your feelings, and I think you should try to trust them a little more." Mary McGee took Val's hands. "You're nothing like your mother, Val. Don't worry about that. Oh, you're like her on the outside. You're tall and slim and so pretty."

"I'm not pretty."

"You are, even though you go to pains to hide it. You have the same beautiful hair as your mother, the same small features, and your eyes are the same unusual color as hers. But there was an emptiness in your mother's eyes and your eyes aren't like that. They're clear and bright and filled with feeling, and they're beautiful. Trust yourself, Val. Trust your feelings."

Val was too filled with emotion to speak. Attuned to her discomfort, Mary hesitated a moment, then sat back. She forced a smile and when she spoke again her tone was light and casual. "I think I'll have a little of that pie myself. I really shouldn't. I've gotten a bit round around the middle lately, but..." She shrugged. "I'm quite famous for my apple pie, you know." Mary paused, her voice softening. "Try the pie, dear, and then we'll talk about the price of cattle and your father's new bulls. I'm very interested in hearing about them."

"Them sissy bulls..."

Mary giggled. "They *do* look like sissies, don't they? But please don't tell your father I said that."

Val smiled, the surprising warmth she felt for this woman expanding inside her. "I won't tell him."

Those four words seeming to seal an unspoken bond between them, Val picked up her fork.

* * *

Branch kicked Caesar into motion, scattering the nearby stock as he rode toward the men working a short distance away and snapped, "What do you think you're doin', Potter?"

Potter looked up, his wiry brows rising under the dusty brim of his hat as he leaned on the muddy shovel in his hand. "I thought me and the boys was doin' what you told us to do a few minutes ago—cleanin' up this water hole before it goes and gets itself polluted."

Branch stared down into Potter's bearded face, his dark eyes hard as flint. "I told you, Wyatt and Simm to clean up that water hole an hour ago, but I haven't seen you do anythin' but lean on that shovel for the past twenty minutes."

"Is that so!"

"You heard it!"

Potter's hairy beard twitched with annoyance. "I ain't never had no complaints about my work from the old man."

"Well, I'm not Stark."

"You sure as hell ain't!"

Branch's expression hardened. "Do you have some complaints?"

Potter sniffed.

"Do you?"

"Yeah, plenty, but I ain't got time to talk about them 'cause my boss thinks I waste too much time as it is."

Turning back to the water hole, Potter jammed his shovel into the slippery slime that lent a putrid stench to the formerly clear water and threw it atop a nearby pile. Ignoring the inquisitive glances of Simm and Wyatt, Branch kicked Caesar into motion, and within minutes, he was at the other side of the pasture.

Noting the limp of a steer that scrambled out of his way as

he approached, Branch drew his mount up short. He stared at the animal's feet. Foot rot! If one steer had it, there were more.

"Whalen!" The dark cowhand turned sharply from the task he had been assigned, and Branch saw resentment in the fellow's gaze that hadn't been far from the surface since that day at the Loco Steer. Short on patience, Branch ordered, "Get back to the ranch and see if there's anything on hand for foot rot."

"I don't know nothin' about nursin' no cows."

Branch's dark eyes pinned him. "You're tellin' me you've never seen a case of foot rot before?"

Whalen's hard expression did not flinch. "I'm tellin' you that Stark always took care of them things himself."

"Well, looks like you fellas are goin' to be in for an education. Now get back to the ranch, and if you don't see anything in the barn that you recognize, ask Red Hand. It's my bet that nothin' much escapes that old Indian."

"That old drunk don't know nothin'—"

"Do what I said if you want to keep earnin' your pay here, Whalen. And don't come back with empty hands if you know what's good for you."

Branch waited until Whalen wheeled his horse with a mumbled response and started back toward the ranch. Turning his horse as well, he made his way cautiously through the milling cattle in an attempt to ascertain the extent of foot rot in that particular section of the herd. He was keeping a mental count that did not lighten his already foul disposition when his thoughts wandered.

It had been an especially irritating day that showed little hope of improving. Branch glanced toward the position of the sun in the cloudless sky, frowning. Just a few more hours…just a little longer, and they'd be back at the ranch and he'd find out what it was that had kept Val from riding out with them today.

Suddenly annoyed with his line of thought, Branch jerked his hat from his head and ran his hand roughly through his perspiration-soaked hair. The light breeze cooled his scalp, a physical relief that did little to soothe the agitation inside him.

Damn it all, what did it really matter? Val's behavior since the night she had run away from him in the barn had been agitating him to no end. He had suffered unexpected torment watching her as she encouraged Simm's attentions at every opportunity, while making certain their coy exchange of glances and short, whispered conversations did not interfere with the performance of their daily work. She had driven him to the point of distraction for three days, only to declare that morning that she wouldn't be riding out with the hands today because she had other things to do. The expression on Will Stark's face had been a clear indication that he had no idea what his daughter was up to, and Branch had been more disturbed than he cared to admit.

Despising himself, he had kept a cautious eye on Simm the entire morning, hardly allowing the clear-cheeked cowboy out of his sight. He suspected the effort had not gone unnoticed by the rest of the men, but that knowledge had not affected his behavior in the least. Branch looked back at the water hole, his eyes burning into Simm's bent back. If that fella thought he was going to go sneaking back to the Circle S to find Val, he was sadly mistaken.

Momentarily shocked by the rancor of his own thoughts, Branch pulled Caesar up short. What was the matter with him? When Val Stark was tormenting him with her nearness, he wished her on the other side of the earth, but when she was out of his sight, he ached to have her near. His emotions were in knots with her or without her, and his mind still hadn't stopped spinning. What *did* he want? Did he really know?

Branch paused, his eyes narrowing with determination the second before he jammed his hat back on his head and spurred his horse into a leap forward that scattered cattle and raised the heads of the men working nearby. It occurred to him as he reined Caesar back to a canter and turned him toward the higher pasture where the rest of the men were working that he might not know what he *wanted*, but he sure knew what he *needed*.

Suddenly determined, Branch took a deep, steadying breath. He'd just make sure that he went into town with the boys tomorrow for their Saturday night prowl. It would make a new man of him.

The setting sun was making its final descent as Will walked toward the barn with a troubled expression. His high hopes of only a few days earlier had plummeted and he had begun thinking that he had only seen what he wanted to see in Branch's expression that time Branch had seen Val and Simm together. The way Val seemed to be encouraging Simm of late would have been heartening, but after hearing Mary's thoughts on the matter, he only felt worse. He was in deep need of another conversation with the woman he loved if he was to survive this complicated mess. The knowledge that Mary's cowhands would be away for a few days while they delivered some stock to a nearby county availed him of an opportunity to spend more than just a few hours with her that weekend, and he was determined to make the best of it.

Will shook his head. Stolen moments at his age.... It was downright ridiculous!

Pausing as he reached the barn, Will squinted into the darkened interior, his eyes focusing on a lamp hanging in the corner where Branch was applying salve to the scar on Caesar's flank. Branch looked up as he approached, frowning, but Will was not deterred.

Stopping beside his surly ranch manager, he watched Branch's careful ministrations as he commented, "I'm sure glad you got that mess in the summer pasture cleaned up today."

"Which mess was that?"

Branch's stiff expression barely changed, and Will hesitated a moment before continuing. Nobody had to tell him that Walker was wound up tighter than a spring of late, and he had the feelin' that it wouldn't make much difference to Walker whether he was the boss or not if somethin' he said made that spring snap. Will decided in favor of caution. "That mess at the water hole and them cows with foot rot. I told the boys to start checkin' out the rest of the herd first thing tomorrow."

Walker looked up, meeting Stark's gaze in silent challenge. "I've got other plans for the men tomorrow."

Stark nodded. "That so? Well, I'm thinkin' it would be smarter to follow through on what you started today."

"Are you sayin' I'm not smart enough to handle a simple case of foot rot in the herd? Maybe you're thinkin' you made a mistake in takin' me on in the first place." Branch's expression tightened. "And maybe you're thinkin'—"

"Yeah, and maybe I'm thinkin' you're spoilin' for a fight and that I'm not about to give it to you." Stark shook his head. "What's the matter with you, Branch? You ain't been fit to live with all week. The men are complainin' that you're drivin' 'em into the ground with work, and you're complainin' that they ain't workin' hard enough. You ain't the same man who came here a while back, and I'm thinkin' it's time *I* should be askin' the questions instead of you. Now if you got somethin' stuck in your craw, it's time to get it out. What's botherin' you?''

Branch's dark eyes narrowed and Stark waited as he drew himself up straight. "Nothin's botherin' me—nothin' you can do anythin' about, anyways. It's been a bad week. I'm thinkin' I've let a few things get to me that I shouldn't have. It isn't anything that a little recreation won't cure.''

Will studied Branch's face. "There ain't nothin' you ain't told me, is there—like any more 'flukes' that are botherin' you?''

Branch shook his head. "No. Either puttin' on guards did the trick, or that whole business was really nothin' at all.''

Will nodded. "That's good, 'cause I've got an idea in my head to go visit Joe Morris, an old friend of mine, for a couple of days. I heard the old boy ain't doin' too well. I figure on goin' early tomorrow, maybe just as soon as the sun comes up.'' Branch made no comment and Will continued. "I'll be back to ride out with you all on Monday.'' Still no comment, and Will could not resist adding, "Yeah, I'm thinkin' that recreation idea of yours is a real good one.''

Branch's head snapped back toward him. His eyes narrowed as he responded, "I'll take care of that foot rot.''

"I know you will,'' the old man replied, raising his eyes to the rafters in unspoken comment as Walker turned back to his horse without another word.

Walking back toward the house, Will suddenly realized that his heart was growing lighter with every step he took. Almost two whole days with Mary—just him and her! They could talk for as long as they wanted without worrying about him havin' to hurry up and leave. Maybe he'd put up that shelf Mary had said she was wantin' in the kitchen. Will grinned. And maybe he wouldn't have time for it. His grin widened.

Humming, a real spring in his step, Will walked into the house.

Emerging onto the porch a few seconds later, Val turned around, her brow raised speculatively at her father's back as he disappeared into the house. She was beginning to worry about her pa. She hadn't heard him humming in years. All that good humor just because he was going to see old Joe Morris for a few days?

Halting, Val looked around and breathed a sigh of relief at finding herself completely alone. She started toward the barn. The long afternoon she had spent with Widow McGee had opened her mind to a whole new line of thought. The widow was right. She was a woman now. She supposed she couldn't deny it or the feelings that had been making her life a living hell since Branch Walker had arrived on the Circle S. The problem was what she was supposed to *do* about it.

Trust your feelings, Val.

The widow's words had rung over and again in her mind on the way home that afternoon, and by the time she'd arrived at the house, the fragile sense of well-being her exchange with the widow had accomplished had been destroyed. She had no doubt in her mind that the widow was talking good sense, but her feelings for Branch Walker were so confused.

Which feelings was she supposed to trust? Should she trust the resentment Walker's arrival and his control of the ranch had evoked—the same feelings that would not be satisfied until he was gone? Or should she trust the feelings that made her shiver at the low rasp in his voice when he looked into her eyes—the feelings that made her mind torment her with his image awake and asleep?

Val shuddered. This was all so new to her. But, as inexperienced as she was, she knew instinctively that Branch suffered a similar agony. She had seen it in his eyes and heard it in his voice.

We can both have what we want if you'll only...

Val shuddered again at the agony she could not expel. She was a few steps from the barn, when she heard Branch's voice coming from inside.

"So it's this way, Potter. We're goin' out an hour early tomorrow mornin'. Stark is takin' off to visit a friend and I want you to take half the men to the north pasture to finish the work he was doin' there. While you're at it, I want you to keep an eye out for foot rot in that part of the herd. I'll keep the other half of the men with me to finish up what we started today."

"We don't need to start out an hour early to get that work finished. The fellas are already complainin' about the way you've been drivin' them lately."

"They won't be complainin' when we come back early so we can have more time in town."

The change in Potter's tone was apparent. "Well, maybe you're right, it bein' Saturday night an' all."

"Right."

There was a moment's pause before Potter queried cautiously, "I don't expect you to go givin' away any secrets, but am I right in thinkin' that you got plans for this weekend, Mr. Boss Man?"

"There's only one thing I've got to say about that." Branch's deep voice held a note of resolve Val could not remember ever hearing before. "I'm goin' to get myself a room at the Trail's End Hotel as soon as I get into town. Then I'm goin' to find myself some real good female company and I'm goin' to make the most of it. When I come back to the ranch on Sunday, you can depend on it that I'll be purrin' like a kitten.''

Potter gave a hoot of laughter. "Looks like you're human, after all! I should've figured there was a good reason for all that hollerin' and growlin' you been doin' of late.''

The conversation continued, but Val heard little more. Her face flaming, she turned abruptly and walked back to the house, her mind in a turmoil and her stomach churning. She slammed the door of her room behind her a few minutes later and stripped off her hat and coat, her throat filled from the heated emotions running wild inside her.

It was a man's world, all right! Branch Walker was suffering the same ills she was. He was feeling the "yearnings" that attacked both man and woman alike when they reached a certain age, just as the widow said, only he had freedom to take care of those needs, while she was stuck with the limitations of her sex—aching.

The knot in Val's throat tightened and she fought the heat of tears. So Branch Walker was going to come back purring like a kitten. The image that assaulted her raised Val's chin with a sharp jerk. Damn it all! Branch Walker wasn't going to defeat her—not this way! She needed to remember her own boasting words when she had made that wager with Potter, Simm and Whalen. She could do anything Walker could do, and do it better! She hadn't put any limitations on that statement then, and she wouldn't now.

A new determination coming alive inside her, Val turned to the mirror and assessed what she saw. She frowned at the image of a plain young woman dressed in unbecoming men's clothing and remembered what the widow had said about her being pretty. She'd take a page from Branch Walker's book. She'd come back from town purrin' like a kitten, too—and she'd have the time of her life!

Chapter Thirteen

Red Hand listened for sounds of movement within the silent house, but there were none. He looked at the sky through the kitchen window. The sun had risen and the workday had begun. The cowhands were gone. Stark was gone. It was time for him to be gone, as well—for the wind to whisper in his ears the secrets of the new day, for the sun to touch his skin with the life it gave, for the breath of the Great Spirit to enter his nostrils, purifying him.

Red Hand grunted. It would not be much longer before he again rode off into the hills to welcome the day and to purge the shadows of the night.

Red Hand's expression flickered. The shadows of the night were dark and filled with pain. In them he saw Singing Woman, lifeless, her buckskins lying limply against her wasted body. He saw Little Badger and Morning Dove beside her, their youthful eyes closed forever by the same sickness that had taken their mother. He saw himself kneeling beside them, empty and alone. It was only when he awakened that he remembered the long journey that had brought him to this place.

At the sound of a step behind him, Red Hand raised his

head. It was she whom he awaited, but he did not turn toward Val as she entered the kitchen and stopped short in surprise.

"Red Hand, what are you doin' here this time of the mornin'? I thought you'd be long gone by now."

He did not respond, and without looking he could see the narrowing of Val's sharp eyes as she continued, "Did my pa tell you to check on me so's you could tell him why I didn't ride out with the men today when he got back?"

Red Hand did not turn until he heard the note of frustration in Val's next two words, "Red Hand..."

"Red Hand make breakfast."

"I ain't hungry."

"Val eat."

"I said I ain't hungry."

Red Hand filled a dish and put it on the table. He continued looking at Val in silence until she sat with a low sound of exasperation. "Damn it, Red Hand! How come you're the only one who ever wins an argument with me?"

Red Hand made no response, but he knew Val did not expect one. She did not speak again until her plate was emptied. He was looking at her intently, when she glanced up and frowned.

"What?"

He did not speak.

"What do you want to know?"

He maintained silence.

"You want to know why I stayed home this mornin' when I usually don't let them cowhands take a step without me trailin' along to keep an eye on them, don't you? You want me to tell you what I got goin' on in my head, even though I know you're readin' my mind right now, like you always do." She paused again. "Say somethin', Red Hand!"

Val's eyes narrowed when he did not respond. "You know, don't you?" Val's narrowed eyes filled with tears. "You know I ain't had a decent day since that Branch Walker came here, and that now he fixed it that I can't even have a decent night without him comin' into my dreams and makin' them a livin' hell. The only thing you don't know is what I'm goin' to do about it."

Red Hand listened and waited.

"All right, I'll tell you! I'm goin' into town, and I'm goin' to find me a man. Then I'm goin' to come back purrin' like a kitten—same as Walker. And then I'm goin' to face Walker, man to man, and I ain't goin' to come up the loser, Red Hand. The Circle S is goin' to be mine again, you'll see."

Red Hand remained silent as Val suddenly stood up.

"I'm a woman now. I ain't no little girl, and it's time I found out what bein' a woman means. Only I ain't goin' to be no man's woman. I'm goin' to be my own woman, usin' a man for a convenience. Fair's fair, to my mind."

Val turned, and within a few seconds she disappeared around the corner out of sight. Red Hand waited in silence until she emerged again and started toward the front door. He nodded as she shouted over her shoulder, "I'm goin' to town."

Red Hand listened to the sound of Val's horse as she rode off, and knew this woman was the daughter of his spirit, who had breathed life back into him with her need. He would listen and he would watch. And then he would do what he must do.

Will's journey was near its end. As excited as a child, he had awakened that morning to predawn darkness, dressed and waited impatiently until the men arrived, equally early, for a quick breakfast.

He had been surprised when Val hadn't come to the table and had finally gone to her room to seek her out, only to find her still in bed. Suspicion reared its ugly head when she complained that she hadn't felt well all night and that she was still sick. He hadn't believed a word and was squinting at her face in the semidarkness of her room, when Val had finally exploded, "Can't a woman even have a few monthly pains without havin' every man on the Circle S know about it! All right, I'll get up and go with the men if you're that worried about me takin' a day off!"

He had stopped her then, riddled with guilt at the lack of color in her face as she turned to the light. The poor darlin' really hadn't been feelin' good, but he had been relieved that it was nothin' that needed his care and that he was free to follow his plans. He had left the house as soon as the men had ridden out of the yard, and now here he was.

Will dug his heels into his mount's sides as the ranch house loomed in the distance. His heart was drumming as he scanned the landscape. There was not a sign of movement anywhere and he was relieved to see that the cowhands appeared to have left on schedule. He glanced up at the morning sky. Mary wouldn't be expecting him this early. He hadn't told her that he'd be starting out at sunup so that they wouldn't waste an hour of the precious time they had to spend together. She was probably still in bed, dreaming sweet dreams.

Will grinned, his heart beating faster. Well, if he was lucky, he'd be joining her in that bed, and he'd be making her dreams a little bit sweeter in no more time than it took to—

Will's thoughts drew to a sudden halt at the flutter of movement in the doorway of the house before the door opened. And then he saw Mary staring in his direction. Her hair was unbound, just the way he liked it, and she was wearing that soft blue dressing gown that smelled of roses. He couldn't see her face real clear, but he knew that she was smiling. He knew that because he was smiling, too. And his heart was pounding....

The sun was setting as Branch rode into Clearmont, a determined man. He had spent a long, aggravating day that had just been one more in a long line of aggravating days since he had come to realize that his feelings for Val Stark were out of control. He had arisen that morning before dawn, as had been planned, certain that Val would be ready and waiting at the breakfast table as usual. But he had been wrong. Val had not been at the table, and when Stark had gone to check on her, Branch had known he was not the only person who'd be stunned into speechlessness when Stark told them she wouldn't be ridin' out with the men for the second day in a row. But the speechlessness hadn't lasted long, and Branch had soon become fed up to the gills with the questions Simm asked about her.

Determined not to admit to the disappointment that was a knot deep inside him, he had finished off his breakfast faster than was good for him. He had then driven his men to indigestion in his effort to get out of the house and avoid thoughts of Val Stark lying in her soft warm bed, that long brown hair stretched across her pillow. He had spent the remainder of the day in much the same way as the previous one, making certain Simm did not get out of his sight.

When he'd returned to the ranch that night, he had been startled to learn that Val was gone. If he was to believe Red Hand, she hadn't said where she was going—but that old Indian didn't fool him. Nothing slipped past Red Hand. He knew what was going on—whatever it was.

A burst of music from the Loco Steer broke into Branch's thoughts as he and his mounted group neared the bawdy establishment, and a hard smile touched his lips. The men riding behind him were laughing and trading quips, their spirits light at the thought of the night to come, but his nerves were stretched tighter than a drum. His smile hardened. But not for long. First that room at the Trail's End, next a nice, long bath, and then he was going to find himself a woman. By the time he went back to the Circle S, Val Stark would be nothing more than a faint shadow in his mind.

His disposition warming at the thought, Branch turned into the livery stable to settle Caesar. It was going to be a night to remember.

It had been a day to remember, and Will was damned sorry to see it come to an end. The rays of the setting sun shone through the bedroom window, flashing hues of pink and gold against Mary's fair cheek as she lay beside him. The bed linens were pulled across them both, and he knew he had never been a happier man.

He strained to remember where the hours had flown, aware that the day had started in this very same spot where they now lay, and he would not have had it any other way. He smiled. Mary and he had walked hand in hand through the pasture and had then waded in an ice-cold stream, laughing like children. On their return home, they had had a serious discussion about the future of the open range, and he had not been surprised to find Mary and him in agreement on almost every point.

Will sighed. He and his Mary were meant for each other.

Inspired to touch her by his loving thoughts, Will slid his hand against the covers and rested his palm against Mary's stomach. He caressed her gently.

Mary turned toward him, her eyes bright as she whispered, "Wilbur, I have something to tell you. It's a surprise that I've been saving for the right moment."

Wilbur smiled. "Is that right, darlin'? What is it?"

Mary's round face flushed. "Wilbur, do you remember how I told you that Charlie and I always wanted a child, although the good Lord never saw fit to send us one?"

He continued stroking Mary's stomach as he replied, "Yes, darlin', I remember."

"Well, Wilbur..." Mary paused, her face flushing a little darker as she looked up lovingly into his eyes.

Will was waiting for Mary to continue, when his breath suddenly caught in his throat. His eyes popped wide as he looked at the rise of her stomach underneath the light coverlet. His hand springing back as if it had been burned, he stuttered, "Mary, you don't mea-mean—"

"Wilbur, what's wrong?" Alarmed, Mary stared at Wilbur's white face for long seconds before her eyes widened, as well. A short, choked sound emerged from her throat. The sound suddenly became full-fledged laughter, and Mary was convulsed to the point where tears ran down her cheeks and she was weak from the effort before she calmed enough to set Will's thundering heart at rest.

"No...no, dear, it's not that. You must know that there isn't a chance in the world that I could be—"

Mary laughed uproariously again. Finally in control a few moments later, she managed to rasp, "I'm so sorry, dear, but you should have seen your face."

"Mary, darlin'." Will managed a weak smile. "You near to stopped my heart."

Mary's smile instantly faded. "Wilbur, I'm really sorry. I didn't for a minute think you'd ever think that I—" Mary started to giggle again and Will's patience began to show the first sign of wear.

"What's your surprise, darlin'? I'm thinkin' it had better be good after all this."

"I think it is good, dear, because you know how much I've always wished that Valentine could be my daughter. Well, I think there's a chance that it might just happen some day—I mean that she might come to think of me as someone she can turn to like a mother." Mary paused and took a deep breath. "Valentine came to visit me yesterday, Wilbur, and I think she really likes me."

"Valentine came to see *you* yesterday? That's where she went?"

"That's right. She came and we talked. We had such a nice visit that I didn't want her to leave. I think she felt the same."

"What did you talk about?"

"Oh, I can't tell you that."

"Why not? I'm her father."

"She confided in me."

Will could feel the color returning to his face in a heated flush. "But *I'm* her father."

"Oh, Will, I'm sorry. If I had thought it would make you angry, I would never have mentioned that Valentine was here."

"I'm glad she came, Mary, as surprised as I am to hear that she did. I just want to know why she came."

"Please forgive me, dear, but I can't tell you anything we discussed. The only thing I can say is that I think everything is going to be all right. I have a feeling in my bones that it's all going to work out."

"Mary…"

"Oh, Wilbur, I'm sorry. Here, let me console you."

Drawing his head down against her breast, Mary stroked his cheek in a way that sent little shivers down Will's spine. Will gave a low sigh. It was real fine to be consoled. It was real fine to have a good woman like Mary love him. But he still wondered—

"Wilbur..." Will looked up to see Mary's eyes glowing. "We might *really* be a family one day."

Remembering the expression on Branch Walker's face that morning, Will didn't have the heart to reply.

Clearmont came alive with sounds of Saturday night revelry as the sun dropped below the horizon. The lights of the main street below reflected brightly through the window of Val's room in the Trail's End Hotel as she directed a nervous glance over her shoulder toward the raucous sights and sounds. Strangely, she felt as if she had never seen or heard them before as she walked a few steps closer to the window to get a clearer view of the activity below.

The street was filled with a seemingly endless flow of wagons and horsemen coming and going. Almost directly across from her, Asa Ledman's store was brightly lit. She could see customers moving through the aisles closest to the window, and at a flashing glimpse of Sally Ledman's slender form, she pulled back spontaneously. Cursing her unconscious display of discomfiture, Val took a bold step forward, knowing she was clearly visible as she continued looking down into the street. The gunsmith's shop was closed for the night, but the barbershop next door with its public baths was seeing a brisk flow of traffic. Beyond it, the blacksmith's shop was dark, but she knew the livery stable and various other small shops would see steady business for some hours yet.

Ending her surveillance of the street, Val turned around and walked to the mirror. She paused to take a deep breath as she surveyed her reflection once more, astounded that an afternoon shopping in the Frenchwoman's store frequented by the Loco Steer girls could have made such a difference in her appearance. She swallowed the lump in her throat as she questioned aloud in a shaky voice, "Val Stark, is that really you?"

There was no response from the tall brunette who stared back at her with startled gray eyes. Val giggled nervously at the thought that the woman reflected in the glass had a right to be startled. She was really something to see!

Val smoothed her hand against the upward sweep of her hair, marveling at the elegant job she had done of twisting the weighty strands into an elaborate hairdo similar to those favored by the women at the Loco Steer. It made little difference to her that she had used at least four pounds of hairpins to secure the shiny mass and that the present discomfort of her scalp put her in mind of a porcupine with its quills reversed. She was pleased with the way her upswept curls emphasized the long length of her neck and the curve of shoulders that were almost bared.

Val's gaze dropped a little lower and she suffered her first pang of disquiet. She wasn't sure she should have let Madame LaRue talk her into this particular dress. Not that the soft red fabric didn't provide an excellent contrast with her dark hair and light skin, but she somehow had the idea that the style was fashioned with a woman in mind who was a little less ample in an area where she had not realized she was ample at all.

Tearing her eyes from the creamy mounds that puffed atop the neckline of her dress, Val turned slightly, smoothing the narrow waistline and the generous flare of the skirt below. She smiled at the red slippers that peeked out from beneath the hemline. They were surprisingly soft and comfortable, despite the height of the heels, and if she were to name her favorite piece from the new equipment she had assembled for this landmark night, she would have to say it was her shoes.

Val picked up the brilliant red plume that the Frenchwoman had included free of charge, and considered its appearance as she held it against the back of her head. She secured it there with another few pins and stepped back to assess herself again. It amused her to note that in her new high-heeled shoes, she probably met the mark of six feet, and she would tower over most of the men in the Loco Steer by at least a few inches. Her amusement momentarily dulled with the thought that there was one man she wouldn't dwarf, but she shrugged and attempted to dismiss the thought.

It would be impossible to miss her, that was for sure.

A burst of laughter from the street below turned Val toward the window again. Well, she was ready, wasn't she? What was she waiting for?

Val reached for the black lacy shawl that Madam LaRue had insisted was the perfect complement to her outfit and snatched up her small beaded purse. She was as ready as she would ever be.

Looking back at the silvered glass one last time, Val saluted the image reflected there as she said aloud, "Glad to meet you, Miss Valentine Stark. You and me are goin' to get to know each other real well tonight. And when we're done, darlin', we're both goin' to be purrin' like a kitten."

Turning determinedly from the mirror, Val walked to the door. She ignored the butterflies that leaped to life in her stomach the moment her hand touched the knob. Pulling the door open and stepping out into the hallway, she mumbled through gritted teeth, "Yeah, purrin' like a kitten."

* * *

The Loco Steer was ablaze with light and alive with music. Turning with his drink in hand, Branch leaned back against the bar with a strained smile. He had entered the crowded saloon an hour earlier, a man with a mission. Freshly bathed and clothed, he had sauntered to the bar, as ready as he would ever be, his gaze roaming the lush beauties circulating through the crowded room. He had bought himself a drink and turned with an eye toward a serious selection of the female delights available. The only problem was that the more he looked, the more his enthusiasm waned. He had started getting curious glances as he turned down one girl after another, and the raised brow and knowing smirk he received from the last one had been a definite insult to his masculinity.

His cheek twitching with annoyance, Branch tossed back another drink. He had never been that picky when it came to women. A pleasant smile and a willing body were usually enough to satisfy his needs. So why had the first girl who approached him "giggled too much" for him to bear? Why had the second one had "a vacant look" that distracted him, and the third one been "too coarse"? Whatever the answers, he was beginning to believe his great expectations were heading for dismal failure, when a delicate arm slipped around his waist and he heard a sultry voice beside him.

"What kept you, handsome? I've been waitin' for you all night."

Branch looked down into the brightly painted face of a blonde who had been otherwise engaged when he had first walked in. She was all woman, from the top of her flaxen-haired head to the tips of her high-heeled shoes, and his superior height lent an appreciative angle to his view of the female flesh exposed in the neckline of her gown. "Well, how do you do, darlin'?'' Branch offered with a smile. "What might your name be?"

"My name's Lulu." The blonde lowered her darkly colored eyelids seductively as she squeezed closer. "But you can call me 'darlin' if you like, 'cause that sounds good to me."

"It sounds good to me, too, darlin'." Branch's smile broadened.

Twenty minutes and several drinks later Branch's voluptuous companion was still rubbing her lush curves against him. She was nibbling on his ear and caressing his manly parts in a way that had already sent several nearby customers for the nearest woman and a room upstairs, but it wasn't doing him any good.

Branch was getting desperate.

He looked around him. Whalen, Potter and Boggs were involved in a game of poker and had hardly looked up since he'd entered. Simm, Wallace and Wyatt were passing the time of day with a few of the girls. Little and Smith had disappeared into the upstairs rooms. All the men were enjoying themselves. So what in hell was wrong with him?

Stifling a moan, he turned with renewed determination toward the seeking lips of the woman in his arms. He attempted to block out the dark-haired, gray-eyed image that popped before him as he ground his mouth against hers, but it was to no avail. The lush flesh of the woman in his arms repelled him, her flowery perfume was making him nauseous and her active hands put him in mind of an octopus he had once seen in a picture book as a child.

Suddenly a chorus of gasps sounded over the revelry surrounding him. Branch raised his head and stared in breathless silence at the beautiful woman begowned in red, standing just inside the saloon doors.

No, it couldn't be!

His eyes were still bulging with disbelief when Simm rose slowly from the poker table and asked in a voice harsh with incredulity, "Val...is that you?"

All movement and sound within the room seemed to stop as the lovely vision spoke in a low voice that was almost unrecognizable.

"No, I ain't Val. I'm Miss Valentine Stark, and I'm pleased to meet you all."

The words had hardly escaped her lips before Val became aware of the tremor of excitement that passed over the room. She dropped her shawl from her shoulders, hardly daring to believe the reaction she received from the wide-eyed men assembled. Simm hastened toward her as she unconsciously searched the room for a familiar blond head that towered above the rest. Her gaze jerked to a jarring halt when she saw Branch standing at the bar, his arms wrapped around a buxom woman as blond as he.

Her trepidation dissolving in a hot blast of fury, Val advanced slowly into the room. So Branch was well on his way to purrin' like a kitten with that alley cat he had in his arms. Well, she was going to find herself a great big tomcat of her own, and then she'd show him what purrin' was really like!

Val halted as Simm appeared unexpectedly in her path. His face was flushed as he stammered, "Val...I mean, Miss Valentine, I'd be pleased to be your escort this evenin'. As a matter of fact, I'd be downright honored to have the most beautiful woman in the room on my arm."

Sadness momentarily tinged Val's anger. She didn't want to hurt Billy Simm, but she didn't want to encourage him into thinking that one night would mean more than she intended it to mean. Her reply was firm but kind.

"I'm engaged for this evenin', Billy." She scanned the room for a suitable face, settling at last on a dark-haired, well-dressed gambler type who was staring lustfully in her direction. "There's the fella I'm supposed to meet. I'm sorry. I hope you'll excuse me now."

Sauntering toward the table where the dark-haired man sat, Val was aware that the entire room watched as she approached him. The fellow stood up politely and she forced her smile brighter. "I was lookin' for a friendly face, and I saw yours. I was thinkin' that we might have met somewhere before."

"I don't think so, ma'am." The gambler's voice was liquid velvet. "My name's Thomas Diamond and I only arrived in town yesterday. I'm just passing through, but it would be my pleasure to buy you a drink, if I may. I've just finished my hand here."

Val's stomach lurched sickeningly as she nodded. "Glad to meet you, Mr. Diamond. That would suit me just fine."

Trembling inwardly as the suave fellow led her to a place at the bar only a few feet from Branch and his hefty blonde, Val faced rigidly forward. She didn't pause for amenities when the bartender filled her glass, but tossed it back with a quick snap of her neck that elicited a chuckle from her companion.

"You handled that real well, Miss Stark."

Val looked up at the fellow coyly. "Call me, 'Valentine,' Tom. That's a whole lot more friendly."

Diamond's smile edged on a leer. "I'm all for being friendly, Valentine."

His arm moved around her waist and Val swallowed hard and faced the bar. "Pour me another, Harry. And keep 'em comin'."

Diamond inched closer and Val gulped against the lump that rose in her throat. It occurred to her as she turned to look into the dark, mustached face so close to hers that the fella looked more like a wolf on the prowl than a cat who was supposed to make her purr. But she supposed she wasn't an expert.

A short glance out of the corner of her eye revealed that Branch's blond companion did not suffer the same lack of experience as her long-fingered hands roamed his muscular physique. Barely controlling the urge to rip the woman's hair out by its suspiciously dark roots, Val tossed back another drink, coughed and looked up into her tomcat's face.

Succumbing to impulse, she tested a low, rough sound in her throat. Diamond's reaction was so intense that she jumped as he jerked her against his side with a "That's right, Valentine. I like it a whole lot when a lady gets so friendly that she purrs."

Val's mouth went dry. Picking up her glass, she responded inanely, "Bottoms up!" shuddering as her tomcat pulled her closer.

Branch was openmouthed with disbelief. He shook his head. This couldn't be happening! He blinked and stared harder at the woman who stood a few feet down the bar. Val Stark wasn't in this saloon. She wasn't dressed in a red gown that revealed more of her womanly charms than he was comfortable seeing on display. And she wasn't standing at the bar with a no-good, low-down gambler who was leanin' far too close and whispering in her ear. No! This was a dream...a damned nightmare that was worse than any of the others that had plagued him since Val Stark had gotten under his skin.

Branch slapped at his companion's busy hands, but she would not be discouraged. He dodged her seeking lips, finally allowing her insistent kiss as he peered over her shoulder at Val's flushed face.

Damn that Val. If she thought she was going to spoil this night for him the way she had spoiled every other day and night since he'd arrived on the Circle S, she was wrong. What did he care if she was making the mistake of her life with the game she seemed to be playing? What did he care if that good-for-nothing she had linked up with was hanging over her, all but salivating? What did he care if she was putting down those drinks like a woman with a purpose?

Branch kissed his amorous blonde hard, his eyes popping open halfway through the kiss to stare again in Val's direction. The urge to kill mounted inside him as the fellow leaned closer to Val, his mouth against her ear. A glimpse of Val's face revealed eyes that had gone glassy, and Branch's lips stiffened into a growl that peeled away his companion's kiss. He felt a knot of tension squeeze tight inside him as Val tossed another drink down her throat, but the last straw was when her sleazy companion leaned down to press a kiss against the white flesh bulging at the neckline of her dress.

A bellow of rage erupting from his throat, Branch pushed himself free of his clinging blonde. His fists balled, his eyes wild, he paid no attention to the path that had suddenly cleared before him as he charged to Val's side. She looked up at him and his heart pounded in his chest as he demanded, "Put on that damned shawl! You're leavin' here right now!"

Val turned fully toward him, swaying as she replied, "I ain't goin' nowhere, especially with you. I got my tomcat here, and he's goin' to make me purr." She turned back to the fellow, who stood possessively behind her. "Ain't that right, Tom...cat?"

The fellow's low "Yeah..." had barely escaped his lips

before Branch was holding him off the floor by the lapels of his well-tailored suit.

Branch grated menacingly into his face, "Is it worth your life, fella? 'Cause that's what it's goin' to cost you to make this woman purr."

The fellow's low peep of denial was music to his ears, and Branch thrust him backward, laughing as the gambling man decided not to gamble and headed out the door at a pace just short of a run.

"Damn you!" Val faced him furiously. "Do you see what you did? I was just gettin' the knack of this whole thing, and you spoiled it. Now I have to go and start all over!"

His chest heaving, Branch stared down into Val's flushed face, knowing he had never wanted a woman more in his life than he wanted this crazy, aggravating, beautiful she-devil who had made his life a living hell. Suddenly aware of the leering faces around him, Branch ordered, "Come on. We're gettin' out of here."

Val's jaw hardened. "I told you. I ain't goin' nowhere."

Recognizing the set of her jaw and the light in her eyes, Branch did not waste further time on words. Flipping Val over his shoulder, he stomped to the door to the cheers and whistles of the crowd around him. She was still pounding at his back with all her might when he turned down the nearest alley, halted midway and stood her on her feet.

Facing her rage, Branch listened as Val stormed, "Don't you look down at me like that, Branch Walker! You don't fool me none. You couldn't stand the way you was feelin' no better than I could, and you was takin' the easy way out. You was goin' to come back to the ranch purrin'."

"Where'd you hear that?"

"What difference does it make where I heard it? It's true,

ain't it? You was achin' inside every time we got close, and achin' more every time you thought about gettin' closer. You was achin' and wantin' and yearnin' just like me, but you wasn't goin' to go on sufferin'. You was goin' to 'take the cure' and get me out of your mind with that painted woman in there. But you can't stand seein' me do the same thing. You want me to go back home still hurtin' bad while you come back feelin' just fine. Well, you ain't done nothin' but put things off a few hours for me, 'cause I ain't goin' home until I'm purrin', too. Purrin' so I don't hurt no more. Purrin' so I can look at you without wantin' to die. I'm goin' to be pur-rin'—''

"All right...all right, Val." All the fight gone out of him, Branch slid his arms around her, his heart thundering as Val fought his embrace. "If that's the way you want it, that's the way it's goin' to be." Subduing her struggles with surprising ease, he whispered against her lips, "But if anybody is goin' to make you purr, it's goin' to be me."

His mouth on hers, Branch pulled Val closer, pressing the long length of her against him, reveling in the womanly soft-ness combined with hard tight muscles that fought him dili-gently as his mouth surged deeper. But Val's wild struggle gradually slowed, and he groaned as her lips suddenly sepa-rated under his and the ardor of Val's response stirred a heated beauty inside him that he could not ignore.

Masculine vitals lagging the whole evening came instantly alive, and Branch pressed his hardness against Val as he tore his mouth from hers long enough to look down into her dazed expression. He kissed her lips briefly as he whispered, "Come with me, Val. I want to make you feel good. I want to hold you in my arms and show you what it's like to have a man love you with everythin' that's in him. I want to make you feel happy and light and free, better than you ever felt before. I want to make you purr, Val, 'cause I know that's the way it's supposed to be between us, and nothin' else is goin' to ease that ache we both feel inside.'' Branch kissed her again, trailing his lips across her cheek in a tantalizing path to her ear as he whispered, ''Oh, Val…I want you more than I ever wanted any woman in my life, darlin'. Let me make you happy.''

Val was shivering in his arms, but Branch knew it was not from the chill in the night air. Her low response was so soft that he barely heard it over the hammering of his heart. He urged softly, ''What did you say, Val? Tell me again, darlin'.''

Drawing back, Branch stared down into silver eyes filled with the awe of awakening desire. His throat was thick with emotion and he swallowed tightly as Val responded, ''I said I want you to love me, Branch.''

The burst of elation inside him almost more than he could bear, Branch crushed Val in his arms. Drawing back, he whispered, ''You're sure?''

Val nodded. ''Oh, I'm sure, all right. I know what I want now.''

Val moved closer, but Branch pushed her firmly away. ''No, Val.''

Gripping her hand, uncertain if he would be able to bear the press of his tortured emotions a moment longer, Branch turned toward the rear entrance to the hotel and drew her along behind him.

The darkness of the alley stirred with movement as Val and Branch faded from sight. The shadows came alive, taking on Red Hand's form as the silent Indian emerged to cautiously follow the path Val and Branch had taken. He paused, watching as they climbed the rear staircase of the hotel. His expression impassive, he waited for long moments after they slipped inside, his only reaction an almost imperceptible nod. The satisfaction he so carefully concealed was fleeting as he returned to the shadows, to a duty not yet fulfilled.

Branch closed the hotel room door behind them as Val looked up at him in silence. He stood so close that she could feel his breath against her face, could smell his tantalizing scent. The taste of his mouth was still fresh on hers, and she had not had enough of it. She wanted more. She shivered.

"Don't be afraid, Val, darlin'." Branch stripped off his coat and hat, then caressed her cheek gently. "I won't hurt you."

"I ain't afraid." Val moistened her lips, allowing her shawl to fall to the floor as her hunger for Branch loomed stronger than any emotion she had ever known. Her voice became hoarse. "I was just…yearnin'."

"Oh, Val…"

Within a moment she was in his arms, tasting his mouth, glorying in the wonder of his embrace, feeling the power of him in every sinew as he consumed her with his kiss. Wanting all he had to offer, Val wrapped her arms around him, pulling him close, clutching, feeling, wondering at the joy of being held and loved by Branch as she had so often dreamed. Her hand moved in his hair as his kiss deepened. The heavy strands were thick and warm, and she reveled in the touch of them as they slipped between her fingers like liquid gold. Her palms moved searchingly against his back, tracing the outline of his straining muscles as his ministrations grew more intense. She hugged him close as his heated kisses trailed the long line of her throat, her shoulders, the full rise of her breasts.

Panting and wanting, Val struggled at the closure of her

dress, only to feel Branch's hands moving capably at the fastenings there. Jealousy burned hot inside her for a brief moment at the efficiency of his movements, but she forced it from her mind as she drew his mouth down to hers. His fingers moving more quickly than before quickly freed her from the confines of the garment, then stilled as her gown fell to her waist. Silent, he stepped back.

Uncertain at his unexpected hesitation, Val would not allow him to see her trepidation as she stood before him. She did not flinch as his gaze touched the line of her shoulders and caressed her naked breasts. When he reached out with callused hands to caress their fullness, she gasped, to be rewarded by the warmth of his mouth as he covered a taut crest.

All manner of wild color exploded behind her closed eyes as Val reveled in Branch's loving, clutching him close. She had wanted this, without knowing what she wanted; she had needed this, without understanding the true cause of her need; she had been certain it would be like this without really knowing. But she had no doubts now. She knew that Branch's arms were the only arms she wanted around her. She knew his lips were the only lips she wanted to touch her in any way. She knew her flesh was meant to meet his in ultimate ecstasy. And she knew, no matter the brief duration of the feelings they might share this night, that she would never love any other man more.

Val gave herself freely to Branch as his mouth met hers again. She worked roughly at the buttons on his shirt, managing to bare his chest to fit warmly against hers. She was breathless with the feelings washing over her with wave after colorful wave, when Branch suddenly lifted her up into his arms and took the few short steps to the bed. She gave a short gasp as she felt its softness beneath her.

Branch was shuddering as he lay Val down on the bed. The incredible darkness of her hair stood out against the white linens and he gazed at the gleam of her faultless skin and the lushness of female curves that were now bared to his view. She was perfect, all woman and wanting him, and he knew that this was the moment he had been waiting for all his life.

Branch's look consumed Val's flushed cheeks and parted lips, and a pang of despair assaulted him as a tear trailed from the corner of her eye. He silently cursed his impatient hunger for her. Val was inexperienced with intimacy and he was going too fast.

His guilt soaring, he whispered, "Don't cry, Val. I won't hurt you, and I won't do anything you don't want me to do." He swallowed before speaking his next words, aware of the price he might be forced to pay. "I—I'll leave if you want me to."

Val shook her head with surprising vigor, another tear falling as she said, "I'm not afraid, and I don't want you to leave. I want you to love me."

"Then why are you cryin', darlin'?"

"I ain't cryin' exactly." Val raised a hand to her upswept hair. "It's just these damned hairpins. I think they're drawin' blood."

Branch's low laugh was filled with relief as he promptly pulled Val to a sitting position and began moving his fingers through her hair in search of the offending pins. But his smile faded more with each pin that fell, and with each strand of dark hair that dropped to Val's white shoulders, his heart beat faster. Jealous of the strands that caressed her perfect skin, he made fast work of his chore so he might brush them away with his lips.

His loving attentions soon beyond his control, Branch

stripped away the last impediments to the meeting of their flesh. He loved Val fully then, tasting every inch of her, guiding her on the breathless journey to passion, delighting in each step as she sighed, moaned and cried out, reacting spontaneously to the splendor that grew to torment with their increasing mutual need.

Warm upon her at last, Branch sought the ultimate joining, aware that he had never wanted a woman more than he wanted Val Stark, that he had never loved a woman more, that there could never be another woman for him from this moment on.

Pausing at the brink, Branch leaned down to whisper against Val's parted lips. "Val, I want you to say it. I want you to say you want me—that you want me now as much as I want you."

Branch stared intently into the velvet gray of Val's eyes as she whispered in return, "I want you, Branch, and I know this was meant to be between us. So hurry up, darlin', because I'm needin' you bad."

With a soft sound of joyous gratification, Branch raised himself above Val. Fitting himself against her, her moistness easing his way, Branch thrust himself inside her. Val's arms strained him close, her legs locked around him, and Branch gloried in the beauty of Val's acceptance. The rhythm of his lovemaking escalated toward culmination and he confirmed in his heart a truth he had always known: that Val was not a woman of half measures; that when she loved, she would love all the way. It was with deep humility that he accepted the incredible fortune of being the man allowed to love her.

Moments later, Val lay still and replete beneath Branch's sated body. The perspiration of their mutual passion was slick between them as he raised his head to look down into Val's face. Her eyes were closed, her lips parted, and he could not resist kissing them lightly as he whispered, "Are you all right, Val? Did I hurt you?"

Val's love-drugged lids slowly rose. Her silver gaze met his as she raised a hand to stroke his hair. "No, you didn't hurt me. I never thought it could be so…fine."

A smile flickered across Branch's mouth as he teased softly, "Well, if it was so fine, let's hear it then."

Val appeared confused. "Hear what?"

At his raised brow, Val gave a sudden low laugh. Her eyes glowing, she then parted her lips and purred.

The hour grew late in the Loco Steer. Shouts of laughter, steady conversation and nonstop music emanating from the upright piano in the corner of the room mingled to reach the proportions of a din. Having occupied his time after Branch carried Val out the door with refilling his glass, Simm clutched the bar with an unsteady hand, oblivious of the world around him. Beside him, Potter, Wyatt and Boggs exchanged quips, while Smith and Little, fresh from their visits to the upstairs rooms, completed a foursome at a nearby poker table.

The topic of Val's entrance into the saloon and her unorthodox departure had been bantered about and worn to death by the delighted spectators until there was nothing more to be said. The subject had slipped from the minds of all as the night wore on—all except one.

Standing at the corner of the bar, Aubrey Whalen grew more embittered with each passing minute. Branch Walker had not come back to the saloon, and nobody had to tell him what Walker and that uppity witch were doing now.

Walker and his heavy-handed ways… Whalen's frustration soared. He had thought at first that Walker might cut Val Stark down to size, but he had been wrong. Walker's arrival had done nothin' more than worsen a situation that had already been hardly tolerable, and it hadn't been long before his grievance against Walker was as deep as his grievance against Val Stark. He had thought that little wager with Val Stark would knock both them high-steppin' fools down a peg, but he had been wrong there, too. The petty annoyances he had arranged with the tainted water hole, the slaughtered calves and the downed fencing—even that job he had done on Val Stark's saddle hadn't worked out the way he had planned. Walker had just gotten more stiff-necked, and Val Stark just went on beggin' even harder for what she had comin' to her.

Whalen snorted, his dark, heavy features growing morose. Yeah, he'd like to show Val Stark what bein' a real man meant. Wherever she was with Walker right now, he knew she wasn't gettin' half of what he had been savin' for her. Whalen snorted again at the heaviness in his loins that was always present at the thought of Val Stark's tall, slender body.

Whalen stood abruptly. Well, if he couldn't get his satisfaction one way, he'd get it another, and he knew just how to do it.

The bulls… If he got rid of them, he'd get rid of Walker and he'd have Val Stark all to himself again. He had the feelin' it would be easier to handle her then. And even if it wasn't, he'd handle her. He'd handle her if it was the last thing he ever did.

Not bothering to look around him, Whalen walked a wavering line toward the doorway. He pushed open the doors and took a deep breath. He'd had a lot to drink, but he'd be cold sober by the time he reached the Circle S. He'd fix them bulls real easy with the stuff he'd bought today, and he'd act as surprised as the next fella when they was found. Then he'd say goodbye to Walker and hello to Val Stark in a way he never had before. He could hardly wait.

Jerking his horse's reins from the rail, Whalen mounted and spurred his horse into motion. The cool night air rushed against his heated skin and he gave a hard laugh. Yeah, he could hardly wait.

Slipping from the shadows nearby, Red Hand watched as Whalen's horse disappeared from sight. The only change in his expression the narrowing of his obsidian eyes, he turned back into the alley behind the saloon. Emerging mounted moments later, he guided his pony carefully onto the street and within minutes faded into the darkness.

A shriek of laughter from the street below roused Val from her semisleep. She turned, momentarily startled to find herself pinned against the bed by the arm Branch stretched across her breasts. His leg was curled around her thigh, as well, and in his possessive posture she recognized the danger of what had just passed between them.

Val closed her eyes. She had outsmarted herself this time, all right. She had told herself that she was as good as a man and equal to a man in every way. She had told herself she would live her life with the freedom of a man because she could not take the chance of being a woman—not the kind of woman her mother had been. But she now knew she was her mother's daughter more clearly than she had ever dreamed.

Val opened her eyes and turned to face Branch. His breathing was deep and steady. She reached over to touch his heavy golden hair, fascinated by its glow in the dim light of the nearby lamp. He was such a beautiful man. His features were strong and cleanly cut, his lips full and loving. She remembered the sensation of Branch's mouth moving against hers, trailing her body, and she shuddered.

The glory of Branch's lovemaking was sharply clear in her mind. Her body still reverberated with its power and she wondered if her mother had experienced this same weakness in the arms of her beautiful traveling man. But she did not want to be like her mother. She did not want to give up everything for the sake of being held by a certain man. She had worked too long and too hard. She could not afford a dependency that would weaken her, for she feared that down deep, her mother's weakness was already lurking.

She had had a night to remember. It would have to be enough. There would be no gambling men in her future. She knew that this man was the only one for her, even if she could not afford the risk of loving him.

Branch moved in his sleep, his arm clutching her closer, and Val fought the heady joy of that possessive gesture. Gathering her courage, she carefully raised his arm from her breast, regretting the loss with every fiber in her body, and slipped from beneath the weight of his leg.

She stood up and dressed quickly, turning only when she was done to look down at Branch, loving him and grieving. Succumbing to the emotion that made the thought of leaving him a physical torment, Val leaned down to press a kiss against his hair. She steeled herself against the pain of departure as she turned and slipped from the room.

A few yards down the hall, Val entered her room. She emerged a short time later in the worn work clothes of Val Stark, telling herself as she walked rapidly toward the stairs that this was the person she truly was—the person she wanted to be.

She walked down the steps, refusing to look back at something that was over and done—something that must be forgotten.

Chapter Fourteen

The silver light of a full moon illuminated the landscape
clearly as the Circle S came into sight, and Whalen cursed
under his breath. It had been a long, uncomfortable ride from
the Loco Steer, during which he had made a mental note to
pay that bearded barkeep back for the bad whiskey he had
slipped on him. Whalen's pale face twitched. He knew that
whiskey was bad because he had been bringing it up all the
way back to the ranch, something he seldom did after a night
on the town.

Whalen's face drew into dark lines. He was going to be
doing a lot of paying back in the next few months, starting
with tonight. He patted his saddlebag with a satisfied hand.
He was glad he had taken the time to make his purchase before
going to the Loco Steer. He couldn't depend on Red Hand's
herbs to get them bulls out of the way for good.

Recognizing the need for caution as he drew closer to the
Circle S, Whalen carefully surveyed the area. His brows knit
into a heavy line when his scrutiny revealed the house was
dark and the area nearby was without a sign of life. He gave
a low laugh. Walker wasn't as smart as he thought he was,
trustin' Red Hand to guard the place while the men were on

the town. That old Indian was probably lyin' on the ground somewhere with an empty bottle beside him, dead to the world. Well, that suited him fine. He didn't need no witnesses when he mixed his special treat for them bulls and served it to them personally.

Whalen moved stealthily into the barn a few minutes later. He lit the lamp and placed it close by as he filled a nearby bucket with some of the special feed Walker had bought for his bulls. With a smile Whalen poured a portion of the contents of the large paper sack into the bucket and mixed it carefully. That fool Asa Ledman had swallowed his story without blinking when he had explained that he needed arsenic for rats that were bedeviling everyone in the bunkhouse. Ledman had even offered suggestions about ways to make the bait more appealing. Yeah, the fella had been downright helpful.

Whalen laughed aloud. Walker had been even more helpful, whether he knew it or not, by fencing in the breeding pastures. Hell, it would be no problem at all to put a bucket where each of them greedy bulls would be the first to find them, and when they'd eaten their fill, he'd just collect them buckets and return them to the barn, and nobody would be the wiser.

Walker would be out of a job soon after that and he would have Val Stark all to himself. When he finished cutting her down to size, she would come begging to him, and he would make her—

At a sudden sound behind him, Whalen turned. His breath escaped in a low hiss as Red Hand loomed unexpectedly in the circle of light from the lamp. He grated harshly, "What're you doin' here?"

Red Hand did not respond, and Whalen felt an unexpected tremor move down his spine. The old Indian's leathery face showed no expression, but there was a coldness in his eyes that Whalen had never witnessed there before, a threat that went unspoken as Red Hand advanced toward him. Red Hand reached for the bucket, but Whalen snatched it back with a growl.

"Get out of here, old man. You're stickin' your nose into somethin' that ain't none of your business, and you're goin' to get it cut off if you ain't careful."

Red Hand's scarred hand slipped to his waist, and in a flash of movement a knife glinted menacingly between them in the dim light. Whalen froze with sudden realization. That old red-skin knew everything! He was goin' to spoil it all—

Red Hand leaped toward him in a blur of motion. Whalen turned in an attempt to dodge him, pulling his gun in the split second before the weight of Red Hand's body knocked him to the ground. A hot, stinging pain pierced Whalen's shoulder and he pulled the trigger, hardly reacting when the old Indian's body jerked with the impact of the bullet, then went suddenly limp upon him.

Gasping with pain, Whalen dragged himself out from under Red Hand's motionless form. He clutched his shoulder as he drew himself to his feet, grunting as his hand came back covered with blood. Swearing under his breath, he kicked Red Hand's lifeless body with all his remaining strength. This knife wound in the shoulder was going to look suspicious if Red Hand suddenly disappeared from the Circle S. There was no way he'd be able to explain it away.

Whalen cursed again, his mind frenzied. He was going to have to get out of here—fast—but he'd be damned if he'd leave the Circle S without getting some satisfaction.

Dragging a bandanna out of his pocket, Whalen stuffed it against his wound and pressed it tight. He laughed under his breath as the bleeding slowed. That fool Indian never was very good with a knife. The cut wasn't much more than a flesh wound and he knew it wouldn't be a serious complication. All he'd have to do is hide Red Hand's body where it wouldn't be discovered for a while and he'd still have time to fix them bulls before he left.

Swearing every step of the way, Whalen dragged Red Hand toward a pile of hay in the corner. He kicked the knife under Red Hand's body and, turning, snatched up a pitchfork and covered him completely. He reapplied pressure against his shoulder as the wound began bleeding again and cursed aloud at the delay it caused. Four more buckets to mix and he'd be on his way. And then, even if things hadn't gone the way he'd planned, he could take satisfaction in knowing that he'd left his mark behind him.

Snatching up the remaining buckets, Whalen went back to work.

Branch awoke, suddenly aware of the empty bed beside him. He squinted in the dim light of the hotel room, momentarily incredulous to find Val gone. The sound of revelry from the street below indicated that the night was still in full swing and that he could not have slept long. He pulled himself to a sitting position in bed, ran an anxious hand through his hair and then laughed. Why was he getting so upset? Val had probably just gone to answer nature's call. She would return.

Branch stood up beside the bed, going over in his mind the interlude of loving he and Val had shared. Everything had been so right—so beautiful. Val had held nothing back from him, and in turn, he had loved her more completely than he had ever loved another woman. He remembered Val's deep, low purr, and his heart raced at the memory of the loving that had resumed after he had drawn her back into his arms.

A growing sense of urgency driving him, Branch reached for his clothes, castigating himself for having held back the words he had so wanted to whisper against Val's lips. But it had been too soon, and he was afraid he would panic her if he expressed the enormity of the emotion he felt for her. Val was so young and inexperienced, and he sensed a deep sense of insecurity despite her surface bravado. He knew his arrival at the Circle S had complicated her life in so many ways that she was not yet equipped to handle. He had been certain the words "I love you" would make her turn tail and run.

Fully clothed, Branch picked up his hat and placed it squarely on his head, realizing there was no sense in fooling himself any longer. Val had run despite his precautions, and he knew why. She had found more than she bargained for in his arms. She had not come to town to find love or commitment. She wanted no part of a demanding emotion that would infringe on the course she had set in her life.

Frustration swelled inside Branch. Well, he hadn't come to town for love or commitment, either, damn it! But it had walked in through the doorway of the Loco Steer in a low-cut red dress and high-heeled shoes. When it had, he'd recognized it and knew he could not escape. That was something Val had yet to learn—that she could not escape emotions that were as deep and powerful as the love they felt for each other. And she did love him. He knew she did.

Branch started toward the door, a dwindling hope rising inside him that he would pull it open to find Val returning to the room, but he knew that he would not. Cursing aloud, Branch stepped into the hall and started toward the staircase. He would check the convenience, the Loco Steer and every other damned building in town in order to find Val, but he had a feeling it was a waste of time.

Branch paused as he stepped out onto the board sidewalk and surveyed the noisy street. His dark eyes were hard. Val loved him. She needed him. She would never be happy without him, and he would convince her of that truth if it took the rest of his life.

Branch took a deep breath, angry with Val, angry with himself, angry with the feeling of loss that still remained after waking to find her gone. He'd find her all right, and when he did…

Val squeezed her heels into Dunbar's sides, urging him to a faster pace. The road was as bright as day in the light of the full moon, the air fresh and crisp. Sound traveled well on clear nights, and the gunshot she had heard a few minutes earlier had been unmistakable.

A gunshot at night…when the only ranch nearby was the Circle S…

The same sense of urgency that had forced the haunting vision of Branch's face from Val's mind caused her to lean low over her horse's neck as the ranch house came into view. There had not been any suspicious incidents at the Circle S lately, but she knew that Red Hand was alone on guard while everyone was away. She also knew that Red Hand seldom used a gun.

Dunbar was covering the ground with elongated strides when Val saw a flicker of light in the barn. Someone was there. Someone who *shouldn't* be there. Val turned toward the barn. Minutes later she drew her mount to a halt a cautious distance away. She dismounted in a flash and drew her gun.

Whalen peered out into the yard from his position of concealment inside the barn, and he snickered at the twist of fate that had delivered Val Stark to him so unexpectedly. He watched as she crept closer, moving swiftly from shadow to shadow as she approached. Whalen's smile twisted into a sneer.

Val Stark thought she was so smart. Whalen remembered the many conflicts between them over the course of the year that he had worked on the Circle S, and the humiliation of her ridicule burned deeper. The only thing that had kept him from leaving was the need to show the fools who had laughed at him so openly that he could cut Val Stark down to size. But he was determined to do more than that before he left now. Whalen laughed low in his throat. This was going to be a night to remember.

Quietly picking up the pitchfork Whalen moved into the shadows beside the barn door. He listened, his heart beginning a heavy pounding as Val Stark's light step sounded nearby. He tensed, waiting. Suddenly bursting out of the darkness, Val leaped through the doorway and he swung the pitchfork with all his might. He laughed at her squeal of pain as the handle struck her arm and sent her gun flying.

Whalen stepped into sight and Val's pain-filled eyes widened. Clutching her arm, she rasped, "Whalen! Have you gone crazy?"

Whalen stepped closer, noting that pain had brought perspiration to Val's forehead and upper lip, and he drawled, "What's the matter, Val? Did you hurt your hand?"

"You bastard! What's goin' on here?"

"I'll tell you what's goin' on." Whalen stepped closer. "Just a little change of plans. But I don't mind changin' my plans to accommodate you. I wouldn't want to go without leavin' you somethin' to remember me by."

"What are you talkin' about, Whalen?" Val looked around

the barn, her eyes searching the shadows. "What was that shot I heard on the way in here? Where's Red Hand?"

"Don't you worry about Red Hand. He ain't feelin' no pain." Whalen's features moved into an expression of mock concern. "But you are, aren't you, sweetheart? Here, let me do somethin' about that."

Without warning, Whalen struck Val cleanly on the chin. He gave a short laugh as Val pitched into his arms, unconscious. His smile drained as he supported her slender body against his chest and whispered into her unhearing ear.

"I knew the minute I saw you comin' that I was goin' to have to make a choice tonight, 'cause there ain't no way I'll have time to take care of them bulls and take care of you, too, before the men come back. But you know somethin'? There wasn't no choice to be made, 'cause I ain't got the same kind of feelin's for them bulls that I got for you." Whalen shifted Val's weight onto his uninjured shoulder as he continued softly, "You don't look as pretty now as you did when you came into that saloon tonight in that red dress, but I know what's under them baggy clothes you're wearin'. And what you got from Walker ain't nothin' beside what you're goin' to get from me. You ain't never goin' to forget this night when I'm done with you." He nodded. "Never."

Minutes later, Whalen tied Val across her saddle, bound and gagged. Quickly mounting his own horse, he gathered Dunbar's reins in his hand and turned back toward Val's unconscious figure. "Come along, sweetheart. I know a little cabin where we can have some real privacy, and by the time somebody gets back here and figures out what happened, we'll have had the time of our lives."

Spurring his horse into motion, Whalen took off at a gallop.

He smiled at the sound of Dunbar trailing unresistingly behind him.

Dawn was a faint glow against the night sky when Branch reached the Circle S. He drew Caesar to a halt in front of the ranch house, uneasiness prickling at his neck as he dismounted. His hand slid automatically toward the gun at his hip. Something was wrong here. Everything was too still, too quiet.

Approaching the house with caution, Branch emerged minutes later, his fears confirmed. The house was empty. Something had to have happened. Val had been seen leaving town no more than a half hour before he started after her, headed in the direction of the Circle S, and he had not passed her on the road. There was nowhere else she could have gone.

Branch's apprehension grew. Red Hand was missing, too, and he knew that the old Indian would never have left the ranch unguarded against explicit instructions without a good reason.

Branch turned toward the barn, uncertain what he expected to find. His hand at the holster on his hip, Branch walked through the doors, surprised to see that a lit lamp rested on the ground, the fuel burning low. Someone had obviously been there and had left in a rush. Branch's step momentarily slowed at the sight of a few buckets filled with feed resting nearby, and he turned to search the shadows more keenly with his gaze. What was going on? Neither Val nor Red Hand would have left a lit lamp in a spot where it could so easily cause a problem. Where were they?

Branch unconsciously raised his hand to massage the knots of tension from the back of his neck. His arm froze at a whisper of sound from the shadows. He remained motionless as he attempted to identify it. There it was again.... Branch jerked his head to the side. It was coming from the corner. Branch's indrawn breath echoed in the silence as a shadowed form suddenly rose from beneath the hay piled there. He snapped into motion as the figure lurched forward and staggered into the light.

"Red Hand!" Branch steadied the old Indian, his heart leaping with concern at the circle of blood that soaked his buckskin shirt. "What happened?"

"Whalen shoot. Him take Val."

"Whalen took Val? Where? Why?"

"Red Hand get 'em."

"Red Hand, listen." Panic was making inroads into Branch's mind. "You're hurt. You can't do anything right now. Just tell me what happened and where Whalen took Val so I can go after them."

"Whalen hate Val, but him want her."

Branch went rigid. "Where did he take her?"

Red Hand shook his head. At Branch's look of desperation, the old Indian added, "Red Hand find."

"How are you going to find them? You can hardly stand."

Red Hand's dark eyes flashed contempt as he repeated, "Red Hand find."

Hastily bandaged minutes later, Red Hand examined the ground outside the barn doors, finally looking up at Branch with eyes as hard as stone. "Whalen carry Val to horse. Him lead Val's horse when him ride off."

Branch stiffened. Red Hand did not have to tell him what that meant. Val was helpless, probably tied and gagged. The thought sent Branch's rage soaring as he assessed the Indian's condition again. Whalen would not leave a trail in the rough country surrounding them that he could follow without Red

Hand's help. Everything depended on the old Blackfoot. He only hoped the fellow was up to it.

Red Hand pulled himself erect, swaying with the difficulty of the effort. Branch's anxieties soared as Red Hand mounted, not waiting for him to follow, and pressed his pony into motion.

Val bit back a groan as the foul-tasting gag was ripped from her mouth. Forcing a bravado to her voice that she did not feel, she met Whalen's scrutiny without flinching. "You're crazy if you think you're goin' to get away with this, Whalen."

Whalen laughed, stepping closer to the filthy cot on which he had deposited her minutes earlier. She had almost forgotten that this old hunter's shack on a deserted portion of the Circle S was still standing, and her heart dropped with the realization that most of the men on the Circle S did not even know of its existence. Appearing to read her thoughts, Whalen replied as he stood towering over her menacingly, "Oh, I'll get away with it, all right. It'll be hours before anybody gets back to the ranch and sobers up enough to start wonderin' what happened to you. They won't find Red Hand's body for days."

Val gasped. "Red Hand's body!"

Whalen's expression tightened. "The old man came after me with a knife." He sneered. "Ain't that a joke? But it didn't take long for me to teach him that a knife ain't no match for a gun."

"You killed him...." Val's voice faded with shock.

"That old drunk ain't no big loss. He wasn't worth much. But you, sweetheart, that's somethin' else. I got a lot of real fine plans for you and me."

Val forced herself not to cringe as Whalen slid his hand across her breasts.

"You looked real pretty in that red dress you was wearin' in the saloon. Real pretty...."

Val gritted her teeth as Whalen suddenly ripped open her shirt, only to growl with disgust as a coarse male undergarment met his gaze. "I like a woman who dresses like a woman, damn it! But maybe you're back to dressin' like this because Walker didn't teach you good enough what bein' a woman is really all about." Whalen's leer grew more menacing. "Well, it's back to school, and I'm the teacher now. Are you ready for your first lesson?"

When Val did not respond, Whalen began unbuckling his belt. He was working at the closure of his pants as he added in a low rasp, "Ready or not, class is goin' to start...."

Red Hand rode ahead of Branch at a cautious pace, swaying revealingly as the morning sky rapidly lightened. Frustration, panic and soul-shaking fear alternated in Branch's mind with the realization that he would be helpless without Red Hand, that if the old man didn't manage to hold on, he'd never find Val in time to stop Whalen from...

Branch cursed under his breath, suddenly furious. This was all Val's fault! Why couldn't she have stayed with him? Why couldn't she have trusted him? Why hadn't she realized, as he had, that they were meant to be together, that they would never be happy apart? Branch briefly closed his eyes against the images that haunted him. He was going to find Val, and when he did, he wasn't going to let her go until she realized that she was only a woman, after all...that she needed him and the protection he could give her against men like Whalen and against situations like the one that now threatened her. And if Whalen harmed Val, he'd kill the bastard.

All thought immediately fled from Branch's mind as Red Hand came to an unexpected halt ahead of him. The old man swayed again and Branch urged his horse abreast of him.

"Red Hand, are you all ri—"

Red Hand raised his hand in a signal for silence, and Branch turned a cautious glance around them. There was no one in sight on the stretch of land that ran level and uninterrupted up to a wooded stand in the distance.

Red Hand dismounted with difficulty and secured his horse on a low-lying shrub. Branch did the same, gripping the fellow's arm as he turned with a warning signal to follow. One glimpse of the old Indian's eyes revealed that he was completely lucid, even if he was weak, and Branch followed without objection as Red Hand dropped to his knees and began crawling toward the tree line.

When they were close enough to the trees to make out the outline of a run-down shack Red Hand slipped his hand to his waist. The glint of a blade caught the pale morning light and Branch realized that Red Hand was certain Val and Whalen were inside, despite the shack's deserted appearance.

They crawled closer, and Branch saw light flicker from within. He heard a whinny and noticed for the first time a lean-to a distance beyond the shack where Dunbar moved restlessly. Whalen's sorrel was tied beside him and Branch's teeth clamped tight with fury as he drew his gun and turned toward Red Hand.

One glance was enough. The circle of blood on Red Hand's buckskin shirt had widened, and it was obvious that the fellow was close to collapse. Branch looked levelly into Red Hand's eyes as he whispered, "You found Val, just like you said you would. Now it's time for me to take over." He saw a glimmer of opposition in the old Indian's gaze, and he added with a hint of steel in his voice, "Don't worry. I'll get him, and I'm tellin' you now...if Whalen hurt Val in any way, he isn't comin' out of that cabin alive."

Waiting only a moment longer for acceptance to register in Red Hand's expression, Branch crawled the remaining distance to the trees. Drawing himself to his feet at last, Branch slipped from shadow to shadow until he was standing beside the cabin wall. All was silent within and Branch's heart began a new pounding, his anxiety edging up to panic with the realization that silent acceptance was unnatural to Val. She would be fighting—vocally, bodily, in any way possible to her—if she was physically able.

Branch edged along the outside of the cabin, his mind flashing tormenting pictures of Val across his mind. She was helpless. She needed him. She was waiting for him to rescue her. Branch paused a moment outside the solid wooden door. His gun drawn, he kicked the door open with a snarl and jumped into the cabin, as the door snapped back against the inside wall with a loud crack.

Fury turned to shock as Val swung around to face him, snapping angrily, "What the— You near scared the life out of me, jumpin' in here like that. Damn it! Couldn't you just open the door like a normal human being?"

Suddenly realizing that his mouth hung agape, Branch closed it and blinked. Was he going crazy? Was Val really standing there, fit and furious because he had startled her? And was that really Whalen lying on the floor of the cabin behind her, neatly tied, packaged and ready to be delivered?

Resting her fists on her hips, Val flashed him a cocky smile. "It's a good thing Whalen ain't no match for me." She looked back at Whalen where he lay wriggling on the floor like a trussed-up calf. His eyes bulged over his gag as she pressed, "Ain't that right, *sweetheart?* Looks like the pupil taught the teacher a lesson this time, don't it?"

Val turned back to Branch. "Anyways, I'm glad you're here. I wasn't lookin' forward to liftin' this beefy fella up onto his horse. I was considerin' leavin' him here and returnin' later with a few of the boys to drag him back."

Val continued talking, but Branch could do no more than stare. Only a few hours earlier Val had lain in his arms, loving him as he had loved her, her slender body shuddering with longing as he worshipped it with his.

Branch blinked again as his mind suddenly corrected his thoughts. No, that wasn't accurate. It wasn't Val who had loved him. It wasn't Val who had purred her contentment. It wasn't Val who had fallen asleep in his arms, her breath against his lips, her body pressed intimately against him. That passionate, loving woman had been Miss Valentine Stark, a person distinctly different from the Val Stark standing before him. This Val Stark was everything she had always said she was—tough, hard, a match for any man, a woman without a drop of love in her....

A sound behind him turned Branch toward Red Hand as he appeared in the doorway at the same moment Val gasped aloud. Reaching Red Hand's side before Branch had a chance to take a step toward him, Val threw her arms around the old Indian's neck. Almost knocked from his feet by Val's enthusiasm, Red Hand accepted Branch's steadying hand as Val drew back far enough to see the circle of blood that stained his buckskin shirt. Her face paled revealingly as she spoke.

"Whalen said you was dead, but I should've known that nobody could kill you until you was ready to let 'em." Val wiped away an unexpected tear and smiled. "They're always underestimatin' us, ain't they, Red Hand?"

The old Indian did not reply, but Branch had the feeling that Val and Red Hand communicated more clearly without words than Val and he had in all their wasted conversations. The pain of that thought and the emptiness of his arms almost more than he could bear, Branch suddenly turned toward the door.

"Where're you goin', Walker? We ain't done here yet."

Branch turned back to meet Val's shadowed gray eyes, realizing he would never be able to read them as clearly as the old Blackfoot obviously did. Jealous, angry and hurting from a frustrated love that he neither wanted nor needed, Branch snapped, "Aren't we? I thought we were. Anyway, if you don't want our friend here to bleed to death, I suggest we start back to the ranch as soon as possible."

Val stiffened. "I know what's good for Red Hand, and I know what's good for me. You just take care of that package I got wrapped up over there, and everything will be fine."

Resenting every step, Branch walked toward the corner where Whalen lay struggling against his bonds. Stripping the rope off his ankles, he jerked the fellow to his feet and shoved him toward the door.

As their silent party rode back toward the Circle S, it occurred to Branch that he had never been so wrong as he had been in evaluating Val's feelings for him. She didn't want him. She didn't even *need* him.

At that realization, Branch had no choice but to accept the fact that everything was over between them.

Chapter Fifteen

Hours had passed since their return from the cabin, and Val was grateful that the chaos that accompanied their arrival had died down to a rumble of disbelief and reiterated hindsight from the startled cowhands. Whalen had been turned over to the law, Doc Pitt had attended to Red Hand's wound and declared it serious but not life threatening and Branch, who had maintained a silent, powerful presence throughout the whole ordeal, had finally retired from the house. Val didn't know where he had gone, and she wouldn't allow herself to care.

Standing in the cramped storage room that had been Red Hand's quarters since he had arrived at the Circle S eight years earlier, Val glanced again at the cot a few feet away. Red Hand was sleeping. At least, she thought he was sleeping. She couldn't be any more sure of Red Hand when he was under the influence of Doc Pitt's sedative than she could be when he was his silent, wily best. But there was one thing of which she was certain. Red Hand had risked his life for her and for the Circle S, and even though she somehow would not have expected any less from him, she knew she would never forget it.

Satisfied she could do no more for him than she had already

done, Val walked back into the kitchen to meet her pa's worried gaze. She attempted a smile. "Red Hand's all right, Pa. He ain't goin' to die or nothin'. He's too tough for that."

"It ain't Red Hand I'm thinkin' about right now." Will Stark's gray mustache twitched revealingly the moment before he took a step forward and hugged his daughter unexpectedly. Embarrassed by his display of affection, Will shook his head. "Damn it, Val, you had a real close call today!"

Val nodded. "You're right, Pa."

Unwilling to answer the questions she knew her father longed to ask, Val looked out the window at the gradual descent of the sun toward the horizon. Not much more than twenty-four hours had passed since she had gone to town, a woman with a mission, yet her life had changed immeasurably in so many ways. She needed time to digest those changes and to come to terms with the feelings running riot inside her. She would talk to her pa some other time—later.

"I think I'll lie down for a while. Call me when supper's ready."

"Supper!" Will turned an uncertain glance toward the storage room as Red Hand's snores sounded opportunely. "Who's goin' to cook? Red Hand sure ain't."

Val's response was frigid. "Well, don't look at me."

Val closed the bedroom door behind her a few minutes later and sagged against it with a sigh. It had been a day she would never forget, and it was only half over. Straightening, Val took the few steps to her bed and dropped down onto it in exhaustion. She closed her eyes, but sleep was edged out by the vision of pain in Branch's dark eyes and the knowledge that she had caused it by deliberately holding him at arm's length.

Val swallowed against the sobs that rose in her throat as she remembered the way her heart had leaped the moment he'd burst through the door of the cabin. Fresh from her ordeal with Whalen, she had wanted to run into his arms and claim the sanctuary that she knew awaited her, but she could not. Something deep inside her had not allowed her to submit to the emotion of the moment when she knew she would regret it.

Damn you, Branch Walker! Val rested a weary hand against her forehead. Why do you have to be so big and blond and handsome? Why do you have to send little chills down my spine every time you look at me. Why do you have to make me melt with hunger when you touch me?

Val groaned. Even now she could not strike from her mind the memory of Branch's strong arms around her, the joy of having his powerful body stretched against hers, the incredible wonder of becoming a part of him.

All right—she loved him!

Finally acknowledging that truth, Val found another question rising to plague her mind. But was love enough? Her mother had loved Pa once, too, enough to give up the city life she relished and to go with him to live on a ranch in the middle of nowhere. In the end, her mother had regretted her sacrifice and had grown to hate her life so much that she'd abandoned it and escaped with her handsome traveling man.

Val shook her head, the memory more painful than she could bear. Would it be the same with her if she sacrificed all she had worked toward, all she had earned? Would she grow to resent Branch as he assumed greater control of her life and the Circle S? Would she grow to hate him?

Val closed her eyes against the agony of her thoughts as weariness began to assert control. She could not trust love— not the kind between a man and a woman. The flaw in her, inherited from her beautiful, selfish mother, was a threat that

would make life beyond enduring. She would not—she *could*
not—take the chance of causing Branch such pain—because
she loved him.

Mary worked efficiently in the small cluttered kitchen of the
Circle S, her feelings torn and her spirits as low as the sun
that was sinking into the horizon. She had arrived an hour
earlier at Will's summons and had been shocked to learn of
Val's experience at the hands of that terrible Aubrey Whalen.
Mary sniffed as she flipped another slice of beef with the skill
of long practice. She had never liked the looks of that fellow,
and she was glad to see him go. She only hoped that Val had
not suffered a scarring experience at his hands.

Tears rose to Mary's eyes at the thought. She forced them
back at the sound of Will's step behind her, but they did not
escape his scrutiny as he turned her toward him with a whisper.

"Mary, darlin', what's wrong?"

His eyes filled with concern, Will attempted to take her into
his arms, but Mary resisted as she cautioned, "Wilbur, please!
Valentine has had a terrible experience and it would only add
to her confusion if she were to come out here and discover us
together."

"Val's sleepin'."

"The walls have ears."

Will smiled. "Oh, Mary. You say the darnedest things."

Mary smiled. "You are the dearest man, Wilbur."

"Not as dear as you, Mary. I can't thank you enough for
comin' to help us out until Red Hand gets better." Wilbur
paused before continuing, his discomfort obvious. "But it
wasn't only cookin' I had on my mind when I asked you to

come, darlin'." Will paused again as he searched for the right words.

"You see, Val ain't done much talkin' since she came back from that cabin. I mean, she didn't tell the sheriff much about what went on when she was alone with Whalen. I'm thinkin' she's holdin' somethin' back that she can't talk about to me. I thought that maybe...I mean if Whalen did somethin' to my little girl that he shouldn't..."

Will's eyes filled unexpectedly and Mary suffered his anguish as he forced himself to continue. "You see, I got the feelin' that Val ain't the same person she was before. I mean, there's somethin' different about her. I thought, bein's that she came to talk to you once before..."

Mary could stand no more. "Wilbur, dear, I understand, and I'm only too happy to help if I can. But I must wait until Val comes to me, you know. I can't force a confidence."

"I know that, darlin'. I just thought it might make Val feel good seein' you here when she wakes up."

Doubts soared within Mary, and she sighed. "I hope so. But even if she isn't happy to see me, I know she'll be relieved to have someone to take over the kitchen until Red Hand is well again. I'm preparing a really hearty supper tonight that I hope will encourage her to eat. She's too thin, you know."

Pausing, Mary forced the concerned frown from her brow before continuing. "We're having steak and eggs, mashed potatoes, fresh biscuits and some of my special sweetened beans that I brought from home. And look here, dear." Mary raised the lid of a pot that bubbled on the rear of the stove. "Applesauce—nice and hot and touched with cinnamon."

Will shook his head. "The boys will think they're in heaven."

Will's smile touched Mary's heart, and she chanced a whispered confession. "I *am* in heaven when I'm with you, Wilbur."

Mary flushed at Will's trailing reply, "Oh, Mary...."

Branch groaned as he stared up at the bunk overhead. Steak and eggs, mashed potatoes, even fresh biscuits and applesauce—Widow McGee had cooked a feast fit for a king. It was the first good meal that had been placed in front of him since he'd arrived at the Circle S, and he hadn't been able to eat a bite.

Branch attempted to swallow the misery that was a thick lump in his throat, but it was no good. He was a fool—so much of one that the situation would be laughable were it not so pathetic. Val's comment to Red Hand in the cabin had been the absolute truth. People did underestimate her. *He* had underestimated her. Val had returned his lovemaking with all the ardor of her inexperienced youth. He had thought that meant that she loved him, but he now knew that he was wrong. Val had simply accomplished the goal she had set for herself when she'd gone into town. She had returned to the ranch "purring."

Branch's low laugh was filled with bitterness. He had made himself believe what he wanted to believe. He had convinced himself that Val was so confused by the emotions their lovemaking had stirred that she didn't really know what she wanted, when the truth was that *he* was the person who was confused. But that confusion had come to an abrupt halt when he'd realized that he'd been as big a fool as Whalen in underrating her.

Branch laughed again, a true quality of mirth entering into the sound as he recalled how Whalen's eyes had bulged when he discovered how helpless he had been rendered by a mere woman.

Branch shrugged, his amusement fading. Val had won her battle with Whalen, and she had won her battle with him. She had subdued Whalen with guile, and had done the same to him with her loving surrender, however brief its duration. He was leaving, and the reason was simple. Disliking Val had been easy, but loving her was too difficult to bear.

Suddenly conscious of the unnatural silence of the bunkhouse, Branch looked around him. Unable to eat, he had left the supper table ahead of the men, relieved that Val had not appeared to witness his poorly concealed distress. He had returned directly to the bunkhouse, grateful to have an hour alone so he might think through his plans for the future, and only just that moment had become aware of the unexpected solitude of the bunkhouse.

The sound of a step at the door interrupted Branch's thoughts and he looked toward it as it swung slowly open on its squeaky hinges. Freezing into motionlessness, Branch gaped. He blinked, then gaped some more. Suddenly springing to a sitting position, he smacked his head on the upper bunk, acutely aware of the hollow sound still echoing in the room as he jumped to his feet. His heart pounding, Branch stared at the apparition that walked toward him as the door swung slowly closed.

Branch's mouth was dry and he ran a nervous hand through his hair as the specter came closer. Was he dreaming, or was the statuesque beauty approaching him, resplendent in a brilliant red dress and matching high-heeled slippers, with gleaming upswept hair that sported a crimson plume and gray eyes glowing above her tempting lips, really Val Stark?

Branch shook his head and took a step backward. No, it

wasn't Val Stark! He had made that mistake before. It was *Miss Valentine Stark,* and he wanted no part of her!

His expression stiffening, Branch commanded gruffly, "Stop where you are!"

The apparition continued its steady progress toward him and Branch panicked. Backed up against the bunk behind him, Branch knew he could retreat no farther, and he commanded with a curious break in his authoritative tone, "I told you to stop where you are, Valentine!"

The specter paused and Branch could feel the brush of its breath against his lips, smell the familiar scent of its skin in his nostrils. He was melting from the heat in the eyes that a few hours earlier had been cold as ice. His indrawn breath shattered the silence as slender arms slipped around his neck, warm breasts pressed against his chest and a voice that sounded like Val's without really sounding like it at all whispered throatily, "What's the matter, Branch? Don't you want me?"

Betrayed by the obvious as she pressed more tightly against him, Branch grumbled a sufficiently unintelligible response, closing his eyes as lush, warm lips met his. He was drowning in the sweet nectar he remembered so well, when his eyes suddenly snapped wide and he awoke to the danger of the moment. Breaking free of the clinging arms that held him, Branch suddenly thrust the wraith from him with an angry growl.

"Oh, no, you don't, Valentine Stark. I'm not going to fall into that trap again!" His dark eyes narrowed. "Whatever your game is, I'm not playin'!"

The mask fell from Val's face with a flash that left him reeling as her gray eyes shot angry sparks. "What're you talkin' about, Branch? What does a woman have to do to seduce a man like you? Hog-tie and gag him?''

Branch's eyes widened. ''Don't go gettin' any ideas, Valentine. You're not goin' to do to me what you did to Whalen. Nobody's goin' to come into this room an hour from now and find me lyin' on the floor trussed up like a sow ready for market.''

Val looked confused. ''Why would I want to do that?'' She smiled. ''I got other plans for you, Branch, darlin'.''

''Branch...*darlin'*?'' Branch shook his head and closed his eyes. Something was wrong here. He was either having the craziest hallucination or the damnedest nightmare he'd ever had in his life! Either way, he knew he somehow had to be dreaming.

Branch peeked open one eye, then the other. She was still there. He swallowed, but his throat didn't seem to work other than to gulp as Val pressed herself against him once more and whispered up against his lips.

''I kinda thought you might be a little angry with me for the way things have been between us for the past few hours. I was a little confused with everythin' happenin' so fast.'' Val stroked his cheek tantalizingly and slid her hand up to entwine her fingers in his hair. He all but groaned under her touch as she continued, ''But I suppose you deserve an explanation.''

Branch nodded. His deep voice was hoarse as he muttered, ''I sure enough do.''

Abruptly gripping his arms, Val steered him backward and pressed him down into a nearby chair. ''This is goin' to take some time, so we might as well get ourselves comfortable.''

Plopping herself down on his lap, Val slid her arm around his neck and tilted his face up to hers. The earnestness in her expression touched Branch's heart as she began hesitantly,

"This ain't goin' to be easy, but I'll try. Well, the whole problem is that I wasn't lookin' to get myself a man. Branch…darlin'. That was the last thing I had on my mind, 'cause I never met any man who was half the man I was—if you know what I mean. I can't tell you how many times I cursed the day you came to the Circle S. You mixed up my life and turned it upside down, and just when I thought I was gettin' the hang of hatin' you, you started changin'. I was hurtin' and achin' when I went to town to take the cure."

Val took a deep breath and Branch began melting inside as the glimmer of tears brightened her incredible eyes.

"But the cure only made things worse, and…well…I got scared."

Not realizing he had raised his hand, Branch brushed away the lone tear that streaked Val's cheek as she continued, "I started wantin' things that I never wanted before, but I told myself that I wasn't goin' to take any chances with my life turnin' out like my ma's. I told myself that I wasn't goin' to cause nobody the pain my ma caused my pa and me. I was lyin' in my room, still drownin' in my sorrows, when my thoughts started turnin' around. I realized that I might be savin' the both of us, but I was cheatin' us, too."

Val looked candidly into Branch's eyes. "I know you love me, Branch. I don't know much about makin' love, but I do know that no man could make love to a woman the way you made love to me without meanin' it. And I think that's what made me run."

Branch stiffened, and Val's eyes narrowed. "You ain't goin' to deny it now, are you?"

Branch shook his head, barely withholding a smile, and Val continued, "That's good, 'cause the truth is, I love you, too."

Branch swallowed, hardly able to believe his ears. He

started to draw her mouth down to his, when she jammed her palms flat against his chest, halting him.

"You had your chance, and you wanted me to talk, instead, so you're goin' to let me finish, whether you like it or not."

Allowing her the opportunity she sought, Branch waited as Val resumed her difficult explanation.

"Like I said, I was lyin' in bed, when it all started coming clear. I thought how I'd been fightin' the odds all my life, makin' my way in a man's world when nobody gave me a chance in a million of succeedin'. I'd done real good, too. It was a matter of wantin' somethin' real bad, and workin' like the devil to get it. I thought about that for a while and I started thinkin' that if I put everything I had into it, I could make things between us work out, too."

Val sighed and her brows drew into a frown. "I started cursin' myself then, 'cause I figured you were probably disgusted with me for blowin' hot and cold with you the way I did, and I calculated that I needed to soften you up a bit before you'd listen to reason."

A smile tugged at the corners of Val's lips as she wiggled her backside on his lap. "But it looks like this here dress I put on just for you didn't soften *all* of you up too well."

Branch did not respond, and Val's smile fell. All trace of her former flippancy gone, she continued softly, "Well, that's all I have to say, except that I want you to tell me straightaway if you think it'll work out."

Val's eyes held his, touching a spot deep inside Branch that he knew was hers alone as she whispered in a halting voice, "I think it's worth a try, Branch. I mean…we might make each other miserable if we get together. That's a possibility. But it's a fact that we'll drive each other crazy in the meantime, just tryin' to keep out of each other's arms, and that wouldn't do neither one of us no good, would it?''

Branch shook his head, a heady warmth growing inside him. He was looking into Val's serious face and seeing his future unfold before him. He was seeing the life they would spend together, the arguments they would have and the time they would spend makin' up in so many ways that he was goin' crazy thinkin' about them. He was thinkin' about the home they would build and the children they would have. He was thinkin' about the hours he would spend holdin' Val in his arms, lovin' and protectin' her, whether she wanted him to protect her or not, and he—

The intoxicating parade of Branch's thoughts halted abruptly as he asked bluntly, "How *did* you get the drop on Whalen?''

A shadow passed over Val's face, and Branch was momentarily angry with himself for reviving an unpleasant memory. However, he somehow had the feeling that if he didn't make her tell him now, she would never tell him at all.

Val's mouth twitched and she gave a little shrug. "Whalen took me by surprise when I found him in the barn. I didn't think he had it in him to do no more than brag and strut, and I didn't think he ever looked at me as more than an irritation who beat him to the draw on everythin' he did. But I was wrong on both counts. He knocked me out, and the next thing I knew I was in the cabin, tied and gagged, and he was bendin' over me. I don't suppose I really thought he'd do nothin' but brag a bit then, either, until he told me that he had killed Red Hand.''

"Killed him!''

Val nodded, a familiar coldness invading her gaze. "That's when I got more mad than scared and started usin' my head.

Whalen started unbuttoning his drawers, and I told him that I had some tricks I could show him with that thing he was so proud of—''

The blood rushed to Branch's face. "Damn it, Val!"

Val's eyes widened. "Well, *he* didn't know that I was bluffin'!"

She paused, allowing a few moments for Branch's twitching to cease, before she continued, "Anyways, I talked him into untying me, and the rest was easy. He couldn't wait to flop down on me, and when he did, I was ready for him. I rolled over, snatched up the gun he'd dropped on the floor and cracked him on the head. And I didn't waste no time tyin' him up with the same ropes he'd used on me, neither."

Val laughed unexpectedly. "He ain't never goin' to forget that headache."

Branch swallowed with difficulty, making a mental note to pay a visit to Whalen in his jail cell the next day.

Val was silent, watching the play of emotions across Branch's face, when his hands suddenly tightened on her arms. She blinked as he rasped, "All right, you've had your say, and now I'm goin' to have mine. You don't know how close you came to losin' the only man who can ever make you happy, Miss Valentine Stark. And that man is me!"

Val's face was solemn. "I know that, darlin'."

Branch's dark eyes narrowed. "Do you also know that I was plannin' to leave the Circle S tomorrow and to get out of this country as fast as I could?"

"That wouldn't have done you no good."

"That so?" The fire of Branch's anger began succumbing to a heat of another kind as Val trailed her lips against his temple and cheek. "What makes you so sure?"

Val pressed fleeting kisses against Branch's lips, raising his heartbeat to thunder in his ears as she whispered, "'Cause you ain't never met a woman like me before, and you never will again. I'm one of a kind, and you wouldn't have been able to forget me."

Branch's lips parted, and he shivered as Val slid her tongue between them. He groaned softly. "What makes you so sure of that?"

Val kissed him deeply, her strong arms entwining his neck as her tongue sought the warm, moist crevices of his mouth. He groaned again, his restraint slipping as he kissed her long and hard in return. Without conscious intent, he scooped her up into his arms and took the few steps to lay her on the bunk from which he had arisen only minutes earlier. He sat beside her, then glanced toward the door.

"You don't have to worry about nobody walkin' in on us." Val's voice was a breathless whisper. "I told them cowboys outside that I'd geld the first fella that took a step toward the door."

Branch gave a short laugh, incredulous as he shook his head and slid his hands under her to the fastenings on her dress. Within a few seconds he had slipped the dress to her waist, and as he gazed down at her incredible beauty, he asked softly, "What about your pa?"

"Him and the widow are busy. I'm thinkin' I might try fixin' things up between them." And at Branch's raised brow, she continued, "Well, Pa's goin' to need somebody to look after him 'cause I'm plannin' on bein' real busy with you."

"You're right on that account. And just for the record—" lowering his head, Branch brushed first one pink, waiting, crest and then the other "—I won't be settlin' for anythin' less than puttin' a ring on your finger."

Val groaned and drew him closer. "We can settle them

details later. But right now I'm thinkin' we've got some pretty good makin' up to do.''

Realizing he was beyond words, Branch crushed Val in his arms. Glorying in the feel of her, knowing he had never expected to love a woman as much as he loved her, he closed his mouth over hers. This woman was his—Val Stark, Valentine Stark—*both* of them. He knew he was a lucky man to get her...uh...them. And if any doubts lingered in Val's mind, he was determined that he'd settle them if it took the next fifty years to do it.

Branch's mouth was sinking deeper into Val's. He was all but lost to the wonder of her, when there were sounds of a struggle outside the door, followed by a long, angry call.

''Valenti-i-i-i-ine!''

Branch's head snapped up, cracking against the bunk overhead. His eyes popped wide. He knew the sound of an angry father when he heard it, and he'd be damned if he'd let that old wild man bust in and find them like this!

Jerking Val to her feet, Branch pulled up the bodice of her dress. He was still working at the fastenings at the back, when the door burst open and Will Stark broke in, followed by a breathless Potter, whose wiry whiskers twitched as he stammered, ''I—I'm sorry, Val. I couldn't hold him back.''

Will Stark surveyed his daughter from head to toe and roared, ''What in hell's goin' on in here?''

Branch gulped, jerking his head to Val as she laughed and explained. ''Nothin' much, Pa. I was just fixin' it so the Circle S can stay in the family after all.''

An unwilling suspicion narrowed Branch's eyes as he looked at Val's pleased expression. ''Val...?''

Val nearly purred as she turned back to his questioning

gaze. "Branch, darlin', I was only jokin'. Did you think I'd really do somethin' like that?"

The thought that he'd never be completely sure of anything when it came to Val, except that he loved her, did not come as a complete surprise. Taking her into his arms to the hoots and cheers of the cowhands who had crowded into the doorway behind Will Stark, Branch also realized that he didn't really care. He had gotten more than he'd bargained for when he'd come to the Circle S. And no matter which way he looked at it, it was the best deal he had ever made.

Epilogue

The early-morning air was cool and crisp, the sky steadily lightening in advance of the rising sun. The ranch yard had not yet come to full life as Clementine Stark Walker walked out onto the porch on her sturdy five-year-old legs, her boots clicking hollowly against the wooden floorboards in the dim light before dawn. A long golden braid hung down her back and she squinted with eyes like gray ice at the whiskered cowboy who stepped into sight and walked toward her as she spoke.

"I'm ridin' out with my pa this mornin', Potter. Saddle up my horse."

Potter's nose twitched and he paused in his approach. "I didn't hear you say 'please,' miss."

"I don't have to say 'please'! Who's the boss around here, anyhow?"

A reluctant smile picked up the corners of Potter's lips. "Well, it sure enough ain't you, little girl."

Clementine's small eyes froze and she opened her mouth to speak as Branch Walker's familiar deep voice instructed from the doorway behind her, "Your ma wants you back in the house, Clementine."

Clementine's face pulled into a frustrated frown. "Pa, I told you that my name ain't Clementine. It's Clem."

"That so?" Branch barely restrained a smile despite his annoyance. "Well, whatever your name is, you'd better get in there before your ma comes out to get you."

"I don't want to go inside. Ma ain't no fun no more." Clementine's light brows furrowed. "I ain't never goin' to have no babies when I grow up."

At the sound of a step, Clementine turned toward her mother as Val stepped out onto the porch. Annoyed, Clementine frowned as Branch slid his arms around his wife and smiled. Her pa was always lookin' at her ma with that silly smile these days. He was always huggin' her and kissin' her and rubbin' her belly, too.

"It's damned sickenin'."

Branch's head turned toward his daughter with a snap. "What did you say, little girl?"

Clem looked up at Branch, her gray eyes wide and innocent. "I said I don't like bickerin'. I'm ridin' out with you this mornin'."

"I don't think you are. You're goin' to school." He turned back to Val and smiled into her pale face. "Isn't that right, darlin'?"

When Val did not immediately respond, he paused, concerned. "You *are* feelin' all right this mornin', aren't you?"

"I'm fine!" Val's gray eyes shot fire. "You'd think nobody ever had a baby before. I did it once before, you know."

Branch kissed his wife's warm lips. Six years had passed since they'd said their vows, and he had never loved her more than he did right now, with her disposition sour because of the restrictions her advanced pregnancy set upon her. He knew that even though she'd be back in the saddle a few weeks after this latest addition to their family arrived, the baby would not suffer for her attention. Val's knack for givin' love came naturally.

Branch sighed. He was a contented man. The passage of six years had allowed the Hereford breeding to become well established on the Circle S, and things were working out even better than they'd planned. The ranch was in good shape. His home life was in good shape; the new house he'd built for his growing family was only a hop, skip and a jump from the old ranch house; he had one daughter who sported his wife's personality too closely for complete comfort and another baby on the way. Life was good. Will Stark and his wife, Mary, were living at the old Circle S ranch house—a union for which Val took full credit—and Red Hand—

Clementine grimaced. "I don't need to go to school, and I don't need to help Ma," she said, anticipating her father's next statement. "Red Hand can help her."

Appearing on signal, Red Hand stood in the doorway. Clementine frowned as she looked up, responding to his stoic expression. "I ain't goin' to school. I'm goin' to ride out with my pa and the boys today."

Red Hand stared into Clementine's small face. He did not speak.

"I said I ain't goin' to school. Simm's goin' to teach me to brand today. He promised."

Red Hand maintained his silence.

"I'm all dressed and ready to go!"

Silence again.

"It ain't fair!"

Turning on her heel, Clementine marched back into the house. Red Hand followed, and Val shook her head. "She's such a stubborn little cuss that sometimes I don't know what to do with her." She looked up at Branch. "She gets that from you, you know."

Branch gave a short laugh as he cupped his wife's face in his hands. "Does she? Well, it's a good thing that I was stubborn, or I'd never have won the prettiest—"

Val frowned.

"The *toughest* woman in the territory."

Val smiled. "You sure enough know how to get around a woman, don't you?"

"I guess that's so, and it isn't so easy gettin' around the size of you these days, either."

Rewarded with a slap for his teasing words, Branch drew Val into his arms and kissed her until her halfhearted struggles ceased. He looked down at her with a thoughtful expression as he whispered, "I love you, Valentine Stark Walker. I always will love you." His gaze grew thoughtful. "Are...are you happy, darlin'?"

"Happy?" Val gave the matter a moment's thought. "I'd be a damned sight happier if you could be carryin' this baby instead of me, but all things considered, I guess I'm happy."

Branch's smile was tentative. "All things considered?"

Val smiled. "All things considered, I think I'm a lucky woman."

"That so?" Branch kissed her again and Val warmed to his loving, secure in the knowledge that it would always be that way. She didn't see any need to reply.

* * * * *

ONCE UPON A TIME...

there was a financial genius who lived in a castle, an archaeologist who was falling for a genie and a beautiful young lawyer on the hunt for a missing heir.

This March 1999, don't miss our newest three-story collection rooted in fairy tale and legend.

CARLA NEGGERS
MARGARET ST. GEORGE
and LEANDRA LOGAN

help you recapture the magic!

Available in March 1999 wherever Harlequin and Silhouette books are sold.

 HARLEQUIN®  Silhouette®

Look us up on-line at: http://www.romance.net   PSBR399

If you enjoyed what you just read,
then we've got an offer you can't resist!

Take 2 bestselling love stories FREE!

Plus get a FREE surprise gift!

Clip this page and mail it to Silhouette Reader Service™

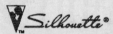
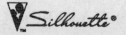

Sultry, sensual and ruthless...

THE AUSTRALIANS

Stories of romance Australian-style, guaranteed to
fulfill that sense of adventure!

This April 1999 look for
Wildcat Wife
by **Lindsay Armstrong**

As an interior designer, Saffron Shaw was the hottest ticket
in Queensland. She could pick and choose her clients, and
thought nothing of turning down a commission from Fraser
Ross. But Fraser wanted much more from the sultry artist
than a new look for his home....

*The Wonder from Down Under: where spirited women win
the hearts of Australia's most independent men!*

Available April 1999
at your favorite retail outlet.

HARLEQUIN®
Makes any time special ™

World's Most Eligible Bachelors

Available April 1999 from Silhouette Books...

The Greek Tycoon
by Suzanne Carey

The World's Most Eligible Bachelor: Extremely wealthy Theo Petrakis was built like a Greek god, and his reputation as a ladies' man—and confirmed bachelor—was no mere myth.

Gorgeous tycoon Theo Petrakis lived life to the fullest, so when he came up against the utterly proper Esme Lord, he found adventure in teaching the American beauty his wicked ways. But one tempestuous night had left them with rings on their fingers and a faint recollection of wedding vows. Was their marriage for real...or just their passion?

Each month, Silhouette Books brings you a brand-new story about an absolutely irresistible bachelor. Find out how the sexiest, most sought-after men are finally caught.

Available at your favorite retail outlet.

PSWMEB8

Based on the bestselling miniseries

FORTUNE'S *Children*™

A FORTUNE'S CHILDREN *Wedding:*
THE HOODWINKED BRIDE

by BARBARA BOSWELL

This March, the Fortune family discovers a twenty-six-year-old secret—beautiful Angelica Carroll *Fortune!* Kate Fortune hires Flynt Corrigan to protect the newest Fortune, and this jaded investigator soon finds this his most tantalizing—and tormenting—assignment to date....

Barbara Boswell's single title is just one of the captivating romances in Silhouette's exciting new miniseries, **Fortune's Children: The Brides,** featuring six special women who perpetuate a family legacy that is greater than mere riches!

Look for *The Honor Bound Groom,* by Jennifer Greene, when **Fortune's Children: The Brides** launches in Silhouette Desire in January 1999!

Available at your favorite retail outlet.

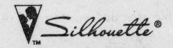

Silhouette®

Coming in May 1999

BABY *Fever*

by
New York Times Bestselling Author

KASEY MICHAELS

When three sisters hear their biological
clocks ticking, they know it's
time for action.

But who will they get to father their babies?

Find out how the road to motherhood
leads to love in this brand-new collection.

Available at your favorite retail outlet.

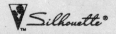